SKINNY

Also by Diana Spechler

Who by Fire

SKINNY

A Novel

Diana Spechler

HARPER ● PERENNIAL

NEW YORK ● LONDON ● TORONTO ● SYDNEY ● NEW DELHI ● AUCKLAND

HARPER ● PERENNIAL

HarperCollins books may be purchased for educational, business, or sales promotional use. For information please write: Special Markets Department, HarperCollins Publishers, 10 East 53rd Street, New York, NY 10022.

FIRST EDITION

Designed by Justin Dodd

Library of Congress Cataloging-in-Publication Data is available upon request.

ISBN 978-0-06-202036-9

11 12 13 14 15   OV/RRD   10 9 8 7 6 5 4 3 2 1

To my Timber Creek kids, and to the grown-ups, too

I put the Special in front of the fat man and a big bowl of vanilla ice cream with chocolate syrup to the side.

Thank you, he says.

You are very welcome, I say—and a feeling comes over me.

Believe it or not, he says, we have not always eaten like this.

Me, I eat and I eat and I can't gain, I say. I'd like to gain, I say.

No, he says. If we had our choice, no. But there is no choice.

Then he picks up his spoon and eats.

—*from "Fat" by Raymond Carver*

Part I │ **Before**

ONE

After I killed my father, he taught me that honesty is optional. But, of course, I'd always known that. This was why I loathed being naked—my choices were stripped away.

It was the first day of Staff Training, forty-eight hours before I would meet Eden Bellham, and I was naked among strangers. Well, naked enough. We all whispered, "I feel so *naked!*" and giggled, awaiting commiseration, because who wants to be the Most Naked Person, to let her body blab her secrets? We stood in bathing suits and flip-flops. We were goose bumps sheathed in towels. We were vulnerable knees, scars with stories, fading bruises, February flesh. We were yellow-tinged toenails, awkward tattoos, scratched mosquito bites, suspicious moles. We were shamefully unshaven. We were birthmarks meant for lovers. We were eyes stealing glances. We were eyes pretending not to steal glances.

Lewis was calling my name.

We were gathered in the politely dim student lounge, which Lewis called the canteen. I separated from the group that was clustered around a bar with no stools, no bottles, no bartender, and walked to the middle of the lounge, where Lewis stood with the nurse, an obese woman with silver hair who had told us to call her Nurse, whose shiny beige leggings carried her cellulite like tight sacks of oatmeal. Nurse was holding a noose of tape measure around the nutritionist's neck.

As I approached, Lewis watched me watch him. The picture of him on the Camp Carolina website, a head and shoulders shot, had depicted a much thinner man. In fact, his face was relatively thin—saggy at the neck, but narrow; clean-shaven; punctuated by wire-rimmed glasses and a gray helmet of hair with a widow's peak so perfect, his forehead was shaped like the top of a heart. It was the middle of his body that betrayed him, like the hoop inside a clown suit.

"Gray Lachmann." He swept an arm across his body and bowed. "Gray from New York City."

"Such a sad name," Nurse said, clucking her tongue. She shook her head and her chins flapped. "Come here, honey." For an alarming moment, I looked at her outstretched arms and thought that she wanted to hug me, to ease the ache of my lackluster name. But then she let the tape measure unfurl from her hand. "Let's see what you add up to."

Nurse wrapped the tape measure around each of my arms, my waist, my hips. She whispered, "These leggings give me a wedgie." She scribbled something on a clipboard.

I let my towel fall to the floor, stepped out of my flip-flops, and stood against a wall. My bathing suit was a brown one-piece, as discreet as a loin cloth. I tried to remember more naked moments, but even the night I'd lost my virginity, I'd been wearing a sweatshirt and also had been spectacularly drunk.

No, this was the moment. This was it. No one had ever been more naked than this.

"I grew up in New York," Lewis said, aiming his camera at me. I smiled into the flash. "In my heart, I'll always be a New Yorker." I envisioned him running to catch a taxi, his balloon belly bouncing, his silver whistle knocking against his chest. "I used to eat at Luigi's. In the Theater District? Back when I was a binge eater." Lewis chuckled. "They have eggplant parm as big as your head. It's worth going." He motioned for me to step on the scale at his feet. "Just for the eggplant. It falls over the edges of the plate . . . How tall are you?"

"Five four."

I watched him punch numbers into a handheld device attached to the scale by a long wire. "You're hardly fat at all," he diagnosed, and for some reason, I remembered my father stealing fries from my plate, poking them into his mouth, saying, "You and your mother with your French fry aversions. Look what you make me do." Then to whoever else was in earshot: "And they wonder why I'm fat, these women."

"Are you going to commit to the diet?" Lewis asked.

I knelt to grab my towel. When I stood, I laughed. "I'm afraid of commitment." My laughter rang false, pinging off the walls like a pinball. I thought of my boyfriend, Mikey, saying, "Leave funny to me, Gray."

"Are you going to—" Lewis scrunched his brow, as if trying to remember something he'd read. "Are you going to *surrender to my program?*"

I could have answered him honestly: I didn't fancy myself the surrendering kind. I recoiled to think of abandoning control, of being caught under the arms and dragged someplace to rest. But the problem with the truth was that inside it lay another truth, and inside that another truth, like those wooden Russian nesting dolls. So instead I asked, "The diet the kids are doing?" I pulled my towel tight around my chest, letting my stomach muscles relax just a bit. I said cheerfully, "Everyone has to start somewhere."

In the past year, I had grown dependent on platitudes: *That's neither here nor there. Qué será será.* People always agreed. They sighed and nodded their heads and said, "That's for damn sure." If there was one thing they knew how to spot, it was wisdom.

"That's what I always say." Lewis rubbed his belly sagely. "Everyone has to start somewhere."

TWO

Mostly, I was not a dishonest person. I had never shoplifted or copied answers on a test. Back in New York, when I felt like breaking plans, I told friends, "I'm staying in tonight," instead of doing what most people did, which was pretend to have a catastrophic disease. And I had been with Mikey for five years without cheating, ever since I met him outside Big Apple Comedy Club.

I was different then, fifteen pounds lighter, a girl with a father, a girl with a stupid office job. And I was so militantly in love with New York City, I once spent a Sunday on the double-decker tourist bus. Mikey was different then, too—a "new jack," fresh out of the box, selling tickets for his own shows in the street.

I noticed him before he noticed me. I was walking aimlessly through the West Village, alone, because I loved Manhattan and its infinite channels. A guy in a red Big Apple Comedy Club T-shirt stood blocking the sidewalk. He was remarkably large, but not large like my father. My father was the fattest person I knew. I'd *seen* fatter people—on television, and in the *Guinness Book of World Records,* like the man who could get through a doorway only if he was buttered; and in person, too, but they were usually confined to wheelchairs.

By contrast, my father was active. He was no triathlete, but he cannonballed into swimming pools; and at weddings, he did the twist so low, his knees would crack audibly. When he waltzed my mother around the living room, she vanished—tiny and insignificant—against his great belly, his sweating round head, his mammoth hands. This guy in the street wasn't fat; he was a relatively healthy-looking giant. And his presence was more assailable than my father's. He looked overgrown—a vegetable that should have been picked and was now too ripe.

"You like stand-up comedy?" he asked me. It was what he was asking everyone. He sounded distracted. I couldn't possibly have appreciated the weight of his question. Had he asked me something more direct, like, "Would you like me to change the course of your life?" I would have whacked him with my purse, shouted, "No!" and run.

But I said, "I love stand-up comedy." I could see in his brown eyes that he knew how to flirt. That was all it was: I wanted to be flirted with. I wanted to pat his wild black hair. I was twenty-two and I didn't know anything.

In those first months with Mikey, I always ran the last few blocks to his apartment because I couldn't get to him quickly enough. I spent hours in Saint Mark's Bookshop, poring over books he had mentioned—books about Taoism and Steve Martin and disasters that might end the world.

In the years that followed, I was a faithful girlfriend, guilty of only the most minor transgressions: a kiss in the back of a comedy club, for example, a few months before I left for camp. Mikey was onstage when it happened, the spotlight in his eyes. He was doing a bit he'd been working out for weeks—a joke about his girlfriend's father dying. It wasn't funny yet. Sometimes jokes took months to smooth out. This one still had wrinkles.

I was sitting beside an older comic who had just been on *Conan O'Brien* and always wore a fedora onstage; a guy full of a bravado particular to men with above-average access to sex. He leaned into me and tipped his hat. He whispered, "If you don't mind my saying so, your boyfriend's a douche."

I whispered, "I mind your saying so," but when he pressed his mouth to mine, I let him. I was sick of Mikey's dead father joke.

And there were those months of correspondence with my high school crush. We exchanged e-mails day after day, spilling words into each other like bodily fluids, until he finally proposed a visit and I had to admit that I lived with my boyfriend. For weeks after that, my heart pounded whenever I checked my e-mail, but my in-box stayed sadly empty of him.

And there were many men in many bars—*Can I buy you a drink? So what's your story?*—men in suits and loosened ties, exhausted bankers sipping single malts; men from whom I would slip away while they checked the score or flagged the bartender; men who touched my necklaces, their knuckles brushing my collarbones. I loved tired men with needy hands.

And who's to say Mikey was the perfect boyfriend? I knew how things went in the comedy clubs. After shows, girls stood outside smoking and fixing their bangs, or they ordered vodka sodas and lingered at their tables. They told Mikey, "You were *so funny."* They thought they'd found the key to happiness—a boy-friend who could make them laugh. They said, "I loved your joke about traffic. I loved your joke about the president. I loved when you said that thing to that person in the audience about his ugly sweater." They got up close to him and thrust out their chests. They smoothed their shiny hair over their hopeful shoulders.

But none of that matters. I know that. I do. What Mikey might have or might not have done—that doesn't matter at all.

THREE

What mattered was this: Before my father died, I spent most of my life dieting, spent most days knowing, at every moment, how many calories I had thus far consumed. As a child, I sat through school days distracted, squeezing my stomach beneath the desk, counting calories in my head as the clock hands made their circles. I did sit-ups instead of homework, my feet trapped beneath the couch.

Each day, I ate my way to sixteen hundred, then stopped, brushed my teeth, and silently recited my dieting mantra in a firm voice unlike my own, the voice of a referee: "You're done."

Before my father died, my answer to, "Would you like to see the dessert menu?" was always, unequivocally "No." I avoided croissants. I avoided white pasta. If I craved pasta, I imagined a loaf of Wonder Bread smothered in tomato sauce, thought, *empty carbs, nutritional zero,* and pictured my stomach rising like dough. I rarely missed a day at the gym. Every couple of months, I'd lose control, eat three slices of pizza, binge on peanut M&M's; but the next day, I'd be right back at it—counting, measuring, lacing up my sneakers.

And then my father died and I inherited his hunger.

At first, I was confused, so I believed what I was told. "Such a stressful time," people said, touching my hair, rubbing slow circles on my back. I believed them that stress was pulling me loose from myself, making me drift up and hover above things, so that all of life looked surreal. It was stress that made me detach enough to eat and eat without stopping.

Shivah felt like an amateur production of an absurd play. My mother and I, like set designers, covered the mirrors with linens. My uncles left their faces unshaven, as if the drama teacher had told them, "In this scene, you must appear grief-stricken." And then there were the actors with bit parts—the chorus, the townspeople, the shopkeepers. The people came in droves. The people loved my father. The people came with food as though they planned to resurrect him.

So there were things to bite into: the edges of casseroles—burnt, black, crumbly, scraped from the glass with spatulas. The sweet insides of blintzes. The cool thickness of cream cheese, a pillowy bite from a bagel, the light smokiness of lox. As I chewed, I let my eyelids drop, like curtains over an unpleasant scene.

Each time I found my plate empty, I wanted one more thing. Perhaps a piece of pie would fill me. When it didn't, I appealed to the spinach and artichoke dip. Once I'd finished that off, I realized I'd been misguided all day; all I needed, in fact, was a dish of mint chocolate chip ice cream. Even when the nausea came, I kept scrounging for the food that would save me.

Then someone made my mother a sandwich. She whispered to me, "I can't taste a thing, Gray. It's sawdust."

Her words weren't out of character. She often waved away food: "It's not worth the calories!" "Who needs pastries?" "I'm stuffed; I couldn't possibly." This was the woman who had taught me to weigh my vegetables on an antique food scale.

But in the wake of my father's death, I wondered: *In what, if not food, was she finding relief? How was she managing these days, these minutes, if not by sinking her teeth into things, filling her stomach, and then waiting, exhausted, as digestion made space for more?*

"I feel like Dad," I told her, as I wolfed a warm slice of cake, covering my mouth with my fingers, ashamed of my feverish chewing.

"Honey," she said, watching me, "if cake's going to get you through this, then go ahead. Eat cake." But the crinkling of her forehead said otherwise. We were not cake-eating women.

This was how my father had chosen to haunt his daughter.

Not by appearing to me in my dreams. Not by brushing the back of my hand with invisible, ghostly fingers. Not by speaking through silence to me, or smiting my enemies, or slamming doors, or making framed family pictures fall mysteriously from shelves and shatter. My vengeful father, in the afterlife, stole my self-control.

The people kept explaining: "Death makes people hungry. Funerals make people hungry." So during shivah, we feasted together—a social, manic, boisterous binge. And then they said the dumbest things:

"We're celebrating his life!"

"He would just love this!"

"I can picture Alan now. Can't you see him laughing at us?"

We ate and ate until we had to lie down, undo buttons, breathe through our mouths. But when everyone left, I kept eating. When I returned to New York, I kept eating. The first time Mikey saw me do it, he stared. "I've never seen you so . . . hungry."

"You're not allowed to say that," I told him. "It's like calling me fat."

"I didn't call you fat. There's a long road between hungry and fat. Want to go out for wings?"

I shook the nearly empty cereal box I was holding. "Okay," I said.

"Holy shit, are you serious? I get to take my girl out for wings? Can we go to a Yankees game?"

"No."

"Want to watch porn?"

"I want . . ."

"What? Tell me. This is awesome!"

"I don't know," I said. My head was filled with noise. I held it between my palms. "I guess I just want chicken."

We went to an all-you-can-eat buffalo wings joint on Avenue B. Mikey finished long before I did, and then watched me intently as I gnawed chicken meat off bone after bone, the spicy sauce searing my lips. He finally set his beer mug down and said, "Am I allowed to ask if you're pregnant?"

This was one of many firsts we would have in the ensuing months: the first time I ate more than he did, the first time he didn't get to finish my dinner, the first time I told him not to touch me, the first time he noticed I'd gone a week without laughing, the first time he watched me clutch my hair in my fists and scream, "I just want to shut off my brain!"

Soon after the day we ate wings, I began to hide my eating from Mikey. As far as he knew, I was the old Gray again—counting calories, steaming my green beans. As far as he knew, I was still the girl he'd met outside Big Apple Comedy Club.

DIANA SPECHLER

All of this led to another first: I began to detest my boyfriend. How could he let this happen to me? After all I'd done for him, couldn't he wire my jaw shut, or lock me up and feed me nothing but water? Couldn't he scoop me up into his arms and carry me to safety?

I did not want to live with this hunger. Quite plainly, I wanted to die.

FOUR

Before I stuffed my body into my bathing suit, walked to the canteen, presented myself to my colleagues, and committed to a two-month diet, I drove through the Carolina Academy entrance, past the engraved wooden sign that said CAROLINA ACADEMY and the construction paper sign taped to it that said CAMP CAROLINA, LEWIS TELLER'S BRAND-NEW, REVOLUTIONARY WEIGHT-LOSS CAMP FOR CHILDREN. I saw a boarding school reminiscent of a farm—green fields, lush trees, and white wooden buildings.

Lewis flagged me down from the dirt path that looped through campus and directed me to the girls' dorm, where I would spend the next two months on the third floor with the oldest girls (one floor above the intermediate girls, two floors above the youngest girls; the boys would stay in another dorm on the other side of campus). I hauled my belongings up to my dorm room, plugged in my window fan, and lay on the pin-striped mattress.

Someone knocked, and then pushed the door open. The girl who stood on the threshold was as tall as a man, with hips that filled the door frame. She had the face of a baby, her skin smooth and pale, her eyes wide and black, and a mass of red hair sprouting, thriving, from her part. Although she was dressed in gym clothes—spandex shorts, a loose tank top over a sports bra—she shimmered like a showgirl. When she smiled, a dainty stitching of white scars spread beneath her lower lip. She said that her name was Sheena, like the Ramones song "Sheena Is a Punk Rocker," and did I know who the Ramones were?

"Yes," I said, "I know the Ramones." I didn't give her more than that. I hadn't come here to make friends.

She said that she was my co-counselor, that she was such a mature nineteen, Lewis hadn't minded putting her in charge of seventeen-year-old campers. "I'm going to lose one hundred pounds," she said. I believed everything she told me. But when she said, "You're skinny," I looked down at my body and saw all of the imperfect pieces of it.

I wasn't skinny—not compared to what I'd been a year earlier, and even then . . . no. No, I had never been skinny. Not compared to the models who wandered around SoHo, their legs like drinking straws from the tops of their boots to the short hems of their shorts. Not compared to my mother, who, when ordering in restaurants, always asked for half of her meal to be boxed up before it left the kitchen; who sometimes ate a quarter of a block of low-fat tofu (uncooked, unseasoned) for dinner, carving slimy bites off with the edge of her fork.

Mikey liked to tell me that untying my bathrobe was like opening a present on Christmas morning, but Mikey was always my most fervent cheerleader. I was average, really, with a face that could have belonged to anyone—a slight bump on the bridge of my nose, raised cheekbones that let me get away with "exotic" (although people more often said I looked "foreign").

My father's eyes had been as dark as secrets. Mine had my mother's green mixed in. My hair was brown and wispy like his. My smile was protracted by dimples like his. My skin, like his, tanned before it burned. When I walked, my toes cracked like his. When I lay in bed reading, my feet rocked like his. In the past year, I had gained fifteen pounds, adding a roll to my stomach, a quiver to my thighs.

I told Sheena, "I'm not skinny."

"Compared to me. I'm spread out like a cold supper." Sheena grabbed a handful of her own ass. Then she held one of her ankles, folding her leg in half, stretching her quad muscles. She wore flip-flops and orange toenail polish. A tattoo on her wide right thigh said *Beautiful* in purple script. "It's fine. I know I'm beautiful. Do you have a boyfriend?"

"I do."

"Is he rich?"

"No. He's a comedian."

"Are you rich?"

I laughed.

She dropped her foot and leaned in the door frame. "People from New York are usually rich. Everyone tells me I should be a comedian. But I'm not really funny. I just have a lot of presence." She looked around my empty room. "I broke up with my boyfriend a few months ago. He was abusive."

This made me sit up. I liked when strangers turned their hearts inside out, proudly presenting their auricles.

"It sucks because I'll never love anyone that much ever again." Sheena examined the fiery split ends of her hair.

I felt her words in my stomach, like food I might get sick on. "Sure you will."

"Probably not." She flipped her hair over her shoulder.

"There are plenty of people to love."

"Wouldn't be the same. Nothing's the same as your first love. We used to sneak into swimming pools together. In a rich neighborhood. We swam in eleven pools one night. We figured out how to get in without splashing. I don't care. At the end of the summer, when I'm, like, a hundred sixty pounds—a hundred sixty's not bad for me; I don't want to lose my ass or anything—when I'm a hundred sixty pounds, I'll go find him." Sheena looked past my head and smiled vaguely, conjuring an image in the bright, hot air. Her eyes were so young. A child's eyes. Here was a person who still saw reason to shape her life around proving something. She would lose weight for the man she loved.

"You don't have to do that," I said.

"Do what?"

"Well, who am I to say, but . . ."

"Are you going to tell me some girl power shit?"

"You seem so interesting. And you're pretty. I would kill for hair like yours. Why hang your life on one hook, you know?"

"I'm my own hook," Sheena said, knotting her arms over her chest.

"Right. Good. Because it's just . . . he could move away."

"He's already moved away. He's in jail."

"He could go blind," I said. "He could die." I pressed both hands to my lips to close them.

"I hope he shits razor blades," Sheena said. "But if he's out of jail by the end of the summer, I'll run into him on purpose. And he'll be like, 'I can't believe I screwed that up.' You know? Like, 'How could I have let her go?'"

"Good idea," I said. "He'll kick himself."

Sheena tipped her head to one side and squinted her black eyes at me. But I wasn't patronizing her. No one would have dreamt of condescending to Sheena.

"You'll look gorgeous," I said, smiling.

Sheena nodded. "I will." She smiled back, her fingers moving over her scars. "I'll be skinny," she said. "I'll be happy."

FIVE

The night before the campers would arrive, fourteen hours before I would meet Eden Bellham, I decided—no . . . I was compelled—to have my final meal. The Last Supper. Once the idea occurred to me—no . . . gripped my throat like strong fingers—I mumbled something to a few people about picking up some things at Walmart. Then I got into the car that had once been my father's, buckled the seat belt that still had an extender on it, and drove to Melrose, the nearest town, to an all-you-can-eat Chinese buffet called Chinese Buffet.

The Chinese part was questionable; the buffet included pizza, spaghetti marinara, cream puffs, California rolls, and flan. Not that the details mattered to me. Three nights before, I'd eaten four pints of ice cream, and afterward couldn't have named the flavor.

I gazed through the sneeze guard at the lo mein glistening beneath the heat lamps, at the unidentified meat shimmering in hot pink sauce.

And I began.

I heaped my plate high with egg rolls and pasta, fried balls of something masquerading as chicken, rice peppered with tiny green and orange cubes that represented peas and carrots. I barely heard the booth sigh when I sat, barely noticed the sticky, synthetic sensation on the backs of my thighs.

Chopsticks are supposed to aid dieters, to lend themselves to smaller bites. I loved chopsticks for the wrong reasons—the pleasing pinching, the length unobstructed by tines. I pulled a pair from its red paper sheath. I cracked it apart. And then I shoveled, stuffed, and filled. I chewed with my mouth open, gulping for air. I felt myself come loose from my body and drift above the table to watch. Rice flecked the front of my T-shirt.

I went back for seconds.

I went back for thirds.

I had brought a magazine—the kind that lobotomizes. I looked at celebrities in expensive jeans. I learned that one was dating another, that one was either pregnant or fat, that one had bought groceries in West Los Angeles. I felt grease and sauce make my chin slick, sweat bead at my hairline, and the heat of Chinese food emanate from my armpits.

I approached the buffet for a round of desserts. And then another. And then went back for more lo mein, remembering the inimitable first mouthful—the steaming, salty relief.

I didn't stop until sickness spread its wings in my gut and reared its beefy head in my throat. I rested my elbows on the table, my hot face in my palms. I spoke silently to myself.

Don't think about how fat you feel. You're no fatter than you were an hour ago. You're just full. You will digest. What were you supposed to do, skip dinner? Don't think about your stomach swelling in your shorts. Don't think about the tops of your thighs; it's natural that they touch. Don't think about how bloated your cheeks will feel in the morning. This will never happen again. Tomorrow will be the beginning.

DIANA SPECHLER

SIX

Here's what it's like to want to be dead: a maze of discomfiting observations.

My body, on the brink of decay, will finally be thin.

When an average-looking woman dies young, everyone pretends she was beautiful.

One should die in something slimming.

Death will be the ultimate appetite suppressant.

For six months after I killed my father, until I discovered Eden Bellham, until I decided to go to fat camp, this was where my head was.

According to medical professionals, my father's assassin was a transmural myocardial infarction, a heart attack that destroys three layers of tissue on the myocardial wall. What a gift that fancy words exist to deflect culpability.

The rift between my father and me, the rift that led me to a girl named Eden Bellham, and eventually to Camp Carolina, had begun four years before, when my parents came to New York to see me and meet my new boyfriend.

"You will love my dad," I told Mikey. "Everyone loves my dad."

I imagined Mikey cracking jokes and my father laughing his wheezy, pink-faced laugh. I imagined them drinking scotch together. I imagined my dad giving him a man hug and saying, "I always wanted a son," or, "These women . . ." (waving his arm at my mother and me) " . . . they don't know how to drink."

I imagined Mikey smiling approvingly, telling me, "Your dad's an all right guy," the way he did on the rare occasion when he met someone he deemed truly cool.

When we gathered for dinner at a seafood restaurant, my father, who always had the loudest laugh in the room, whose hugs were magnificent and crushing, sat in his suit coat and yarmulke, frowning, sipping whiskey on ice. When I remember that night, I remember his yarmulke—a black spot centered on his scalp like a pupil.

For the first decade of my life, my father's Judaism was incidental. But when I was eleven years old, he quit his job as an insurance litigator, became a high school history teacher, got involved with the Lubavitcher Chasids, and started spending time at the Chabad House. Without explanation, he hung a framed photograph of the Lubavitcher rabbi in our living room. He began running errands for the rabbi. He cleaned the rabbi's car. He bought tefillin and wrapped it around his arm every morning when he woke up.

Other things did not change. For example, although he frequently invited me to the Chabad House, he never forced me to go. He chose to ignore the kosher laws and continued to eat bacon double cheeseburgers and popcorn shrimp. To me, his system of practicing Judaism seemed a nonsensical combination of stringent and dismissive, a vaguely annoying hobby that had little to do with me.

But now I sensed, without much evidence, a connection between his yarmulke and the way he spoke to Mikey. "Where do you see yourself in ten years?" he asked.

"Dad!" I said.

"See myself?"

"Yes. What's your ten-year plan?"

Mikey shifted in his seat, inching closer to me. "Well, I don't know." He looked at my face. "I guess I'll be doing what I'm doing now."

"Which is?"

"Comedy?"

"Comedy. Ah." My father swirled the ice in his glass, having managed, somehow, in the space of a second, to make "comedy" sound absurd, effete, as if Mikey had said, "In ten years, I plan to be dancing and spinning in a meadow."

"Well, I'm a comedian," Mikey said unhelpfully.

I looked at Mikey, whom I had up until this moment considered the embodiment of masculinity, the most attractive man I was sure I'd ever meet. Why had I never noticed how unkempt his thick black hair was? Who went to dinner with his new girlfriend's parents without taking the time to comb his hair? Were his *fingernails* dirty? And why did he always look in restaurants as if he didn't know how to be comfortable in restaurants, as if civilized life were beneath him, as if he'd been born to dine on garlic knots from Brooklyn pizzerias?

I looked at my mother, who was, as usual, tiny beside my father. I looked at our matching meals: sashimi, garden greens, no dressing. Why couldn't she stick up for me? Why couldn't she say, "Alan, leave the kids alone"? Why couldn't she change the subject?

The next night, against my better judgment, I took my parents to one of Mikey's shows. By then, I'd seen Mikey perform five or six times, so I was aware that, like any new comic, sometimes he wooed the crowd, and sometimes he left them cold. But back then, I could still sit in the audience and feel an ache between my legs just from watching his hand grip the microphone. I wanted to show him off.

That night, his audience was filled with drunk people who wouldn't pay attention. He couldn't contain the heckler in the front row. He tripped over his words. One by one, his jokes fell flat.

The next morning, when I met my parents at a diner before they left the city, my father said, "Gray, if I ask you a question, will you promise to answer honestly?"

"I guess."

"The picture in our house of the rabbi . . . you remember it?"

"Yeah. Why?"

"Have you ever dreamt about him?"

"Huh?"

"Alan . . . " my mother said.

"Sometimes he appears to young women," my father said, "in their dreams."

"Gross," I said.

"When they're about to make the mistake of marrying out of the faith."

I looked to the front of the diner, to the door and the sunlight on it. It was a beautiful day. A man climbed up from underground, his arms full of swollen trash bags. I felt how heavy they were. I looked back at my father. "Is this a joke? Are you joking?"

"Gray," he said, "we do not approve."

My mother, hunched in the corner of the booth in a purple tracksuit, blew daintily into her white mug of tea and didn't look up.

"I love him," I said, and I felt a little jolt in my chest. I had never told Mikey that I loved him. We hadn't known each other long. But suddenly, it seemed urgent that my father understand: "I love him," I said, with more energy this time, and in repeating it, I was making it true, making a fortress of Mikey and me that my father couldn't penetrate.

My father cut into his omelet. Cheese oozed out in a sickening, oily spurt. "You'll want children, won't you? Then what? Who will support them?"

"What is this, the 1950s?" I said, but I could hear my voice break, feel my throat tightening. I brushed away tears, filled with shame. "I love him," I said again, and this time it felt like a fact. I hated my father. I loved Mikey. Nothing had ever been clearer. "He loves me." Stupidly, helplessly, I added, "We love each other." I pushed my untouched breakfast away, scrambled egg whites and vegetables that shone menacingly with grease.

"Look. Gray." My father wiped the corners of his mouth with his napkin and leaned toward me. "There are many people . . . artists . . . who want to make it, but don't. Not everyone makes it."

"People can't just give up on their dreams," I said.

It was perversely gratifying, getting behind these clichés. No one could stop *me* from loving and dreaming.

"In real life," my father said, spearing a few hash browns with his fork, "*most* people have to give up on their dreams. Do you know how competitive stand-up comedy is? He's no Lenny Bruce. He's no George Carlin. And what are *you* going to do, spend your life lolling around in seamy comedy clubs?"

"Guess so," I said. "We'll even *live* in comedy clubs, because we'll be too poor to pay rent. One day, we'll raise our children in them."

"Now, Gray," my mother said, but my father cut her off.

"You might think you don't care about money," he said, "but you will. Eventually, everyone cares about money."

"You gave up law to pursue *your* dream!" I said. "And it's not like Mom's slaving away at some corporate job."

My mother worked as a floral designer, her slim fingers cutting tulip stems at an angle, accenting bouquets of white roses with hyacinth.

"We're not rich," my father said slowly, "but my salary is steady. I always put food on the table."

"So what are you suggesting? Should Mikey be just like you? I'm sure a steady salary has made you blissfully happy."

My father jerked back like I'd spit in his eye. The strange thing was, until that moment, I'd never thought much about my father's happiness. He laughed a lot. But he often made mean jokes at the expense of others. He often aimed to make people feel as if his life were more fulfilling than theirs. I looked at his belly inside his button-down shirt. It strained against the plastic buttons and touched the metal edging of the table. I understood, uncomfortably and suddenly, that my father was unhappy. And at the same time, I realized that I must have known for years. How else would I have been able to say what I'd just said? You don't always realize it until you're under attack: You are intimately acquainted with your loved ones' weak spots.

My father's lips tightened into a knot. He huffed heavy breaths through his nose. When he opened his mouth, I thought he was going to yell. But instead, his voice was measured. "Mikey isn't Jewish."

"So?"

He stared at me, narrowing his eyes, blurring me into nothing. I stared back. I didn't speak. And that was when he exploded.

DIANA SPECHLER

"What the hell is the *matter* with you, Gray? *'So?'* Are you a *child? That's* all you have to say? *'So?'*" He paused, panting, and gripped the edge of the table with both hands. "Do you know the first *thing* about Judaism? How your people have *suffered? Do* you? Answer me! You don't have any idea about anything!" he shouted.

I could feel strangers' heads all around us, swiveling. My father would have loved for me to pound my fists on my plate, upsetting the silverware; to scream until my lungs ached; to kick him under the table. So I didn't react. I sat motionless. All I could feel was my heart, buried deep inside me, panicked.

My father's breathing sounded labored. Finally, he leaned back in the booth, spent, balled up his napkin, and threw it on his plate. "I should have done better," he said, shaking his head. "I gave you too much leeway. You should have been wearing long skirts. I should have started years ago making *shidduch* for you."

"I'm out of here," I said, sliding out of the booth.

My mother said, "Gray, don't go. Let's talk."

"You haven't said a word," I said. "I'm done talking."

I left my parents in the diner. I thought, *Mikey will make it as a comedian.* I thought, *I am about to change my life.*

I never told Mikey about that fight, but I didn't have to. He knew he'd bombed—onstage and in person—with his girl-friend's parents.

Back then, he was getting only three or four spots a week, many of which were open mics. Humiliatingly, open mics cost him five dollars a pop. For his other spots, he was forced to "bark," selling tickets in the street for several hours before a show to earn seven minutes of stage time. It was a thankless and demoralizing cycle: "Until I get good,

I won't get work. But if no one will give me work now, if I can't even get onstage to practice, how am I supposed to get good?"

He studied comedians on HBO. He sat in the back of the Comedy Cellar and watched the regulars perform under the low ceiling that made them look larger than life. "Gray," he would say, "these guys have been doing comedy for twenty-five years. I *can't* wait twenty-five years for a break." He chain-smoked. He angrily tended bar on the day shift. He gripped his pen like a weapon and wrote vitriolic jokes. Sometimes he would say to me, "Tell me if you think this is funny." He would run the heel of his hand up the spine of his open notebook and read to me from its pages.

Sometimes I thought his ideas were funny; other times, I worried. He wrote one joke, for instance, about his girlfriend having too many pairs of shoes. How could he not know that was a cliché? And if he didn't know, didn't that mean he was, like my father had predicted, never going to make it? And if he never made it, would I one day have to tell my father, "You were right. Mikey didn't make it. And like you warned, I now want money and a baby"?

"I don't think that's so funny," I said about the shoes.

Mikey's face crumpled a little, but then he sighed. "You're right. It's hack." We were on the 6 train, heading to one of his "bringer" shows—a racket even more degrading than a standard open mic, requiring comics to contribute seven friends to the audience in exchange for five minutes of stage time. The subway was crowded. All around us, people sat staring blankly at the floor or reading the same best-sellers. We stood, sharing a pole, gazing at each other. "I think I just wanted to write something about you. I missed you today when you were at work."

I leaned my face on his chest and smiled into his T-shirt. Even when Mikey couldn't make me laugh, he could usually make me smile. I thought of my cubicle at the advertising firm where I spent my days crunching numbers, of the tiny letters spelling GO FUCK YOURSELF STRAIGHT TO HELL that some previous inhabitant had scratched into the wood. I looked up at Mikey. "What if I barked *for* you? I could sell tickets in the street."

"I can't ask you to do that, Gray. No." Mikey tucked my hair behind my ear.

"You didn't ask."

"No girl of mine is going to work in the street."

"Oh, please," I said. "Don't repress me."

I made a deal with the owner of Big Apple Comedy Club: For each ticket I sold, I would get a cut of the price and Mikey would get stage time. I started barking on Saturday and Sunday afternoons. At the same time, Mikey was barking for shows at other clubs. We started doubling his weekend spots.

"Let me run a few shows a week," I told the club owner. "Give me the nights you aren't filling up. I'll sell every seat in the club."

I started approaching other clubs. "Let me run your Friday night early show . . . Let me run your Sunday night show . . . Let me run all three of your Saturday shows."

Within six months, I was able to quit my office job, which my father's friend had given me. By then, I was running three shows a night—twenty-one shows a week at clubs all over the city. Mikey was performing in all of them. I traded, too: I would book a comedian who ran another show if he would book Mikey on one of his shows.

Within a couple of years, Mikey could hold his own at Caroline's, at Gotham, at Comic Strip Live. He could work a crowd with perfect reflexes. His size became his niche, and he took a stage name: Big Mike. And then came a starring role in a potato chip commercial. A brief appearance on HBO. A less brief appearance on Comedy Central. The Montreal Comedy Festival. He quit bartending. He passed his audition at the Comedy Cellar. And gradually, the clubs I was booking started paying him the way they were paying comedians who had been in the circuit for ten years. Colleges started booking him. Corporate parties. Even a few casinos. He bought a used car for all the road work. He was making it as a comedian.

Two years had passed since I'd seen my father. He had long since stopped calling, but my mother still tried to run interventions.

"He misses you," she would call to say.

"He can let me know when he's ready to change."

"People don't change, sweetie. You're asking too much."

And then a third year passed. Three whole years I withheld myself from him.

Until two weeks before my twenty-sixth birthday, when he called me and I answered.

"Come home," he said. He sounded older than I remembered. "Won't you please come home?"

My father died on my twenty-sixth birthday in the parking lot of Morgan Rye's Steak House. It was June. The sun had only just begun to set. I'll never forget how the sky was bleeding—messy red-pink smears across the wide blue face of twilight.

Nearby, an old woman stood caged in a walker. A child holding a shiny balloon asked, "What's more important, the clouds or the trees?" Overhead, an airplane moaned in exertion. A woman yelled, "Dang it! I forgot my doggie bag!" And the last sound that came from my father was a sigh. It sounded like other sighs—the one he'd released after finishing his steak, the one he'd always heaved upon sitting in his armchair, his first-sip-of-scotch sigh, his that's-some-good-jazz sigh. Often, when I think of that night, I remember my father, sighing.

SEVEN

Three weeks after the funeral, just before I headed back to New York, my mother told me that my father had left me in charge of his will. "We all know I'm no good with that stuff. You, on the other hand . . ."

"This makes no sense," I said. "I suck at finances."

"You do not. You're a whiz with organization. Practical matters."

"I don't feel like dealing with practical matters."

"I know," my mother said. "I don't want to do anything. I want to crawl into a hole."

So did I. I wanted to lie in a wooden box and be lowered into a hole. In between my sleepless nights, I was filling my days with food. Already, my pants were leaving indentations on my waist, the sides of my bras were bulging, and my cheeks looked vaguely inflated. Hunger felt so much like panic, and fullness like despair.

I did not make an appointment with Saul Weiss, the fiduciary of my father's will. Instead I went back to New York and made silent deals with my father: *If you switch off my appetite, I will stop booking comedy clubs. I will tithe to Jewish charities. I will wear long skirts. I will leave Mikey. Please. Please. Please.*

But he only laughed and laughed—a deep, echoing, dead-person laugh—and turned up the volume on my hunger.

I shut down my business anyway. Laughter sounded dark and desperate; I no longer wished to sell it. A friend got me a job tending bar on the Lower East Side, at Little Mermaid Grill, land of the maritime kitsch wall decorations, of the clam rolls and fish-and-chips and popcorn shrimp (the greasy, fetid aromas of which seeped into my hair, soaked my clothing, followed me home); where I had to wear an androgynous blue polo shirt like a cabana boy, where the weekend crowd consisted of loud, hair-gelled Jersey guys who demanded Jägerbombs, and whose girlfriends wore stilettos that matched their dresses and ordered Malibu Bay Breezes or Vodka Red Bulls.

At Little Mermaid, I indulged in self-pity, silently narrating my life in the third person, past tense: *This was the night a man from Long Island reached across the bar and grabbed for her breast.*

This was the shift that was so slow, she sat in the alley on an overturned bucket, smoking the fry cook's Parliament Lights.

Were she to die just before a Friday rush, Little Mermaid would have to close for the evening.

This was the month she split the seams on two pairs of pants.

I ignored the voice mails that clogged my cell phone—comedians who hadn't heard the news, creditors after my father's money, daily warnings from Saul Weiss.

I had no energy for any of it. I had energy only for food: egg rolls that burned the roof of my mouth, pizza with crusts that scraped my throat, Cheetos that left indelible stains on my hands, and nameless birthday cakes from the bakery counter. At a friend's apartment one day, catching sight of her bottle of prescription muscle relaxers, I shoved my hands into my pockets to keep from grabbing it, tipping my head back, opening my mouth, and bingeing.

Six months passed like this. It occurred to me that I should ask for help, that I should sit down with someone who cared about me and confess what I'd done to my father, confess that I couldn't stop eating. I knew I had a problem. Happy people didn't spend their days eating; they ate when their bodies required it.

But bingeing on food is not like binge drinking. I was not the sad, mysterious girl at the bar. I had no stories about waking up in a duck pond or making a ruckus with a tambourine. I was no skinny, tortured smoker, wearing a nicotine patch like a badge on my arm. There is no sexiness in a family-size bag of Bugles, no trophy for speed-eating fettuccine Alfredo, or for missing, day after day, the *ding-ding-ding* in the brain that says "full."

In the apartment, I would wait until Mikey was gone before running down to the corner bodega. Or I would order Chinese delivery—so many menu items, the bag would arrive with three sets of chopsticks, as if I were having a dinner party. I would make pasta and cover it in cheese. I would buy jumbo-size packages of Chips Ahoy! cookies, two for the price of one. I would eat the second package of Chips Ahoy! cookies. I began to recognize other bingers. Their clothes were ill-fitting. Their foreheads looked worried. In the snack aisle of Duane Reade, among the processed, chemical-filled, cheerily wrapped food-like things, we avoided one another's eyes.

It occurred to me that my father had had secrets, too.

• • •

In mid-December, my mother called me. "You didn't take care of the will! You said you did. Months ago! Saul just called me. Who do you think has to bail you out if you get hauled off to jail? You want to put me through that? You want to burden Mikey?"

I made the call to Saul Weiss, an old law school friend of my father's.

"I know this is unpleasant," he said, "but other people are waiting for your father's money. You need to—"

"Who?"

"Well, for one thing, your father left a trust for a woman in Virginia."

Such a funny word—"trust."

"Why?"

"I don't know. I really don't . . . I could guess. But . . ."

"Does my mom know about this?"

"I'm not sure."

I closed my eyes, the phone pressed to my ear, and asked Saul for a name.

EIGHT

A small gift—that the woman receiving my father's money was Azalea Bellham; it took seconds to learn from the Internet that she was a social worker and therapist in Bridger Heights, Virginia. Her shoddy website displayed her head shot—her mirthless smile, her 1980s hairdo (a thin gate of bangs with more bangs above them, blown back and sprayed). The home page said, "Sometimes reaching out is the most difficult step to recovery. Call me." The website linked to her blog, which, for the next six months, I would refresh on my computer screen seventy times a day: Tales of a Single Mother.

The first post I read was called *When Life Throws You Lemons, Make Lemon Meringue Pie Cupcakes: A Recipe Even Your Teenager Will Love!* A handful of readers left comments like, "I tried this recipe with white chocolate sprinkles. Perfect refreshing dessert after a lazy summer barbecue!"

Azalea wrote in a vague way about raising children, spouting clichés as if she'd learned about child rearing from bad sitcoms ("Do you ever get the feeling that your child has gotten too smart? LOL!"), but she never mentioned her own child.

Until, one day, she did.

I was reading comments on a post she'd written about children and the Internet. In response to a commenter's lament about her son's password-protected blog, Azalea wrote, "My teenager left her blog up on her screen last night. Who knew my kid has a blog??? Apparently she hated the grilled Hawaiian and hazelnut chicken I made for dinner! Fifteen-year-olds!"

Fifteen.

My heart jerked in my chest. Fifteen years ago was the period I'd always thought of as my father's midlife crisis—when he switched careers and began to pray.

I googled "grilled Hawaiian and hazelnut chicken." And I found Azalea's daughter. And I realized that when I was eleven, Azalea must have told my father that he had a second child.

Azalea Bellham's daughter didn't reveal her name on her blog, but I read her posts until I gathered enough information to narrow my Google search.

Eden.

On her blog, Chef Girl, Eden focused primarily on her cooking classes, on the recipes she was trying, on her dreams of becoming a chef and her opinions on various shows on the Food Network. But some posts were simply expressions of teen angst. She thought her mother was an idiot. She hated everyone in her high school. She hated girls who shopped at Anthropologie, who dyed their hair, who paid for French manicures. She hated boys who loved those girls. She knew that her real life would begin in culinary arts school and she wished the time would just hurry up and pass.

I clicked on her pictures over and over—Eden with her southern cooking class; Eden holding a baby; Eden alone at a desk, alone on brick steps wearing a sweatshirt with a hood, alone on a bed and in a car and in a Santa hat.

Eden's skin was dark. Her eyes disappeared into slits when she smiled for the camera. She had a thick stomach, fat arms, and skinny legs. She was fat on top and skinny on the bottom, her weight a virus that hadn't finished spreading.

Yes, I saw my father in her. He was in her forehead when she squinted at the sun, in her mouth when she half-smiled. He was everywhere in her body.

I stood and went to the kitchen. I had the apartment to myself and had just made lemon meringue pie cupcakes. Seeing them cooling on the counter, I felt my body grow fatter, as if a bicycle pump were inflating me. I carried the tin back to the computer and opened Eden's blog again. She had just posted something new.

I clicked on the link titled *Aspiring Chef Spends Summer Eating World's Worst Food*.

"My mom is making me go to fat camp. I hate her. She read an article that said kids with one parent are fatter than kids with two parents, especially if the one parent works, and that makes no sense because how can a parent with no husband not work? Where would money come from if my mom didn't work? And also is it my fault that I never met my father?"

I paused to reread that sentence.

"Is it my fault that my mom works? Is it my fault that diabetes runs in my family? No. So why do I have to go to fat camp???"

At the bottom of the post, a link: Camp Carolina, a brand new, revolutionary weight-loss camp for children.

I opened my eyes and looked down at my desk. I'd eaten the first three cupcakes so quickly, steam was still rising from the half-eaten fourth one. I shoved the rest of it into my mouth, then typed the Camp Carolina website into the address bar on my screen.

A skinny child holding a red hula hoop stared back at me. As I chewed and swallowed, I grabbed a fistful of my own thigh. *Step out of your "before" picture,* the caption said, *and into your "after."*

Before reading that, I'd never been sure that the dead could communicate with the living. But my father had handed me his will, handed me his secret. And now here he was, speaking: If I wanted to recover, I'd have to confess to my sister. Sisters wore the same winter coats. They sat side by side in the back of the station wagon. They fought over the hairbrush. But our father thought there was still time for us. Who else could forgive me for taking his life? If she absolved me, he would, too.

I looked down at the muffin tin, the rows of empty holes. My father stood behind me, casting his shadow. I would have known him anywhere. Of course he'd hated Mikey. Not because Mikey wasn't Jewish, but because he was my boyfriend. He had already lost one daughter. He'd been afraid of losing me, too. He rested his hands on my shoulders, his chin on the top of my head. I felt the weight of my father, compounding the weight of me.

Part II | **Surrendering**

NINE

Before the campers arrived, Lewis gave the counselors a tour of the kitchen. "Meet the kitchen ladies," he said, holding his arm out to three women in hairnets. We waited for him to tell us their names, but he didn't, and they didn't seem to care. They leaned on the stainless-steel countertops, wearing white aprons and bright blue eyeliner. They each looked in need of a cigarette. One wore a gold necklace with a *#1 Mom* charm.

"The kitchen ladies have a very important job," Lewis said.

They watched him with empty faces.

"Making sure the kids get only what they need. One man can't do everything." Lewis jabbed a thumb at his fleshy chest. "We're all working together. As a team. Fixing the problem."

One of the kitchen ladies picked her teeth with a long finger-nail. "Some high-class problem," she said. She was scrawny and hunched. Her voice was gravelly, her North Carolina accent so thick, her lips barely moved when she spoke.

My stomach muscles ached from my high-class problem—my urgent gorging on lo mein and cream puffs. I longed to step into the kitchen lady's body, to become a woman who ate food slowly just three times a day, sometimes forgetting half of her pastry, thoughtlessly holding a forkful of rice while she finished telling a story.

"Here's the fridge," Lewis said, opening a metal door. He parted the plastic strips that hung like vines. A gust of cool air hit our faces. He closed the fridge and pointed to another door. "Here's the dry storage, where we keep our canned goods." Then he flung his arms wide. "And there's a stove, and there are cupboards, and look: pots, pans, Pam spray, spatulas. You have access to this kitchen," he said. "But if you're doing my program, you must be very careful. If you're surrendering to my program, I suggest you never enter this kitchen at all."

TEN

The campers arrived like a storm. They wore cropped halters that gave way to thick white rings of stomach, tube tops, miniskirts, and skintight jeans. They had the stretch marks and loose skin of the elderly. They flapped and jiggled and wrapped their arms around their middles. They had neon hair and acne. They had rows of tiny metallic rings running from their earlobes to the tops of their ears.

The parents who dropped them off were fat. The fathers had sweat stains in the armpits of their T-shirts, mirrored sunglasses, and guts. The mothers wore stretch pants and tunics, voluminous sundresses with orthopedic shoes. And then there were the parents who weren't fat: mothers who were gracefully slender, dressed in trim cigarette pants and fitted sleeveless blouses; their cool, manicured hands steering their children by the napes of their necks, as if to say, *Here we are, just where I've always thought you should be!*

Sheena and I had five campers between the ages of fifteen and seventeen. Since our hall had eight rooms, our campers were the only ones who didn't have roommates. Although it was a privilege borne purely of logistics (our group was the smallest; each of the other five groups was roughly twice the size of ours), Lewis wished to be extolled for it.

"Lewis Teller's luxury hotel," he said to me, clapping my shoulder. "Don't say I don't take care of you!"

There was Spider, whose skin was dry and pink and diseased, who had a habit of crossing her arms to scratch at her rough, flaky elbows. Although she didn't look the least bit Japanese, her T-shirt displayed a Japanese flag and was tucked into pleated shorts.

"I want to make sure you understand," her father told me, "that Spider's allergies can kill her." He handed me a computer printout list of seventeen items titled "Spider's Allergies and Intolerances."

"Does Nurse have a copy of this?" I asked. "Does Lewis?"

"You bet." He wasn't much taller than I, and he stood close, staring into my eyes as if to inject something into them. "But I want you to have one, too."

"One time my ears got all fat and hot after I ate birthday cake," Spider told me. "Remember that, Dad?"

Spider's father turned from me to make Spider's bed. "I do," he said. "I'll never forget it."

I flinched when he snapped the top sheet open; it floated to the mattress like a shroud.

There was one unfortunately named girl: Harriet, who was hairy. She and her parents stood in a cluster, communicating inaudibly. They moved as a unit. They looked like triplets. They hugged good-bye in a circle.

And then there was Miss, short for Mississippi, who

had beautiful, creamy blond, hair-commercial hair and an angry white freckled face. Her mother and father looked nervous, more like personal assistants than parents, their arms weighed down with Miss's belongings—an enormous stuffed panther; a hand mirror that looked to be framed in sterling silver, with Miss's initials sharply engraved on the handle. "We want Miss to be *comfortable*," Miss's father said. "Miss is very special." He put an arm around his wife's shoulders.

"You're going to make everyone think I have a dick," Miss said.

And there was Whitney, who was black and tough, her skin the brown of expensive oak furniture. Whitney was at Camp Carolina partly because she was shapeless—no waist, no neck, no discernible ankles—and partly because she was from the Florida Panhandle, where a hurricane had swallowed her home. Now her family lived with relatives—nine people in a three-bedroom house.

"We thought we'd give Whitney a change of scenery," her mother whispered to me. She held my elbow when she said it. "She has a touch of PTSD."

"Who doesn't?" I said, cheerful as ever, but I stepped away a little. We stood together in Whitney's doorway, watching her talk on her cell phone and unpack her bag. "I'd like to see the Panhandle sometime," I said.

"Really, doll?"

"I wouldn't mind a warmer winter," I said.

I didn't care about the Panhandle. I didn't care about Whitney. I didn't care about itchy, allergic Spider; or Miss, who would bite like a rabid dog; or Paleolithic Harriet, who might have been carrying a club, who kept her eyes down and spoke in grunts.

All morning, I'd been watching the stairwell at the end of the hallway, waiting for Eden Bellham to appear.

Whitney's mother sighed, her eyes on her daughter. "You wait until we get back on our feet," she told me. "Then when we're all set up in a new house, you'll come down and stay with us." She started to swallow rapidly, like something was stuck. "Whitney, get off the phone, would you? Say good-bye to your old mother."

Before the parents had even left, before the last of the campers had arrived, Whitney stood in the hallway and made a speech. "I don't like females," she boomed, raising her index finger like a politician. "I don't like females in my space, and I don't like female issues. The problem with females," she said, setting her fists on her hips, "is hormones." Her forehead furrowed. She barely had eyebrows, but the wisps of them met above her nose. "Please keep your hormones out of my hair." We all looked at her hair. It appeared to be chemically straightened, her ponytail secured by yellow plastic balls.

"Are you a misogynist?" Spider asked Whitney.

"What's a misogynist?"

"It means you're sexist against women."

"I'm a feminist."

"You can't be a feminist."

"Says who?"

"Says me. Because you're a misogynist."

"What is this chick's *problem*?"

"I was named after a feminist," Spider said.

Miss turned to Spider. "You were named after a bug."

"Spiders are air-breathing Chelicerate Arthropods."

Miss returned her focus to Whitney, and the two of them engaged in a telepathic exchange, like a pitcher and a catcher, Whitney squinting, Miss nodding, tightening her ponytail,

DIANA SPECHLER

scratching her chin. And then Whitney reached for Miss's freckled white hand, and the two of them marched into Whitney's room, closing the door behind them. That was how they would spend most of the summer: together, locking everyone out.

Eden was the last to arrive. Until she did, I didn't quite believe she'd show up. Until I saw the touchable pieces of her—tangles in her hair, brown concealer on her pimples, silver hoop earrings—I didn't quite believe I was going to spend my summer at a weight-loss camp.

ELEVEN

Eden and I had the same bathing suit. After the campers' first dinner, I watched Lewis take her "before" picture in the canteen. She stood where I had stood a few days earlier, wearing that brown U-back one-piece, her hair tangled and falling to her elbows, her skin dark and acne-pocked, her arms crossed over her stomach. How could I have missed them in pictures—the dark, twinkly eyes that had once belonged to my father?

That morning, when Eden had arrived with Azalea, I'd hurried down the hall to hide in the bathroom, leaving Sheena to show Eden to her room. But first, I got a good look. Eden was twice Azalea's size. Azalea was as small as my mother, her hair carefully frosted and coiffed, her eyes an anemic green. It had never been a secret that my father liked his women thin.

"Of course he has the kids weigh in *after* dinner," Sheena said now into my ear. "They'll be at their highest weights. Just watch, on the last day of camp, he'll weigh them in before breakfast. Then it'll look like everyone lost more, and Lewis will be like, 'It's my *program*! It's because everyone *surrendered* to *my program*!'"

"I didn't even think of that."

"Girl!" Sheena jammed an elbow into my ribs. "What, do you *trust* everyone?"

"Uncross your arms," Lewis told Eden.

Eden held her arms away from her body.

Before coming to camp, I'd bought that bathing suit, my first one-piece, because in a bikini, I felt too exposed, my love handles bulging like soft white frog throats.

But first, I had agonized. To donate one's bikini to Goodwill was to relax into a life of obesity, to set off on the road to a bathing suit with a skirt, and then to a sarong over a bathing suit with a skirt, and then to something terry cloth with a zipper. Waving good-bye to my bikini-wearing days meant I'd soon be nothing but crumpled flesh and cellulite, varicose veins and Birkenstocks, waddling down a beach in an XXL cover-up printed with a sexy, skinny girl in a bikini.

"Basically all of my friends are black," Eden was saying, apropos of God knows what. "Either black or Latino. Minorities. I just really click with minorities." Her eyes were on Whitney, who was leaning an elbow on the bar, talking quietly with Miss. Of all the girls, Whitney was the prettiest—the pink of her full lips striking against her dark skin, the gap between her two front teeth not a flaw, but a mark of her beauty. She was tall, her fat distributed evenly, so that unlike some of the other girls (Miss, for instance, whose sickly white ass and thighs spread endlessly in either direction), weight loss would have left her well shaped. I could picture her skinny—statuesque like a runway model.

Whitney and Miss glanced at Eden, then looked back at each other, widening their eyes, tightening their lips around their laughter.

"Everyone thinks I'm Puerto Rican," Eden was saying, as Nurse measured one of her arms. "God, I don't even know why I'm here! I shouldn't be here. My mother made me come because we have a family history of diabetes and heart problems."

My breath snagged in my chest.

Sheena whispered, "She's crazy as a peach orchard bore."

I touched my heart to still it. "It's the first day. It's awkward. She wants to be liked."

"Everyone wants to be liked. That girl's deranged."

I watched Eden. A gold six-pointed star hung from a chain around her neck. I wondered what she knew. For the first time ever, I wished I'd let my father drag me to the Chabad House. I wished I had some knowledge that I could pass along to Eden. Instead, most of my knowledge of Judaism came from dumb things like Bar Mitzvah parties.

Grab my waist, Eden. This is how Jews do the conga.

When Lewis finished taking her picture, Eden wrapped a towel around herself, hiding the star, hiding her unwieldy torso, her scrawny legs. All at once, I felt a surge of hope.

My sister and I were going to be skinny.

Already, we had, at different times, in different states, walked into J.Crew, tried on the same bathing suit without removing our socks, turned this way and that before unflattering mirrors, picked our wedgies, shrugged our shoulders, and drawn identical conclusions.

TWELVE

Toward the end of the day, the worst I had was a mild headache. A small pang of hunger. Or . . . not hunger. A longing to eat. But the longing was contained—the flame of a cigarette lighter. I hoped that in a structured environment, where people were feeding me, controlling my portions, counting my calories, I could, as Lewis liked to say, surrender to the program.

That morning, breakfast had been microwaved waffles, two per person, with low-calorie syrup. A box of cereal. Low-fat yogurt. Lunch had been English muffin pizza, and dinner dry chicken and green beans. All summer, every lunch and dinner would include unlimited trips to the salad bar (but only one serving of fat-free dressing) and a cup of sugar-free, fat-free Jell-O, Lewis's favorite treat.

I could do this.

It wasn't until nighttime that I felt the familiar pull of food. Maybe it was because the kids were asleep, so I had no access to Eden. Or maybe it was because the off-duty counselors (one-half of the staff would be on duty every other night, the other half on alternate nights) gathered on the steps that led to the cafeteria.

No one wanted to say it first: "Let's raid the kitchen." We weren't campers. We should have had self-restraint. If anyone, I could have said it: "I'm going to get a snack." After all, although I was toting around fifteen more pounds than I would have liked, the other counselors were Fat. Their necks looked like stacks of doughnuts. The rolls of their stomachs were both horizontal and vertical. Their thighs were so large, their legs appeared to turn out below the knee, creating an arrowhead of space between their calves.

But if I couldn't make it even a day, if the program failed me (or rather, if I failed at the program), if I entered the kitchen, seeking out the hidden key that would unlock the dry storage room, if I couldn't stop eating the way I'd been eating, I would have no choice but to do the one thing that I knew would make me stop.

But how? Tap Eden's shoulder and say, "Guess who I am? Guess what I did?" We needed time to get acquainted. I wanted her to like me. I had to try to "surrender." So I said nothing to the other counselors. But as I recalled images from the kitchen tour—the wide metal refrigerator door, the cardboard boxes of 100-calorie snacks stacked against the wall—I kept losing track of the conversation.

When I tuned back in, I heard a counselor named Brendan say, "I was so high, I saw a whole village in a fountain." He chuckled, covering his face and glasses with his hands. "If they'd invited me in, I would have gone."

Brendan attended college. I knew this because his entire wardrobe consisted of clothing that advertised North Carolina

State University—roomy basketball shorts, T-shirts that stuck to his sweaty skin. The day before, when Lewis had told the counselors that we would each have to teach a "specialty class," Brendan had volunteered to teach rock climbing on the climbing wall in the gym. "Fine," Lewis had said, without asking Brendan, "Are you qualified to teach rock climbing?" Perhaps he assumed that Brendan—who weighed three-hundred-plus pounds—would at least be able to hold down the belay rope.

"I have nothing to teach," I'd told Lewis.

Lewis had nodded. "Water aerobics."

KJ, another boys' counselor, had offered to lifeguard and to teach swimming lessons.

"Perfect!" Lewis had clapped his hands and rubbed them together. "A lifeguard!"

KJ had scratched the bridge of his nose in a way that said, *I am not, in fact, a lifeguard.* "I have really quick reflexes."

Sheena had volunteered to teach yoga, even though the extent of her familiarity with it was a yoga DVD she had memorized. "If you don't mind me teaching the same yoga poses all summer . . ."

Lewis didn't.

Mia, one of the counselors for the youngest girls, was dubbed "the nutritionist." Nutrition was her college major, but she was only twenty-one years old, not a nutritionist at all. Regardless, she would teach nutrition classes. "Not that they should listen to me!" she'd told Lewis, patting her soft stomach, her southern accent calling to mind tea parties, long white gloves, floral church dresses.

"I once got so high, I ate a whole box of Pop-Tarts!" she said now.

Mia's arms were so fat, she didn't have wrists—just creases separating hands from forearms. I felt a gulf between us. I had once eaten two boxes of Pop-Tarts sober, tearing one silver foil packet after another, not bothering with the toaster, feeling the sweet grains of sugar and cinnamon on my teeth.

My father had been different. He'd always eaten not as if he were running a race, but methodically, thoughtlessly, all day long, the way other people breathed.

Mia continued: "Don't start, any of y'all. I know a future nutritionist has no business eating Pop-Tarts. But it's my favorite breakfast. Can't help it." She pinched her own chubby cheek. "Evidently."

I never ate Pop-Tarts for breakfast. In the morning, I was always determined, waking to the thought, *Today, I'll get back on track.* Sometimes I would fast until noon. Often, I stayed in control until nighttime. It was always later in the day that things would fall apart.

As another counselor relayed a story about smoking a joint with a teacher, Bennett, the assistant director, appeared at the base of the steps.

"Lord, he's gorgeous," Mia muttered. It was what she said every time she saw Bennett.

Bennett was a personal trainer. He looked like a high school athlete, but with crow's feet like crackle glazing around his blue eyes. His body was built exclusively of muscle. He wore soccer shorts and T-shirts with the sleeves cut off, revealing the rolling hills of his triceps and biceps and a red heart tattoo on his upper right arm with a name inside: *Camille.* Looking at Bennett made me clench my hands into fists, not because I wanted to touch him—not exactly. I wanted to press my fingers to the glass that should have encased him.

He emerged from the dark as if he'd been cloaked in it. Someone said, "You scared me!"

And then my longing to eat was gone. In its place was the thought that Bennett could have found me in the kitchen, could have turned on a light and caught me eating as if someone were timing me. I'd been caught once before—some months earlier in an East Village diner. I had ordered three entrées, and had begun to eat from all three, when two girls I knew from college walked in, pointed at me from the doorway, and rushed to my table.

"Gray Lachmann!" they said together.

They wanted to catch up, to tell me who had married whom. I didn't invite them to sit. They kept glancing at the seat across from me, as if surely, at any moment, I'd no longer be alone.

I wrapped my arms around my stomach and looked away from Bennett. But then he sat beside me.

"Hey, Angeline."

I turned to him. "It's Gray." He smelled like summer and muscles. I looked at the simple curve of his ear. I told him again: "My name's Gray."

"I'm all brushed up on what your name is." Bennett leaned back on his elbows, his T-shirt stretching taut against the bulk of his chest. "What's everyone doing?"

Brendan said, "We're telling high stories."

"What are high stories?"

"Stories about getting high."

Bennett looked at me and grinned. I grinned back. In that moment, we were old together, sealed by the superiority of adulthood. Bennett had fourteen years on me. Forty-one, he had told me during staff training, laughing, as if it were preposterous that he, Bennett Milton, could have entered middle age.

"Angeline," he said, his arm so close to mine, I could feel the coarse blond hairs of it. "She rides in a long gray limousine. And she struts around New York City. I can just see you struttin' around New York City."

"I don't strut."

He bumped my arm with his. "It's a song."

"I think strutting requires high heels. I never wear high heels."

"That right?"

"New York City. We're always walking. I wear flip-flops." I lifted one of my feet to show him my black rubber flip-flop. My toenails needed a trim. A couple were jagged. I curled my toes to hide them. "If it's cold out, I wear sneakers."

"Sneakers? That what you Yanks call tennis shoes?"

I looked hard at Bennett, pleased with his means of communication—an amused, detached acceptance of anything I said. This was not a man who would bother to know my brain. If I told him, "I'm a murderer!" he would probably say, "Well, *are* you now." He probably loved baseball games. He probably played Frisbee. He probably liked to watch people walk by and note, "You know what I enjoy? People watching."

"What are you doing all the way down here anyway, Angeline?"

This was not lost on me: My hunger was gone. From the second Bennett appeared beside me, I'd felt no desire to eat. I smiled and thought, *Perhaps this is a sexy, mysterious smile.* But then I started to sense that Bennett was bored (after all, I had just held forth about footwear); that he had better things to do than watch me fashion a mysterious smile—beautiful people always had better things to do, didn't they?—that he was going to get up and walk away.

And so, to keep him beside me, I spoke. "I like to mix things up," I said. "Nothing wrong with a little change."

THIRTEEN

In the pool later that week, teaching my campers water aerobics, I finally wore a bikini, a red one I'd had for years. After just a few days on the program, I already felt bikini-worthy.

No, I'm not telling the whole truth: After just a few days on the program, surrounded by obese people, I felt confident that no one would balk at my love handles.

I shivered in the morning that was lit by a cloudless sky. Whitney the hurricane survivor, who had announced on the first day, "I don't do water," was in Nurse's office, sick with vague symptoms, so I was staring at four of my five campers, and they were staring back.

No, again, I'm not telling the whole truth: I was staring only at Eden, who was wearing our brown bathing suit.

"Hook your legs over the wall," I said. "Like you're going to do sit-ups." I paused. "Because you are."

Harriet raised her hand like a student. "Won't our faces go under?" Her hair was a dark, wiry puff, a silhouette of a bush. She was wearing her glasses, long black shorts, and a black T-shirt that billowed around her in the water like ink.

"Yes," I said. I hadn't thought about it. "So don't forget to regulate your breathing accordingly . . . Fifty crunches."

"Fifty?" Miss, in a turquoise tankini, made a visor for her eyes with one hand. Her yellow hair was pulled back into a fat braided ponytail, the tip grazing the water's surface.

Was it a good idea, the tankini? Granted, it covered the stomach without screaming to the world, "I know I'm not deserving of a two-piece!" But perhaps it revealed an ugly indecision; or an even more neurotic self-consciousness than a one-piece could reveal: *I am affecting an illusion of thinness.* Or *I am affecting an illusion of self-confidence.*

"I am *not* doing fifty crunches," Miss said.

"Twenty then," I said because Miss made me nervous. She had the enviable quality of self-possession. She could say nothing and hold eye contact, her thin lips disappearing. She could wait for the other person to look away first. She had an impressive assortment of condescending faces. Her few humane expressions were reserved for Whitney and Sheena.

"The sun's in my eyes," Spider said. "I could get a migraine. I'm prone to migraines."

Spider was prone to everything—hives, asthma, diarrhea, hay fever, eczema, belting out Japanese songs loudly and off-key. She had EpiPens, inhalers, Tums, and nasal sprays. She wore some of these antidotes on thin ropes around her neck, a shield of medicinal jewelry.

"Then keep your eyes shut," I said.

"This is *gay*," Miss whined.

Spider turned to her. "For your information, 'gay' is a misnomer. Unless you think water aerobics has a sexual preference."

I looked through the chain-link fence around the pool to the nearby grass, where Bennett was refereeing the boys' sumo wrestling class. Sumo wrestling was Lewis's invention, or else it was something he had learned at another camp (he'd worked at weight-loss camps all his life, he liked to brag). Campers wrestled wearing hollowed-out rubber tires around their waists while Bennett watched, holding a plastic whistle between his teeth. Whenever Bennett engaged in any activity—blowing a whistle, scratching his arm, dribbling a basketball—he looked as if he'd been built and groomed to do exactly that one thing.

I scanned my brain for hunger. Gone. Glimpsing Bennett was like mainlining speed. Couldn't I hire him just to stay close to me, paying him per week what I would otherwise spend on food?

"I wish Sheena taught this class," Miss told me. She was standing with her hands linked behind her head, watching the other girls as if they were doing sit-ups for her amusement, and they were failing her.

"Thanks," I said.

"Just being honest."

"Who asked you to be honest?"

"Are you, like, whipped on Bennett or something?"

"No," I said. "Please do your crunches."

"You keep looking at him."

"How do you know? I'm wearing sunglasses. Want to know what I'm looking at? I'm looking at everyone but you doing water aerobics."

"He's got, like, a twelve-pack. He's so hot."

I turned away from Miss. Eden's eyes were squeezed shut and wrinkled like peach pits, her mouth forming an O when she took in air, her black hair fanning out on the surface of the water whenever she stopped to catch her breath.

In one of my early memories, my father hurls me into a public pool. "It's the only way she'll learn to swim."

And I will always know how it feels to drown—sinking to a white floor with open eyes, the sound of my heart in my ears. Sure, he rescued me, but first he made me sink.

There was the red towel he wrapped me in, there was his fist squeezing water from my hair. "She's all right," he said. "My tough girl. Created in my image, this one." I coughed like I would cough forever. He patted my back and told me, "Your father will always save you."

"But what if you're not there?"

"Where would I be?"

"At work?"

"Then you'll close your eyes and think of me," he said, "and you'll know exactly what to do."

FOURTEEN

"You hate fat people," Lewis said that afternoon. He was sitting on the center of the couch in the library, which he called the rec hall. The couch was velour and floral with torn cushions. Lewis's arms were spread open across the back. His legs were open, too, giving us a spectacular view of the fat on his inner thighs from where we sat on the linoleum. Sheena was off teaching yoga to one of the boys' groups.

It had been quickly established that Sheena, not I, was the cool counselor, partly because she wasn't much older than the campers, but for other reasons, too. When Sheena laughed, she would collapse, draping her arms around whomever had been funny, rewarding him with the heat of her affection. She liked to be the boss of every activity. Everyone listened to her and followed her instructions.

Unlike Sheena, I had been grown up for too many years and was accustomed to working only with adults. I didn't know any

kids, except a few cousins whom I rarely saw. With my campers, whenever I spoke, I sounded like my mother. ("Isn't it just a
beautiful day?" "Look at those birds! Aren't they funny?")

"We *are* fat people," Harriet said, flipping through a book
she'd pulled from a dusty shelf.

"But you don't really believe that." Lewis plucked his T-shirt
from between two rolls of fat, then returned his arm to the back
of the couch. His armpits were sweating through his sleeves.

"No," Harriet said, "I'm pretty sure I believe it."

"No," Lewis said. "You don't."

Lewis was not necessarily combative, but opinions that
weren't his were immaterial things. Even if someone voiced
an opinion he shared, he was less likely to say, "You're right, I
agree," than to offer up a story about himself as proof that origi-
nally, he had authored that opinion. He would have liked to pat-
ent his opinions, especially the ones that contradicted his other
opinions. Add to that: His stories rarely made sense. He would
forget in the middle of the telling what his point was. And the
point usually became, *I am wonderful.*

In this vein, he scheduled each group once a week for Conversations with Lewis. It was group therapy, although Lewis wasn't
a therapist. Or a nutritionist. Or a doctor. In fact, he didn't have a
bachelor's degree, which he considered an extraordinary achieve-
ment. Lewis was immensely, ceaselessly impressed with his own
ability to don so many hats—shrink, genius, general world expert,
champion of myriad things—without ever having wasted pre-
cious time or money on something as worthless as an education.

"This summer," he said, "you'll write letters. This is one
of the things that makes my camp unique. This therapeutic,
letter-writing exercise. Letters to fat people. About why you
hate them."

Spider said, "I don't hate anyone."

"Everyone hates," Lewis said. "We are full of hate." His face brightened. "*Fat* with hate."

"If you hate people, that means you wish they were dead." Spider was fiddling with her EpiPen necklace. "Like Sasuke. She wants everyone dead."

"Who's Sasuke?" Harriet asked.

"An anime character who is full of hatred."

As if it weren't enough to have peeling skin, allergies, and terry-cloth wristbands; as if it weren't enough to love early mornings and to insist on frequently using sign language even though no one was deaf and no one knew sign language, Spider was passionate about Japanese anime. She sometimes used Japanese words, or at least words that she claimed were Japanese. At the first dinner, she had brought anime chopsticks to the cafeteria, but Lewis had confiscated them. "Mealtime is not a game," he had said.

Now Spider stuck her EpiPen into her mouth and sucked it like a pacifier.

Miss whispered, "Spider, keep sucking that thing. It's good practice for blow jobs." I was close enough to hear her, but I pretended I didn't. Miss tapped Spider's shoulder. "Since you're allergic to latex, you won't be able to have sex until you want to get pregnant. So you have lots of years of blow jobs ahead of you."

Whitney was kneeling behind Miss, holding Miss's hair in her fingers, twisting it into long, skinny braids. "Um, Miss?" Whitney said. "Ever heard of the Pill?"

Miss giggled, but stopped abruptly when Spider chimed back in: "Ever heard of abstinence? It's only the most effective form of birth control."

"My neighbors used to have this really angry dog," Whitney said. "It drooled white froth from its fangs and they would leave the thing tied up all day to a rail in their front yard. If you walked by, it would bark and try to pounce at you, but it couldn't because of its leash. And then one day it was doing that to some kids, trying to pounce, and its head popped off."

"No way!" Spider said.

Whitney finished a braid and tucked it behind Miss's ear. "That's what happens if you hold everything in. It's healthy to hate. You have to let out your aggression."

Lewis said, "You will let out your aggression with these letters. It's the first step to accepting your bodies."

"We're supposed to accept our bodies?" Spider said. "Isn't the point of this camp to lose weight?"

"I once got attacked by a dog," Eden said, and I wrapped a hand around my arm, as if sharp teeth had punctured my skin.

Whose dog? I wondered. *And then what happened?* But Eden was looking at Whitney, who was ignoring her. Eden was always looking at Whitney, and Whitney was always ignoring her. Eden pulled a strand of her own hair out to the side and started braiding it the way Whitney was braiding Miss's. She hadn't inherited our father's social deftness. She was the girl waiting to have her breasts autographed, the sycophant banging on the glass with both fists. She was not a misfit like Spider, who seemed as oblivious to her own social status as she was to her constant camel toe. She was not a misfit like Harriet, who was so unsightly—dressed in black, wearing wire-rimmed glasses that shrunk her eyes, her hair like steel wool, her body enormous, her odor pervasive, her skin furry—her whole existence was an apology.

Eden was cloying—loud and eager, or else sullenly quiet. She said all the wrong things. When she talked with Whitney, she tried to sound like someone from a rap video. Once I'd heard her call out, "Where my bitches at?" No one had replied. Sometimes she said, "S'up," and sliced the air with her hand. She favored a baseball cap sideways, long basketball shorts, and roomy tank tops. She listened to hip-hop at top volume and tried, unsuccessfully, to dance the way Whitney danced—spontaneously, frequently, and with remarkable skill. But when it came to dancing, Eden had no skill. All this and a Jewish star necklace.

I wondered which parts of her would have been different had she grown up with our father. Her name, for one thing. When my mother was pregnant with me (following years of attempts and eventual acceptance that she'd never have a baby), she suggested to my father, in a fit of passion, that they name me Silver, whether I was a boy or a girl. "It's the shiniest name I can think of," she said.

But my father was superstitious. "Silver is a thing to steal," he said. And so they settled on Gray. My father never would have agreed to Eden, a name that invoked perfection. I suspected that Azalea had chosen it to harm him.

I knew from Azalea's website that she'd gotten two master's degrees in Virginia, and from the dates, I'd inferred that she must have left Massachusetts while she was pregnant. Perhaps the affair had ended the way many do—the cheater returning to his wife, closing out his mistress as if she never existed, convincing himself that she never existed. Perhaps my father had vanished suddenly, leaving only a stray sock in the corner, a razor on the lip of her sink. Perhaps Azalea strained her ears day after day, listening for the phone. Perhaps morning after morning, she woke, blessedly blank for the first few seconds, before the memories of being discarded descended, so heavy on her body that she couldn't move from bed.

What I would have given for a recording of the phone call—Azalea telling my father, "I'm pregnant with your child," or, "I just gave birth to your child," or, "You don't want me to tell your wife about us? Then you'd better start paying up."

I did not blame Azalea Bellham. I could not resent her. I knew how it felt to simultaneously love and hate my father.

"These letters will set you free," Lewis said. "If we're all honest, we can admit that we feel, deep down, that we're not fat people. The fat people we are . . . they've invaded our bodies. They've taken over. Secretly, you believe that you're skinny." He paused. Then he asked, "Don't you believe that who you really are is the thin person locked up inside you?"

"No," Harriet said.

"Yes," said Lewis.

"I just don't care," Eden said, glancing at Whitney. "I don't care about any of this. My mom made me come here. I don't even overeat. I basically just chew gum all day and then have a healthy dinner. I'm not, like, one of those people who eats all the time. This camp is so pointless for me."

"So leave," Miss said.

"I probably will," Eden said.

Her words made my palms sweat. I knew about mothers and only daughters. If Eden complained that she hated it here, Azalea would drive down to get her.

"I'm a chef," Eden continued. "I should be cooking this summer, not starving myself. I know how to make healthy food. I'm not the type who's always cooking everything in butter."

"You're not a chef," Miss said. "That's so retarded." Her hair was now coiled into tiny Medusa twists all over her head. "You can't be a chef in high school."

"Why not?" I said.

"Because," said Miss.

"If Eden says she's a chef, she's a chef."

"No, but I see your point. I guess I'm not really a chef," Eden told Miss, who ignored her.

Lewis resumed as if no one had spoken. "You don't know this yet," he said, "but getting old feels the same way. You will never believe that you're old. You'll walk around picturing yourself young. Right, Gray?"

I moved my eyes from Eden to Lewis. "I'm not old."

"See?" Lewis said. "Every day you'll think that you might wake up and be eighteen, that you'll pop out of bed and do the things you used to be able to do. Then you'll catch a glimpse of yourself in a reflective store window. Or in someone's car mirror. And you'll be filled with uncontrollable hatred."

Spider said, "But hatred is—"

"And hatred makes everything worse. It makes you older, fatter, and uglier. It gives you back pain. It makes you do hurtful things to the people who love you."

I looked at Eden again, to see if she was listening. She was watching Whitney and chewing her lip.

"One day you'll have to let go," Lewis said. "Anger will not serve you."

FIFTEEN

Dear Fat People,
    Please get me out of this retarded, gay-ass camp.

                                                        Miss

Dear Quina, Chouji, and Don Corneo,
    Even though you're fat, you're three of the coolest anime characters. Quina, it's so cool that you can eat almost any kind of monster, and everyone thinks it's funny to call Chouji a fatass, but I bet they don't laugh so hard when he turns them into a giant meatball and flattens them, haha. Don Corneo is fat, but you know what? Every girl falls in love with him. So there!

                                                        Love,
                                                        Spider

Dear Fat People,

I wish you weren't all related to me and getting your genes all over me. I want my relatives to be swimsuit models.

Not yours,
Eden

Dear World,

What if everyone was blind? You wouldn't know who was fat and who wasn't. I learned on TV that if we were all blind, we would smell each other. Instead of hating on someone for having a double chin, we'd hate on him for smelling like butter. I used to know this kid who was really skinny, but he always smelled like butter, and everyone hated on him in real life and also would have hated on him if everyone was blind, but you know what? I didn't care what he smelled like or looked like. I don't care what anyone looks like, smells like, or even tastes like! (Kidding!) I think we were all created equal.

Whitney

Dear Fat People,

I don't have anything to say. I don't like writing when I'm on summer vacation.

Good-bye,
Harriet

Dear Fat People,

Now is the time to stop pointing fingers.

You cannot blame your fat on bad genes. Maybe you have a fat relative, but you do not have only fat relatives. And even if you do, that is no reason to give up and be fat. Remember: Had you been born in a different era, all of your relatives might have been racist, or claimed Earth to be as level as a ballroom floor, or watched you burn for being a witch. Anyway, do you really aspire to be just like your relatives?

You cannot blame your fat on your thyroid. Seriously. Stop it. You don't even know what a thyroid is. Thyroid problems are far less common than fat people want to admit.

You cannot blame your fat on your bad knees that keep you from exercising. If you exercised, you wouldn't have bad knees, because you would not have extra weight bearing down on them, making them, as you say, "bad."

You cannot fix fat with a fat-sucking vacuum, or with ultrasound vibrations or lasers, or with a surgery that shrinks your stomach to the size of a pearl. These are just Band-Aids, and Band-Aids fall off. You love food so much, love the pressure of it on your back molars, the richness of it on your tongue, the satisfaction of swallowing the messy, chewed-up ball of it, you will find a way to return to the eating you crave, and then the fat cells will find each other, and bind back together like long-lost lovers, and your stomach will pop its staples or snap its band, and inflate again like a beach ball. You don't believe that? Well, it's true. The way you got fat in the beginning is the way you will get fat again.

If you don't do something now, if you don't make honest and drastic changes, the way you got fat in the beginning will be the way you get fat all your life.

And please? Don't be proud of your fat. When you claim to be proud of something unseemly, the whole world knows that you're lying. You're acting proud instead of ashamed because some fat woman with a national platform gave a fat-pride pep talk into a microphone. Do not say, "I'm so much happier since I stopped trying to be skinny." Do not say, "I'm enjoying life!" when you're really enjoying high-calorie foods in appalling quantities.

Do not say, "America is flawed because women are expected to look like models." America is absolutely flawed, but only models are expected to look like models. Other women should simply avoid obesity to prevent diabetes, muscular problems, and congested arteries. And yes, women are expected to be attractive to men, but this is not an expectation to scorn. Please. You want to be attractive to men. You are not Camille Paglia. You are not Maya Angelou. You are not the kind of woman who roars.

Okay. There are men who like fat women. Fine. So? There are also men who like women to dress up as teddy bears. There are men who are turned on by balloons, by licking dirty bowling shoes, by the thought of becoming an amputee. There are men who get off on dragons having sex with cars.

Dragons. Having sex with cars.

You cannot blame your fat on your ethnic background. Granted, if you are Asian, you store more fat in your organs, but you also belong to a healthy culture. And don't blame your fat on your religion. Yes, 30 percent of Southern Baptists are obese, and the Mormons deploy "wellness missionaries," and sure, I know the Jewish jokes—the jokes with no edge; the soft, plump, low-muscle-tone jokes about Jewish mothers overfeeding their children and Jewish holidays revolving around food. But these are not excuses. Excuses are worthless. Either change your life, stop slinging blame, stop stuffing food into the cracks in your heart, or give yourself over to the shortened, uncomfortable, sweaty life of the obese.

SIXTEEN

A week into camp, Eden and I had exchanged thirty-six words. On my end:

"Cute sandals."

"Do you like that?"

"Do you, um, play any sports at your school?" (Why not? I was counting "um.")

On her end:

"All my friends have the same ones. We got them together."

"No."

"I could if I wanted to, but I don't."

Now it was Sunday. "Lazy Sunday!" according to Lewis, which was supposed to make everyone feel happy and indebted. Every Sunday would be Lazy Sunday, which meant no official wake-up time and no scheduled activities. The campers' only responsibility before 11:00 brunch was to wander into the cafeteria at their leisure so Lewis could weigh them. ("*I* do the weigh-ins," I'd heard him say, patting his chest. "*Me.*")

"You lost four pounds," Lewis told Eden.

From a nearby picnic table, where I was pretending to read a magazine, I looked up to see Lewis hand her an apple from a basket. After a week of such drastic diet change (controlled calories; no added salt; low-fat, low-sugar everything), some campers had lightened considerably, as if the pores in their skin were saltshaker holes. After weighing each camper, Lewis had loudly announced his or her progress— "Congratulations! You've lost thirteen pounds!"—and then beamed smugly, shifting his weight from foot to foot. He clapped each one on the back and asked, "Does my diet work or does my diet work?"

Never mind the thirty-minute speech he'd made during staff training about how the "program" was not a diet, that "diets" were unsustainable, ineffectual, whereas the "program" was a "way of life." Despite that speech, he often used the word "diet." Then he would switch back to "program." Then to "diet."

What was the program anyway? No one was exactly sure.

We knew the Monday-through-Saturday schedule. First, wake up and head to the cafeteria, where Bennett led stretches on the steps (bending to touch his toes so his calf muscles flexed, raising his arms over his head, inadvertently flashing his sculpted stomach). Then the campers had to make it around the loop, the half-mile dirt path that encircled the Carolina Academy campus. There were those who could jog it and those who could not. Some broke a sweat walking, and then sat down abruptly on a rock or on the ground, panting and sweating, complaining of "injuries." The campers loved injuries. They loved to say, "I can barely move my arm," or, "My hip might be broken." They loved to sit and scowl.

Next came breakfast, and after breakfast, the campers were supposed to clean their rooms. None did. My campers lounged on their beds, or crowded into one another's rooms and talked about their real lives, all implying to one another that at home they weren't fat.

After "cleanup," the whole camp met in the gym for Bennett's calisthenics class, which Lewis called "cals," during which Bennett led the campers in "wall sits," which made them look compellingly constipated, and "Indian runs," which Spider deemed a racial slur and renamed "international runs." Then the campers had two activities before lunch, and after lunch, "rest hour," another activity, and a snack (sugar-free ice cream, sugar-free Popsicles, a 100-calorie snack pack, or, on the very worst days, an apple). Then there was one last activity, and then free time, when everyone except hairy-Harriet-who-hated-hygiene showered. Then everyone ate dinner, enjoyed another hour of free time, an evening activity of Lewis's design, one more snack, and then bed. All told, the campers were engaging in roughly five hours of physical activity a day, and consuming eighteen hundred calories.

And that, as far as anyone could tell, was the program.

"That's it?" Eden asked, stepping off the scale. "Four pounds?"

"That's good," Nurse said. "Four in one week?" She plucked a sweaty-looking bandanna from a table and started fanning her face with it, blowing her silver bangs apart. "Lord, it's hotter than the back of a knee."

"But everyone else . . ."

"Water weight," Nurse said. "Next week, you won't see anyone losing fifteen pounds. Basically, everyone was pissing weight this week. You know what I'm saying?"

"I don't care," Eden said, "but my mom will think her money's gone to waste."

"Well," Nurse said, "if you don't have as much to lose . . ."

"I have plenty."

As I watched Eden push her feet into her flip-flops and wiggle her toes, I floated up and out of myself, as if she and Nurse were speaking metaphorically, their meaning slightly out of my reach. But they were just discussing Eden's body. So I could have chimed in, said something encouraging, something to win Eden's favor. *I'm sure your mother is proud of you!* Or, *Four pounds is a whole Chihuahua!* But every time I opened my mouth around Eden, I said something pointless. And why should that have surprised me? Avoiding the important subject always rendered all other conversations inane.

I sat silently, watching Eden, until the cafeteria door swung open, and all eyes in the room turned to Whitney, who paused grandly on the threshold before making her entrance. Holding her arms away from her hips and splaying her fingers, she planted one foot directly in front of the other like a starlet. Miss followed, wearing sunglasses and frowning. Kimmy, a camper from the intermediate group, trailed behind them, her hair pulled into two high pigtails, each braided and adorned with a pink ribbon.

Kimmy had freckles so even, so perfectly sprinkled across the center of her face, they looked manufactured. Sometimes she brought her teddy bear to breakfast. The evening before, I had heard Whitney, her elbow threaded through Miss's, tell Kimmy, "You're our daughter, okay?" and Kimmy had removed her thumb from her mouth just long enough to say, "Sure."

"Kimmy!" Lewis said, opening his arms.

Kimmy let him wrap her up in a hug, squishing her into his thick torso. Her cuteness was a source of universal joy.

"Who loves you?" he said.

"Ew," Miss said. "That's so pervy."

When she was free, Kimmy jammed her thumb back into her mouth, surveyed her surroundings, and locked her eyes on Eden. "*Nuh-uh!*" she squawked around the obstruction of her thumb. She poked the center of Eden's T-shirt with her free hand. "No *way!*"

Eden crossed her arms over her chest, over the navy blue block letters that spelled BRIDGER HIGH SCHOOL. I knew what she was thinking, and I agreed—cuteness was sinister. When I was a child, a puppy bit off part of my fingertip when I tried to touch its droopy ear.

Kimmy removed her thumb from her mouth and flashed the artificial smile of a birthday party clown. "*I'm* from Bridger!" she said, bouncing up and down on her toes, her braided pigtails bouncing as if they'd contracted her enthusiasm. "And my sister goes to Bridger High School! Do you know Lily Jackson?"

"No."

"Yes, you do!"

"No, I don't."

"You have to!"

"Why do I have to?" Eden's eyes darted around the cafeteria—to the door through which she could escape, the windows she could break, the tables beneath which she could hide.

Beside her, Whitney and Miss were arguing over who should weigh in first: "You go." "No, you!"

"Everyone knows her," Kimmy said.

"Obviously that's impossible."

Kimmy watched Eden's face as if she wished she had something more interesting to look at. "Everyone except you, then."

Eden started backing away. "Me and my friends don't notice anyone. We're, like, oblivious to random people." She scratched her nose as she headed toward the door. "I wouldn't notice your sister. Even if we had all the same classes."

"Okay." Kimmy looked increasingly bored, her thumb sagging between her lips, her eyes moving languidly around the room. Boredom was the trophy of the cool, inaccessible to kids like Eden, who were always alert, watching, copying, alive with the anxiety of constant performance. Eden's affectations of boredom—flying her eyelids at half-mast, kicking the ground with the toe of her shoe—were spoiled by her glimpses at Whitney, her mirroring of Whitney's mannerisms, her laughter that chimed in a beat too late.

Eden hurried toward the door, running a palm over the letters on her shirt, as if to erase them.

At Camp Carolina, everyone had secrets. Kids hid gum in the backs of their drawers (even sugarless gum was forbidden, since Lewis had labeled it an appetite stimulant). To their walls, above their plastic mattresses, they taped pictures that made them look carefree. They cut the size tags out of their clothes. They hid in Nurse's office—limping theatrically to the haven of air-conditioning and television and couches—where Nurse indulged them with Icy Hot and pills, ice packs and heat packs, and visualization techniques like, "When you're walking around, pretend you're picking your way through dung. Cow patties. Pretend they're only under your right foot. Then you won't put undue weight on that poor ankle."

Most people are incompetent hiders. The language of the body contradicts their words. They barricade their hearts with their arms. They open their eyes too wide. They peel the label off the beer bottle or nibble the skin from their lips.

I watched Eden open the door, and then I watched through the window as she ran toward the dorm as if something were chasing her, her loose knot of hair knocking the back of her head.

How fitting that my father's daughter was a keeper of secrets.

SEVENTEEN

I should explain how I got to camp. After reading about Camp Carolina on Eden's blog, I e-mailed Lewis my résumé, telling him that obesity ran in my family, that although I didn't have relevant work experience, per se, fat was personal to me. Plus, I was enthusiastic; I could think out of the box; I was a hard worker. I told him I would do anything he needed. He hired me without even a phone interview.

And just like that, I felt alive again. My despair released me, like a tight wool scarf unfurling from my neck. It wasn't death I'd wanted anyway, I realized, just some alternative to what life had become.

Now I had it. Of course, I was still eating. Eating and eating, ceaselessly eating. The eating got worse as the winter wore on, but I clung to its expiration date. When summer came, I would go to camp. Compared to the campers, I would be thin. And then Eden and I would be together, filling up not on food, but on each other. I would gain Eden's confidence and lose fifteen pounds. I would confess to her what I'd done to our father. She would forgive me. He would forgive me. I would be skinny. I would be happy.

Our sister bond would form the way one would in a movie. Eden would catch me in the right light, and glimpse the family resemblance in my eyes, or around my mouth. She would reach out her hand to me, her tears mirroring mine. "I always felt that something was missing," she would stage-whisper, "and all along it's been you."

Sometimes this daydream made me sigh with contentment, even as the eating persisted. Sometimes when I ate, I thought of Eden, imagining our hands moving simultaneously, mechanically, from plate to mouth, plate to mouth.

I told Mikey and anyone else who cared that I was going to camp to help obese children. I was going to help their hearts, so they wouldn't wind up like my father.

When June arrived, I took the Chinatown bus from the Lower East Side to Boston for my father's unveiling. Although only a year had elapsed since his death, the house was unfamiliar. Gone were the days of my mother's wish to "crawl into a hole." She had found unforeseen energy, and become an atypical widow: She hadn't kept her husband's clothes hanging, disembodied, in his closet; his shoes, untied, lined up by the front door. Within weeks of shivah, she'd had a Goodwill truck come to the house. A team of cleaning people. My father's Sears catalog armchair, which she'd always hated ("A chair filled with two decades of my husband's flatulence!" she used to say. "This adds something to our living room?"), had finally gone to the dump. She had replaced all the bedding. She had even repainted the shutters.

We drove twenty miles from home to leave pebbles on his new headstone. The cemetery was in Lexington, where my father had once taken me in the middle of the night to stand on cool grass and watch the reenactment of the Battle of Lexington and Concord.

"Do you remember that?" my mother asked, as we made our way through the cemetery. "You were so little. Dad scooped you out of bed and brought you here in your nightgown."

It was hard for me to imagine it—my father and I that close, my head resting on his shoulder. All I remembered were the gunshots, women in bonnets kneeling beside fallen soldiers, screaming theatrically into the dawn. And I remembered going out for breakfast afterward, my father ordering us both pancakes topped with ice cream. This was back when I still loved pancakes and ice cream without complication.

My mother and I stood at my father's stone. "Gray has decided to go to fat camp," my mother told it. Then she turned to me, as if my father had just yelled, "Susan! Stop her!" She took my hand. Her fingers were cool and small, the bones as thin and snappable as uncooked spaghetti. She looked worried, as if she were seeing me for the first time and she wasn't sure she liked what she saw. Her black pants were too big, her white silk top wrinkled. She was wearing too much blush and blue eyeliner that looked all wrong. She had aged visibly in the last year, her body now withered, rather than delicate; her hair dyed too light a shade of brown, her skin as fragile-looking as the paper of a cocktail umbrella.

"Why *have* you decided to go to fat camp?" she asked.

What could I say? I had wicked secrets. I almost spoke them, almost let the ground around us absorb them, as it absorbed the nutrients of corpses.

"Is that what they call it?" my mother asked. "Fat camp? Is that politically correct?"

I released her hand and dropped to my knees. With my finger, I traced the letters of my father's name. ALAN LACHMANN. "Dad," I said. I ran my palms over the smooth, rounded top of the stone. "I want to honor your legacy. It's my mission to shrink fat American children. This is my commitment to your memory, and my duty as a Jew."

Behind me, my mother began to giggle. Which, of course, had been my real mission. But her laughter stalled quickly. She had become one of those people—who could indulge distraction, but never sustain it. That was the person I was afraid of becoming, one permanently crowded by a sadness that was always waiting, checking its watch, tapping its foot, sighing, "Are you done laughing yet? Are you through smiling? I'm still here, you know. I'm still everything."

Later, when she hugged me good-bye outside my father's once-shiny blue Cadillac, I let her pretend that she wasn't crying.

"I only keep this car for you," she said. "I'd like to get rid of it."

"After this summer."

"It's probably not safe."

"I'll be fine, Mom."

"Are you?" She held me away from her and looked me up and down. "Are you fine?"

"Of course," I told her. "I'm fine."

I drove back to New York in my father's car, and then stuffed it to bursting, adding to its weight until the tires looked squashed. I couldn't see out the back window.

"Why are you taking the vacuum cleaner?" Mikey asked, rubbing the back of his neck. "Why are you taking your printer? Your winter clothes?"

"Because at the end of the summer, we'll look for a bigger apartment. We'll move to Brooklyn or Queens. We need change," I kept telling him. I'd been telling him for a year. Whenever he asked what I meant, I told him I hadn't sorted out the details. "I'll need a new job," I said, cramming my down coat into the trunk.

"Queens?" He looked confused.

"Or Brooklyn."

"What does that have to do with your printer?"

"I'm already packing," I said. "May as well pack everything now. Have it in the car. Be ready to move."

I wasn't making sense. I often pretended that Mikey was dumb. He let me pretend; he usually preferred that to arguing with me.

"But what if I need to vacuum?" he asked, surveying the car.

"When do you vacuum?"

Mikey was shirtless in cargo shorts, his belly pooching over his waistband. His hair was a mess. I stopped myself from smoothing it down. He kissed me and asked, "Are you sure?"

"It's only eight weeks."

"Eight and a half."

"It's summer. It will fly."

"You could put *me* on a diet."

"Right."

"You could padlock the fridge."

"Very funny."

"We could have energetic sex. Burns tons of calories. I've been reading up on it."

There were two parking tickets under my windshield wiper.

Mikey plucked them out and shoved them into his pocket. I climbed into the driver's seat, started the car, and cranked down the window. The car was a billion years old. Foam stuffing sprouted from the seams of the leather seats. Each door had a knob lock that could be pulled up and pushed down. When I was a child, my father had driven me to school in this car.

Mikey put his face in the open window. I licked my finger and smoothed his cowlick. "I hate when you do that," he said, but he didn't flinch. His dark eyes were wet, the whites threaded with red. He kissed my cheek. "I know you're keeping something from me."

I started the ignition.

"Gray."

"What?"

"Just promise you won't do anything stupid."

"Like what?"

"Like . . . I don't know . . . drive on switchbacks at a hundred ten."

"I've never done a hundred ten. I don't think this car goes to a hundred ten." I offered him my pinkie. He hooked it with his. "I promise."

"If you die, I'll sleep with your friends. I'll take advantage of their grief. I'll tell them it's what you would have wanted."

"Cute."

Mikey stood and shook a cigarette from his pack. "Well," he said. "Then think twice before speeding." He put a cigarette between his lips, cupped one hand around the end of it, and flicked his lighter.

"I love you," I said.

Mikey took a long drag and turned his head slightly to the right to exhale, keeping his eyes on my face. "I love you, too," he said, shrugging. "You're my girl."

I pulled out of the parking spot and drove to Second Avenue. When I signaled left, my hands trembled. I saw Mikey in my side mirror, smoking and then disappearing when I turned. His arm was partly raised in a wave, his fingers splayed, his head cocked.

Michael Vincent Cosenza, forgive me. Deep down, I understood I wasn't fooling you a bit.

EIGHTEEN

The day after the first-week weigh-in, the whole camp rode in a bus to Adventure Gardens on the border of the Carolinas. My campers wanted to ride the Scorpion, the roller coaster whose tracks looped through the sky like fancy black script. Spider was running toward it, shrieking, leaping through the air. She stopped ahead of the rest of us to bend over and catch her breath, her hands on her knees. Then she rose and turned to us. "The fifth-highest roller coaster in the world is in Japan. Three hundred eighteen feet!"

"I'm dizzy," Harriet told me.

Harriet was always dizzy. During any form of physical activity, she would tell me, "I'm dizzy," and then sit down and look affronted. Harriet wore only black. She wore winter clothes under the North Carolina sun. She frequently folded into herself and tried to disappear. She rarely spoke, but when she did, she liked to say, "I hate myself." Occasionally, she would say, "I wish I were dead."

I would ask, "Do you want to go see Nurse?" and she would clench her fists and pucker her face. She often told me she hated me. "I hate you," she would mutter through the thin lines of her lips.

Sometimes, I hated Harriet back. Other times, I thought of Mikey, because Harriet would have amused him. Since I'd arrived at camp, when Mikey called, he sounded far away. When he made the jokes he'd always made, the sensation that rose in my chest was the opposite of laughter, not a release, but an obstruction. He asked questions that felt impossible.

"How fat are they?"

"They're all different. Jesus, Mikey, what do you think?"

"Are we talking, like, motorized wheelchair fat?"

"There's one kid in a wheelchair. One of the boys. Everyone calls him Pudge."

"Did you come up with that? It's so inspired. It's like naming a Dalmatian 'Spot.' No. It's like naming a Dalmatian 'Dalmatian.' Pudge. I love that. Pudge!"

"The assistant director helps him up every morning while everyone's walking around the loop." I was careful not to name the assistant director, careful not to say, *Bennett who looks like art, Bennett who gave me a nickname, Bennett who barely knows me, but keeps me full like you never did.* "They do stretches together."

"The loop. All this new lingo. You're like a Trekkie. Do they have diabetes?"

"Can we talk about something else?"

"Sure. Do they have heart attacks?"

"Hilarious. Good-bye."

It had become an exhausting game—this way in which we didn't communicate.

Now I glanced at Harriet as we walked. "You don't have to ride."

"Yes, I do. Everyone is. They'll make fun of me."

"They won't even notice."

I was thinking they would, if anything, make fun of her for her persistent body odor. Already, I'd heard the girls complain that Harriet didn't shower. Even Sheena had told me that I should talk with Harriet about hygiene. "I'd talk to her myself," she told me, "but I don't want to get near her."

But what could I say to Harriet, the girl who slept in a sweatshirt, the biggest girl at camp, who was almost as wide as she was tall? This was the girl who had refused to go to weigh-ins on the first day in a bathing suit, who had cried in her room until I'd agreed to arrange a private weigh-in for her with Nurse. This was not a girl who would shower in a dorm bathroom.

"It's not like anyone's looking in her shower stall!" Sheena had said. "What does she think this is, a peep show? Good Lord. Let her rot. Let her grow mold."

"I'll either stay down with you or I'll ride with you," I told Harriet now as we neared the crowded metal ramp. "There aren't many other options."

The day was hot, the sun as invasive as stage lights. The air smelled like fried dough and powdered sugar—a rubber band snapping a wrist. No one was allowed to buy amusement park food—expensive chocolate-vanilla-swirl ice cream cones, pizza slices dotted with sausage, funnel cake, tapestry-size soft pretzels. At noon, the whole camp would meet in the parking lot and eat brown-bag lunches beside the bus.

"Look!" Spider called. She was standing at the end of the line for the Scorpion, pointing to a thick yellow stripe of paint on the ground. "I'm half in North Carolina, half in South Carolina. I exist simultaneously in two states."

Eden stood next to her, straddling the line. "Cool," she said.

I joined them. "It *is* possible to be in two places at once," I said, but Eden lost interest and wandered toward Whitney.

Spider smiled at me. "I thought it was funny, Gray."

"Thanks."

"We're on a precipice."

"That's right," I said. "On the brink."

As the line inched forward, I glimpsed the cardboard policeman holding a stop sign that read STOP! TO RIDE, YOU MUST BE AS TALL AS MY SIGN. I looked for other warnings—a cardboard policeman holding his arms open: *To ride, you must be able to fit between my arms.* But my campers were not the only fat Adventure Gardens patrons. Surely, roller coasters accommodated fat people. Perhaps they were even designed for fat people. Fat people were everywhere. In front of us, an obese family of six shared one giant lollipop, passing it around, licking, passing, licking, passing. My stomach surged in the heat.

"I'm *dizzy.*"

"Harriet," I said, "you act like it's my fault. Like I'm tilting the earth."

"Well, it wasn't *my* idea to go on this stupid ride."

She was standing close enough to me that I could smell her body, sour with old sweat, and feel humidity, like danger, coming off the layer of hair on her skin. I stepped away from her. She stepped closer.

Sheena, Miss, and Whitney were, as usual, clustered together. Sheena had doctored their red Camp Carolina shirts—cutting open the side seams, refastening them with safety pins, cutting each neck into a deep V. Eden had cut a slit up from the bottom of her own shirt, and then tied the two pieces together in the front, but it looked wrong. She was hovering around the edges of their threesome, searching for a hole she could worm through.

When the seven of us reached the front of the line, Whitney and Miss ran for the front car, Eden followed Sheena to the back car, and Spider ran to the second car to sit with a stranger. "This isn't even a giga-coaster," I heard her tell her seatmate. "It's way under three hundred feet. I'd put it at two hundred. Two fifty. But I love all roller coasters. I want to go on the environmentally friendly roller coaster. It's in Europe somewhere. You have to pedal to make it go. In *fact*," she said, leaning forward toward Whitney and Miss, "it's probably good for weight loss. I should tell Lewis. We could take an all-camp trip to Europe next summer. We could make it into the newspaper. 'Campers at Weight-Loss Camp Pedal Pounds Away.'"

"Where would you like to sit?" I asked Harriet.

With both fists, Harriet clutched the hem of the black sweatshirt she wore over her red camp T-shirt. Her lips were pursed and she wheezed angrily through her nose, fogging her glasses, ignoring me.

The Scorpion was shiny black. Each car had two bucket seats, separated by a metal divider; a metal lap bar; and a harness that came down from the top to lock in each passenger's upper body. I walked to the third car and sat in the far seat. A few seconds later, I felt Harriet swaying above me. I looked at her legs. The hair on her shins was full-grown, the skin peppered with tiny red scabs.

When the attendant, a skinny teenager with a bowl cut, wearing black leather cuffs around his wrists, came to lower my harness, he paused, scratched his ear, and pointed at Harriet. "She's not gonna fit," he told me.

I turned my head to look up at Harriet, who was standing on

the metal floor of the car above her seat, turning in tight, frantic circles, like a dog assessing a patch of grass.

"How much you weigh?" the ride attendant asked. His voice rang through the air, echoing as if he'd yelled inside a canyon.

Harriet whimpered.

I got to my feet and looked ahead of us, behind us. But all of the other cars were full. The obese family was strapped in, their lollipop gone. Sheena and our other campers were strapped in. Everyone was waiting for the Scorpion to inch and jerk up the tracks. Only Harriet was too big. "Come on, Harriet," I said. "I don't want to ride. Let's sit this one out. Will you go back down with me?"

Other passengers craned their necks to see us. Ahead, I saw Whitney and Miss laughing, their fingers splayed at their mouths.

I thought Harriet would step out of the car, back onto the metal platform. I thought she would run down the ramp to escape. Instead, she bent abruptly into a lumbering squat, trying to force her hips between the door of the car and the seat partition.

But the attendant had gauged the size difference correctly. "She's not gonna fit," he said again. He tapped my shoulder.

I wrenched away from him. "Stop it," I hissed. "We're getting off. Just go away."

The attendant raised his hands as if I might shoot. "No need to get your Wranglers in a wad. Not my fault she's over the weight limit." He moved on to the next car and started lowering the harnesses. "But get on out," he called back to me, "so I can let the next two people on."

Harriet had switched tactics. She had turned sideways and was trying to wedge herself into the seat like a thick coin into a slot. I thought of her in her bed at home, eating an Entenmann's cake under the covers. I had done that once some months before, alone in the apartment after work: eaten an entire Entenmann's All Butter French Crumb Cake in bed. Then I'd gotten out of bed, gotten dressed, and run to the store for another one.

"Come on," I said again to Harriet. I was suddenly very tired. I did not want this cameo in someone else's trauma. I looked back at Eden's car and saw the side of her head, the shiny black of her hair like a censor. She was talking to Sheena, who was looking away. Sheena should have been dealing with Harriet. I should have been sitting with Eden.

I took a step back from Harriet, out of this flashbulb image that would become an indelible memory; one she would, two decades down the road, relay to a blank-faced therapist, or to a lover while sharing a cigarette in the dark.

She paused in her efforts, looked at me with hate all over her face—in her slightly crooked glasses, her vaguely quivering lip, her clenched forehead—and then stood, finally, and fled. She ran to the ramp where she had to squeeze past the line of people, who would move aside, watch her pass, and imagine her eating under her covers.

I followed.

"Excuse me," I said to each person. "Excuse me. Sorry. Excuse me."

What was I apologizing for? I wasn't fat. I had been acting like a fat person for just over a year. I had gained fifteen pounds. Okay. Sure. But I had fought it. I had gone for long runs by the East River. Some days, I had fasted, taking in nothing but water. I had shown *some* self-control. I touched my stomach. I touched each of my arms and felt the lightness in my step.

"Coming through. Please step aside," I said like a security guard, or a person carrying a beer keg aloft.

At the bottom of the ramp, I followed Harriet to a bench. She sat with her legs spread, her elbows on her thighs. She took off her glasses and put her face in her palms. I sat beside her. The glasses sat between us, reflecting a cruel sun. I squinted up at the roller-coaster-car-size people screaming through the sky.

"Do you want to talk?" I touched Harriet's coarse hair. It was so hot, I curled my fingers in.

When she didn't answer, I understood. It was like times I'd lain in bed, sick, knowing I'd feel better if I ran to the bathroom to vomit, but too afraid of vomiting to do anything but lie there, squirming, hot and tangled in synthetic sheets, comfortable inside discomfort.

NINETEEN

Like everyone else's, my body was diminishing. Week two and I could feel there was less of it. According to the scale, I had lost seven pounds. But my clothes said I had lost more.

"Are your tits shrinking?" Mikey asked me on the phone.

They were. In the cups of my bras there were wrinkles, where once the fabric had been taut.

"Come home. I'll massage them back to health."

"I've never felt healthier," I said, and it was true. Since the night at Chinese Buffet, I had eaten only what I was given.

"Are you going to turn into one of those girls who's always wearing a sports bra?"

"When wasn't I one of those girls?"

"Listen. If you want to sleep with Richard Simmons, I'll give you a pass. I know how summer can be."

He did know how summer could be. We'd fallen in love in the summer.

Five summers later, our love was tired, but fresh love was in bloom all around me. After dinner, Whitney and Pudge sat on the stone steps that led up to the cafeteria, Pudge at the bottom in his wheelchair, Whitney beside him on the first step. In Whitney's presence, Pudge looked regal, a king on a throne, holding court. Sometimes Whitney leaned her face against his shin and he palmed the top of her head as if to bless her.

And Miss had begun wearing Brendan's North Carolina State hat, her thick blond ponytail pulled through the hole above the size adjustment strap.

Spider asked me, "Are counselors allowed to have girlfriends who are campers?"

I didn't know. Camp Carolina was light on rules.

"Brendan might want to have sex with Miss, and she's just a kid."

"Brendan's a kid, too," I said.

"No," Spider said, "Brendan's in college."

Brendan and Miss walked around the loop together every morning, Miss in a white hooded sweatshirt, unzipped, hood up; Brendan trying not to pant, pushing his undersize glasses up the sweaty bridge of his nose.

"Doesn't Brendan just scream 'virgin'?" Sheena said to me one morning as we made our way into the cafeteria for breakfast. "He's got a big red bow tied around his cock."

"He's only nineteen," I said.

Sheena snorted. "I'm nineteen! I've been having sex since I was eleven."

"That's disturbing."

"Gray, sometimes I think I'm so much older than you."

I would like to think that she was right. I was young. I didn't know anything. But I would just be excusing my own summer love.

Look, I would never have talked to Bennett if he hadn't talked to me. Would never have asked for his time had he not offered it first. He was a man who could twirl a whistle on a shoelace, who could lift a soccer ball with the front of his foot and with the slightest flick send it neatly to his fingertips.

I saw myself in contrast to him—a girl who spent too much time and money in Manhattan bars, who kept her head down in the street instead of smiling a southern hello. I was the girl who couldn't throw, who couldn't catch, who knew words like "reps," "sets," "electrolytes," "core strength," "body mass index," and "medicine ball" only because I was terrified of fat, not because I was an athlete.

He called me Angeline. He sang to me, "Lookin' at the bright lights, searchin' for the silver screen." And what a thrill it was not to be Gray, to be a whole new angelic person, to be some girl from some song. When he said, "Angeline, come help me set up the gym for kickball," or, "Hold the stopwatch while the kids run sprints," I felt anointed. This was not high school. I was a twenty-seven-year-old woman. But in the glow of Bennett Milton, I felt nothing short of anointed.

I told myself, *There's nothing wrong with having a crush.* I told myself, *I'm allowed to have friends of the opposite sex.*

Then I thought of Mikey saying, "Don't you know by now that men don't want to be your friends?"

Usually when he said that, he meant comedians. Comedians, back when I was booking clubs, were interested only in what I had to give them. I knew that. "I'm not naïve," I always told Mikey. But sometimes after I'd talked with an audience member at a club or a friend of a friend at a party, he would say, "New friend, huh?"

"That guy's really cool," I'd say. "He—"

"Gray. He's not *cool*. He's trying to fuck you."

"You think everyone's trying to fuck me."

"Nope. Just that guy."

"You always say that."

"You know how he asked you about your college major?"

"Yeah?"

"And about your favorite movie?"

"Yeah?"

"That's male code language. Allow me to translate: 'I'm trying to fuck you.'"

But Bennett never *tried* to do anything. His whole existence was one effortless, fluid movement—a sea turtle gliding through the water.

"Who's Camille?" I asked him one night.

I was what Lewis called "Head O.D." O.D. stood for "on duty," and Head O.D. was in charge of the whole camp until midnight, which meant I had to sit on the cafeteria steps, holding a useless flashlight and a walkie-talkie that barely worked in case one of the other on-duty counselors radioed in from the dorms with a problem. From the steps, I could see part of the loop, and beyond that, the library, the girls' dorm to the right, part of the boys' dorm to the left. And always against the white of the buildings, trees as green as putting mats.

Bennett and I sat side by side, drinking water from Camp Carolina water bottles, surrounded by crickets and stars. I felt the way I constantly felt with Bennett—as if he was about to get up and walk away. The feeling always compelled me to ask him a lot of questions.

Bennett glanced down at his tattoo. "I swear, I have to get that thing removed," he said. "I've been meaning to do it. But it's not cheap."

"How not cheap?"

"Maybe a thousand. Or more." He inspected the tattoo more closely, ran his finger over the letters of Camille's name. "It's a lot of ink."

I looked at his arm. The heart throbbed red and full.

"Not much gets by you," Bennett said. He leaned back on his elbows.

"Plenty gets by me."

"Think so?" He yawned.

There it was, my favorite part of talking with Bennett: how our banter would seem to be building momentum, until he would throw out an absentminded stock phrase, like a crisis line operator reading from a script. So different from Mikey, who was always on, always waiting for his chance to be funny, his skin buzzing with anticipation.

"You been into Melrose yet?" Bennett asked. "We should drive into Melrose one of these nights. Get some ribs. Pitcher of beer."

Two weeks ago, I could have devoured multiple rib cages if given the chance, and then licked every last drop of barbecue sauce from my fingers. But with my eyes on Bennett, I felt no hunger. Ribs were a meal that hungry people ate.

"The personal trainer eats ribs?"

"Don't tell the kids," he said.

I laughed, and then I saw it for the first time: the cross around his neck. It was small and wooden, dangling from a leather thong at the base of his throat.

"Know what I'm famous for with my friends? Ask me about the specials at any fast-food place. Go on. I always know."

"KFC."

"Free medium soft drink with any plated meal."

"What's a plated meal?"

"A meal on a plate."

"Makes it sound healthy."

"Never claimed it was healthy."

"Mia was telling the kids the other day that they should always eat off a plate. Where you get in trouble is if you start eating out of the bag."

"Because you won't know when to stop."

"Knowing when to stop is half the ba—" I cut myself off. I was so very sick of my platitudes.

"Give me another," Bennett said.

"I don't know. Burger King?"

"A free vampire collector's glass with any value meal."

"What's a collector's glass?"

"A glass for collectors."

"But who would collect—"

"Do you know what a value meal is?"

"Isn't it . . . No, actually."

"Bunch of items that cost less all together than they would individually."

"How gestalt."

"Pardon?"

I shook my head. "So you're one of those hypocrite trainers," I said. "I can't believe you eat fast food." I almost nudged him with my elbow, but I stopped just short of touching him.

"I'm not a real personal trainer yet. My test isn't until October."

"So come October, you'll stop eating Burger King?"

"Come October, a lot of things will change. I'll strike out on my own, for one thing. I'm already getting to the end of my rope with Lewis. This camp is a mess. Do you know how many employees here are unqualified?"

"How many?"

"All of us. Pretty much. Look, I know plenty about fitness.

Still, though. He couldn't find a real trainer? Not that I'm complaining. Just saying. You know, Mia doesn't have her RD certification. She's practically a kid. And Brendan sure as shit shouldn't be anywhere near that climbing wall, and KJ, let me tell you, is no lifeguard. Then there's Nurse, who's, what, fifty years old? And hasn't gotten her nursing certification yet. That woman's crass as all get-out. She thinks Couth is her uncle, she's so country."

"You don't like Nurse?"

"I like everyone."

I leaned back on my elbows like Bennett. Above us, the stars winked.

"And you," Bennett said. "Do you know what water aerobics *is*?"

"No."

"How'd you even hear about us, all the way down here?"

"I was reading about weight-loss camps once," I said, crooking my nails to study them. I added, "On the Internet," as if to substantiate my credentials.

"Don't even get me started on Lewis," Bennett said. "For some godforsaken reason, that man thinks he's better than everyone at everything. He's sure that one day he'll prove it."

"I love your accent," I said.

"I don't have an accent."

"'Godforsaken.' What does that even mean?"

"Beats me," Bennett said, sitting back up and rubbing his knees. "Watch. That man is going to go down. I don't know when. I don't know how. But you watch. It won't be pretty."

"I know about narcissists," I said. I sat up, too. "They tend to self-destruct. I used to work with comedians."

Bennett stopped rubbing his knees and stared at me. He wore a Carolina Hurricanes baseball cap, worn and faded; a Rolling Stones T-shirt with a lips-and-tongue logo; cutoff khaki shorts; his black-and-white-striped soccer sandals. "I like how *you* talk," he said. "It's so fancy."

I thought, *Dumb jock*. Then I felt guilty for thinking it. Then I felt turned on. Then I sucked air and words into my chest. And when I opened my mouth, I said, "I like that idea. Ribs and beer. Melrose. Pick any night when I'm off duty."

My heart pounded like wild fists, but Bennett just yawned and stretched his arms. "I forgot I even said that," he said. "I must be tired."

"Oh," I said. "Well, we don't have to."

Bennett laughed. "You want ribs? Who am I to deny Miss Angeline?" He stood. Stretched. Gave my ponytail a noncommittal tug. Then he jogged down the steps and vanished.

TWENTY

The second Saturday of camp, the youngest girls decorated the cafeteria for the social (Lewis's Camp-ese for "dance"). Before it began, Miss sat against the wall in our hallway in the dorm, wearing jogging shorts and a T-shirt, complaining, "This is going to be *so gay*," as everyone else walked around in towels, borrowing one another's clothes, battling the humidity with blow dryers. Whitney had her music cranked up, and Eden was dancing in the hallway, piling her hair up on top of her head, letting it fall as she twitched her hips. When no one joined her, she danced to the bathroom to shower.

I was sitting outside of Eden's room, pretending to do something important with my cell phone.

"So gay," Miss went on. "So retarded. Who are you all dressing up for anyway? There's no one hot at this whole camp, except Bennett, and he's, like, a dad."

Spider slid down the wall across from her, wearing a mustache of white foam.

"You're bleaching your *mustache*?" Miss said.

Spider pointed to it, and then said something in sign language.

Whitney came out into the hall wearing skintight jeans and a hot pink tube top. "Maybe you should wear a North Carolina State bikini," Whitney said, nudging Miss's arm with her foot. "Brendan would get such a trombone in his pants."

When Whitney and Miss began to giggle, Spider, across from them, waved her hands frantically, pointing to her mustache bleach. Finally, unable to contain herself, she jumped to her feet and ran.

From inside the bathroom, she roared, "Trombone!" and exploded into laughter. "Whitney! You made my bleach fall off!"

Harriet stepped into the hallway wearing a black turtleneck dress.

"You're going to sweat to death," I told her.

"No, I won't."

I returned to my phone, pretending not to notice Eden walking out of the bathroom in her towel and flip-flops, another towel twisted around her wet hair.

"Harriet, are you going to a funeral?" Miss asked.

"No."

"I see. Are you a ninja?"

Harriet pulled her turtleneck over her mouth and nose, and then headed back to her room.

"Sorry. I mean, are you a mime? No. I didn't mean that. Are you a stagehand? Are you going to change the set between acts in the dark?"

Whitney snorted, but her laughter stopped abruptly when Eden pointed to her and said, "I was totally going to wear jeans, too."

Whitney sighed and leaned against the wall, a brown roll of fat inflating like an inner tube between the button of her jeans and the bottom of her cropped shirt. "Of course you were."

"I'm obsessed with jeans," Eden said.

"Congratulations," Miss said. "You just won the Most Retarded Sentence of the Week Award." She stood and whispered something into Whitney's ear, and Eden watched for a second, blinking rapidly, and then wandered into her room.

From the bathroom, Spider called, "Don't say 'retarded.' It's insensitive."

"I can say whatever I want," Miss called.

"It's a free country," Whitney said.

I stood, facing Miss. "You don't have to be mean."

"Who was mean? I'm not mean."

"Harriet looks pretty," I said.

"She's gorgeous," Miss said, yawning. "I must be jealous."

"You didn't have to make Eden feel bad."

"Eden jacks my style!" Whitney said. "She tries to talk like she's black all the time. It's *annoying*. She said the *N* word yesterday. I'm sick of dumb white bitches thinking they're black. Eden's a racist."

"She's not a racist."

"This is why I hate females."

"That makes no sense," I said.

"There are so many dumb bitches at this camp."

And then a scream came from Eden's room, so loud and shrill, my vision blurred. Spider ran out of the bathroom, her face scrubbed clean. She was wearing nothing but day-of-the-week underpants. Tuesdays. Ever since the drastic weight losses from the first weigh-in, it was not uncommon for everyone, except Harriet, to be stripped down to underwear.

Sheena popped her head out her door. "What the hell is going on?"

Harriet reappeared, too.

Eden burst out of her room, still screaming, still wearing her towel, her wet hair now loose on her arms and back. "Someone put cockroaches in my fucking bed!" She stopped screaming and wrapped her arms around herself.

"There are no cockroaches in this part of the country," Spider said, scratching at a peeling patch of skin on her cheek. "Earwigs, maybe. But cockroaches are city dwellers."

Eden closed her eyes and balled up her fists at her sides. "Cockroaches. In. My. *Bed*."

I looked around. Whitney was looking at the floor. Sheena was looking at Miss, who was twirling a yellow lock of hair around her finger, watching Eden with a face as blank as a plate. Harriet was crying.

"Harriet, what's wrong?" I asked.

"I hate when people scream," she muttered, and then she stomped into her room and slammed the door.

"What is everyone's problem?" Sheena said. "We're at camp. Bugs get inside sometimes. Deal with it!"

"We're at a boarding school!" Eden said. "It's not a real camp."

"Maybe it was a hate crime," Spider said.

"Y'all are drama queens," Whitney said.

Whitney and Miss linked elbows and scurried into Sheena's room. Sheena followed them in and closed the door.

Eden turned to stomp into Spider's room. I heard the squeak of the mattress springs when she threw herself on Spider's bed. "I'm not sleeping in my room!" she shouted. "Ever again!"

"I'll trade with her," Spider said.

"You don't have to do that, Spider."

"I like earwigs." She scratched her forehead. It was pink from all the scratching. "I wouldn't mind having an earwig farm."

"Yuck."

"Want me to get them and take them outside?"

I watched the pink spread across her forehead. I nodded. "I hate bugs," I said. I thought, *My sister and I hate bugs.* "But it's not your job, Spider. So don't do it if you don't want to, okay?"

"Everyone thinks earwigs crawl into people's ears," Spider said. "And lay eggs in their brains."

I shuddered.

"But that's an urban legend. Or maybe a rural legend."

"You're not afraid?"

"Of *bugs*?"

I looked at the antidote necklaces draped around Spider's neck. "You're brave," I told her.

Spider lifted her arms away from her body and then dropped them as she made her way toward Eden's room. "People are so afraid of things that aren't even scary."

I went to Spider's door and placed my palms on it. For a second, I thought I felt a heartbeat. "Can I come in?"

Eden didn't answer.

"Spider's in your room getting the bugs out of your bed."

After another minute of silence, I opened the door and stepped into Spider's dim room. The air smelled medicinal. A Japanese flag hung in place of blinds, suspended by the breeze from the window fan. Below it, Eden was sprawled facedown on the bed.

"I don't want to talk about it," she said into the pillow.

I sat on the edge of the bed. "We don't have to."

"I don't want to *talk*. At all. About anything."

"Okay," I said. "But don't you want to go to the social?"

Eden rocked her forehead right and left on the pillow. *No.*

I looked at her wet hair and pictured my father's hand cupping the back of her head. I could hear his voice saying, "Cheer up, sleepy Jean."

I thought of Eden's mother, her eyes locked with our father's. I wondered how they'd met. How much time had they spent together? When he died, had she still loved him? Had he loved her? Had he kissed the great wave of her bangs? Had they sat side by side in an air-conditioned movie theater, his palm cupping the nape of her neck? Had he held her beneath a summer-night sky? Had he pointed to the heavens, his belly at her back, and whispered into her hair? ("See how the moon loves the stars? Don't I love you like that?")

I didn't touch Eden. But I wanted to give her something. I could have just said it. Told her what I'd come to tell her. It certainly would have taken her mind off the cockroaches or earwigs, or whatever they were.

But when I opened my mouth, nausea rose inside me. I could do it. No, I couldn't. I had to. No, not yet. Not yet. Yes, now. Now. I inhaled sharply. But suddenly it felt like a lie. *Eden, I'm your sister.* It was ridiculous. What was I thinking? This was the first time I'd been close to her. This was not The Moment. She would scream for Sheena. I would be taken away in a straitjacket.

I slowed my heart by remembering that I had time. The program was working. I felt . . . surrendered to it. I could wait out the summer. By August, everyone would say, "Gray and Eden are like sisters." We would be like sisters. Then I would tell her.

In the meantime, I offered a fortune cookie fortune, since that was what I did best. In fact, I gave her my father's words: "Most people," I said, "are schmucks."

TWENTY-ONE

In the cafeteria, blue paper streamers ran from one wall to the other, balloons gathered at the ceiling, and construction paper posters on the walls read DANCE! and SHAKE IT! One read LOVELY LADY LUMPS. Pudge had gotten out of his wheelchair and was lying on his side on the stage in a colossal red T-shirt and matching red do-rag. His knees were slightly bent, his head propped on his palm. He looked like a fat lady from a painting waiting to be hand-fed grapes. Someone had plugged an iPod into speakers, and Pudge was playing DJ.

The youngest girls looked ready for Easter in long pastel dresses. One girl wore a white bow in her hair. The intermediate girls wore cutoff jean shorts or miniskirts, the bolder ones sporting tube tops and halters. The boys arrived with hair still damp from the shower and short-sleeve button-down shirts already darkening at the armpits.

No one was dancing. The campers stood in girl clusters and boy clusters, or sat at the one picnic table that hadn't been stacked up against the wall.

Lewis stood beside Pudge on the stage. "Isn't anyone going to dance?" he called. "This is a social! Dance! Dance!"

Spider tapped my shoulder. She was wearing terry-cloth wristbands and holding a round hairbrush. Her T-shirt was tucked into her shorts, which were hiked up to her ribs. Of my five campers, Spider had the least weight to lose. She was more puffy than fat, as if her body were a shrine to her allergies. "Will you do my hair?"

"Now?"

"I was going to ask you before."

I looked at her hair. What could I do with it? It was as dry as rope, frizzy and heavy and straggly. It looked as if it would easily burn—wheat in a bad harvest year.

"I could braid it," I said, taking the brush.

"French braid?"

"People still wear French braids?"

"My mom French-braids my hair."

"I haven't seen a French braid in ten years."

"It's my favorite hairdo," Spider said. "I like how it starts from the top."

"Do you know who Bob Marley was?" I asked her.

"Yes."

"Do you know that when he died, they found thirty-seven new species of bugs in his hair?"

"Is that true?"

"I don't know. Probably not."

"Don't tell Eden that," Spider whispered. "I think she's phobic."

She followed me to the picnic table, where I sat on one end of the bench. She sat on the floor at my feet, wrapped her arms around her body, and scratched hard at the eczema on her shoulders, sending tiny dry skin flakes fluttering into the atmosphere. When I took her hair in my hands, she sighed and her shoulders relaxed. She stopped scratching.

Bennett came out of the kitchen carrying a blue cooler. "Snack!" he yelled above the music, and the kids moved toward him. As he doled out sugar-free Popsicles, he looked over the sea of heads at Spider and me. "Popsicle?" he mouthed.

I shook my head, finished Spider's braid, and snapped the elastic into place. She hopped to her feet and ran to Bennett. My fingers found their way to my hipbones. I'd been touching them constantly, speaking to them silently: *Welcome back, dear hipbones. I hope your past year was better than mine.*

Bennett handed out the last of the Popsicles as I stood and crossed the cafeteria. "Angeline," he said when I reached him. His dimples sank into his cheeks, sucking all the air from the room.

I looked away, my face hot, and saw Miss, no longer the critic, alone in a corner with Brendan, holding both of his hands. He was bent down, whispering into her ear.

"I'm off duty tonight," I told Bennett. "I don't even have to be here now. Sheena's here. So."

"That right?" Bennett closed the white lid of the cooler and sat on it. He rested his elbows on his thighs and grinned up at me. Then he hooked a finger through a belt loop on my jeans. "You okay, Angeline?"

The Popsicles campers were licking looked like icicles. This was what happened when I was with Bennett: Sweets were stripped of sugar; food became nonfood.

"I just want to get out of camp for a bit." I raked my hair off my face, making a ponytail with trembling hands. When I realized I didn't have an elastic, I let my hair fall. "I've hardly left camp in two weeks."

"Do that again," Bennett said.

"What?"

"That thing with your hair. That was sexy."

I wiped my palms on my back pockets. I was empty of words. My stomach growled.

Bennett hopped off the cooler and pinched my waist. "Well, let's get you out of camp," he said. "Can't have a city girl all cooped up like a hamster in a cage."

Carolina Academy sat nestled in the Blue Ridge Mountains, in between Melrose, the ugliest town in America, and Falling Rock, the prettiest. Melrose was the land of all-you-can-eat buffets, gas stations, and cell phone stores. Falling Rock was all beautiful cliffs and gorges, sky that stretched pink and ominous, and windy roads that made your ears clog and pop, clog and pop, as if the human body was ill equipped for such splendor.

The bar Bennett chose in Falling Rock was in a dim Mexican restaurant, the walls decorated with straw sombreros; photographs of customers drinking margaritas from tall plastic vases; and colorful ponchos, sleeves spread—invisible people waiting for hugs. We sat side by side on bar stools. Bennett ordered a Corona and a shot of Patrón Silver. The bartender wore a thick, long braid down her narrow back. She was thinner than I had ever been, and her thinness looked thoughtless, like she was a woman who would eat a few nachos and then smoke a cigarette.

"Chilled?" she asked Bennett, holding up her shaker.

"Nah."

"Salt?"

"Won't be necessary."

My impulse was to show possession, to touch Bennett's hand, the pale green veins beneath his skin like the cords of a leaf, his black waterproof watch, the blond hairs on the backs of his fingers, the smooth clipped panes of his nails. But to touch him was to admit to a decision. The outer corners of our knees brushed together through our jeans, and I felt Bennett as acutely as if we were naked.

"So," Bennett said, and I leaned closer to him. I loved that word when it came from a stranger. From someone close, "so" meant, *We need to talk and it won't be pleasant.* From Bennett, it felt like fingertips grazing the outermost cells of my skin. "It's high time you told me what you're doing here," he said.

I hesitated, unsure of what he meant. Here with him? Here at camp? Here in a town elevated 3,500 feet above New York City?

"We should all sit down sometime," Bennett said, "the whole staff, and tell our stories. Bet we'd hear some crazy ones."

Yes. These were the conversations I wanted to have. Bennett was so different from the cynics I knew in New York—the harried servers, the stand-up comics.

"Everyone's here to lose weight," I said. "Everyone's in college. Or just out. And they're overweight. And here's an opportunity to get paid to diet for two months. That's everyone's story."

"Not yours."

"Not yours, either." Behind the bar, the liquor bottles stood at attention, guarding a gilt-framed mirror. A poster tacked to the ceiling showed a cowboy on horseback, mid-lasso. "What do you think he's trying to catch?" I finished my Stoli and soda as Bennett took his shot. The bartender replaced our empty glasses with full ones.

Bennett tilted his head back and squinted one eye at the poster. "A cow?"

I smiled. Mikey would have answered with a joke. He would have said it loudly enough for everyone around us to hear.

"It's like us at camp," I said.

"Lassoing cows?"

"God." I covered my face. "I have this friend who teaches special ed and she always makes jokes about her students . . . What's it called? Battlefield humor? So tasteless. But now here I am, no different."

"Don't be so hard on yourself."

I lifted my face from my hands. "I hate when people say that. I'm not hard enough on myself."

"You're a good person, Angeline."

"There's no such thing as a good person."

"What have you done that's so bad?"

I paused. "I don't know."

"Killed anyone?"

I laughed. It sounded shrill.

"See? You're fine."

"Three-legged dogs turn my stomach. I can't even look at them. A good person would adopt one. And one time this spring, I was leaving work, and it was pouring out, and I took someone's nice umbrella from the umbrella stand by the door and left my cheap broken one. I still have the nice one. It has a big yellow sun inside. I love it. I don't even feel guilty about it anymore."

"If you weren't a good person, you wouldn't be working at a weight-loss camp."

"What would I be doing? Tanning? Robbing banks?" I traced the rim of my glass with one fingertip. "A lot of bad people act good. There are pedophiles who become religious leaders. Socio- paths who become psychiatrists. Maybe you overestimate me."

"Maybe you underestimate yourself."

"So you're one of those motivator personal trainers. You're like Richard Simmons."

Bennett lifted an eyebrow. "Huh?"

"Nothing." I shook my head, clearing the image of Mikey as if from an Etch A Sketch. "What are *you* doing here?"

"Asked you first."

"Guess you did. Okay." I looked at him and lied. I told him the carefully phrased half-truth—no, tiny fraction of a truth—I'd told everyone before I left New York: "My father died last summer. He was obese. It killed him. I want to help obese children."

Bennett pressed his lime into the mouth of his beer bottle with his thumb. "My son's got a weight problem," he said. "I wanted him to come to camp, but he wouldn't. And his mother's no help."

My eyes moved to his tattoo. His sleeve covered most of it, but the point of the heart peeked out. "Is Camille his mother?"

Bennett swigged his beer, then wiped his lips with the back of his hand. "Yup."

"Were you married?"

"Married. Working in sales. The whole nine."

"I used to work in sales, too," I said.

I had a brief, bright memory then of barking in the West Village, before my business took off, before I hired a street team to bark for me. In a way, that had been the best time—the beginning, when I was doing everything myself, when I thought I could make anything happen.

Barking had come to me intuitively. I knew what to say to unlock strangers' wallets. I would study each person's face, how he held his arms, where his feet were pointing, and I would infer what he needed to hear, when he wanted me to laugh, and at which point in the conversation I should casually touch his arm or step a little closer to him, making a mirror image of his toes with mine. I targeted large groups, sometimes selling ten tickets in one shot. I knew to compliment a woman's accessories, a man's height, a baby's distinctiveness. I learned quickly never to waste time on a person wearing headphones or a man holding a woman's hand.

Unlike most barkers, I didn't hate barking. I liked being on my feet all day, burning calories. I liked when men would say, "You're too sweet to be selling things from the sidewalk." They would ask, "Are you a comedian?" and I would say, demurely, "No, I'm just the face."

"The face," they would say. "Well, it's a pretty cute face." And they would reach into the back pockets of their jeans.

"I can see you in sales," I told Bennett.

"I sure never could."

"You'd be good at it. You're convincing."

"I'm not trying to convince anyone of anything." Bennett moved his leg away from mine, and then looked past my head to a baseball game on a television in the corner. I stared at the space between our knees. "I studied exercise physiology in college. Played soccer." He looked down at his beer bottle and scratched at the label. "Division one. But . . ." His mouth turned up at the edges. "Miss Angeline," he said. "You know what?"

"What?"

"I hated sales. Last year, I woke up one morning and said, 'Enough.' You ever think that? 'Enough already'?"

"No," I said. "I've never thought that in my whole life."

Bennett inhaled as if to say something else, but then his face paused between expressions.

"I'm kidding," I said.

He chuckled, scratching his head.

"Sorry. My boyfriend always tells me I'm not funny. Sometimes I forget."

The word "boyfriend" exploded in the air between us like fireworks.

"Your boyfriend sounds . . ."

"He's a good guy. It's just . . . he's professionally funny. 'Professionally funny.' I'm 'humorous, at best.'" I stopped talking. I was making Mikey sound like an asshole, when in fact, I was the one drinking tequila with a strange man, touching my knee to his, playing with my necklace to draw attention to my cleavage.

"You ever been to Durham?" Bennett asked.

"Durm?"

"Dur-RUM. I slur it all together like the southern boy I am. And here I thought you were the one with the accent. Durham's the diet capital of the world. That's what they say. But still North Carolina's the twelfth fattest state in the country. Mississippi's number one. Never move to Mississippi."

I touched my middle, fingering the rolls. They were shrinking, but still supple like living things. In Mississippi, they would flourish. I wondered if Bennett could see it—how close I was, at every second, to becoming obese. *Don't move to Mississippi. Don't think about lasagna. Don't miss a day of spin class.*

"Are you suggesting I visit the diet capital of the world?"

"I live there."

"So *that's* why you have a perfect body."

Bennett grinned. "This ol' thing?" He patted his stomach. "Anyway, there's this facility there that's like a fancy fat camp for adults. I wandered in there to see about employment. Lewis was working there. That's his winter job. He answers phones. We got to talking and he told me he was starting this camp." Bennett took a long sip. "Ahh," he said, holding up his bottle to look at it. "I do love a cold beer. Is there anything in life better than a cold beer?"

I saw part of him through that bottle, manageably blurry, less significant through glass.

"So what happened with Lewis?"

"What happened?" He lowered the bottle to the bar. "He hired me. Rest is history. I'll see about getting my boy here next summer."

I didn't want to think about next summer. I didn't want to think about a person who belonged to Bennett. I didn't want to think about the fall or the winter or anything but this evening—the cautious, burgeoning lust and the alcohol and the ceiling fans that did little to make the restaurant less stuffy. I didn't want to think that my plan might not work, that I might leave camp in August only to resume the uncomfortable dance I'd been doing with food the past year, regaining weight when all the bistros and bodegas and bakeries of New York City were once again at my disposal.

I didn't want to think about a day when my jeans would no longer feel loose and the man beside me would not be Bennett with the Hurricanes cap and the southern accent and the V-shaped torso and the cross around his neck; a man who didn't grasp sarcasm; a man who appeared and disappeared second by second, like a series of beeps; but Mikey, who knew—almost—everything about me, whose unrelenting knowing of me weighed as much as a whole other person.

"How old's your son?"

"Eleven." Bennett leaned to the side, reached into his back pocket, pulled out a brown leather wallet, and flipped it open. A child with his blue eyes beamed back at me. Freckles flecked his nose. If I could have taken a cookie cutter and trimmed away the layer of fat around his face, then he would have been perfect.

I squeezed one eye shut and imagined him thin. "Adorable."

"I agree." Bennett flipped his wallet closed and stuffed it back into his pocket.

I pressed my paper cocktail napkin to the outside of my glass, blotting the condensation.

"You're going to break my heart, aren't you, Angeline?"

I shifted my gaze to the crumpled napkin in my fist and dropped it on the bar. When I glanced at Bennett again, he was looking right at me.

I laughed. "Me?"

"You're going to make me fall for you. One of those summer loves people write songs about. And then you'll head back to your big-city life. I can see it now." Because his smile was confident, his words sounded not desperate, but flirtatious. And how could he have been desperate? He was a sculpture come to life. What could he possibly have needed from me?

"What are you talking about?" I was still laughing. "I have a boyfriend."

"I know you do."

"So you're kidding, right?" I was leaning my elbow on the bar now, resting my face on my fist. In my other hand, I held my glass. I finished my drink in a long gulp, set my glass on the bar and my cold hand in my lap. Bennett touched the inside of my wrist and I shivered. His cologne smelled nothing like Mikey's; it was lighter, airier, a slow fan on a summer day. I caught intermittent whiffs of it, and then couldn't smell it at all. "I can't sleep with you," I said.

"Who says I want to sleep with you? I wouldn't sleep with you."

"Because I'd break your heart?"

"No."

"You'd sleep with me, Bennett."

"I wouldn't."

"Why?" I touched my stomach again, sucking it in.

"If I slept with you, you'd call your boyfriend tomorrow and drop him like a hot rock. You'd tell me you'd been planning to anyway, that it had nothing to do with me. Am I right?"

"I'm not leaving my boyfriend. We've been together forever."

"You'd leave him, and then you'd say to me, 'I'm just looking to have fun for the summer.' You'd act cool as a moose, but if I agreed to a fling, you'd want a relationship. And then you'd want to get married. And I've already been down that dark alley."

His words made me uneasy, like an unexpected mirror. Here was a man who knew about hunger, who had a handle on wanting.

My rolls were growing, pressing against the waistband of my jeans. Nearby, I heard the urgent sizzle of fajitas and smelled soft strips of chicken, sautéed onions, steaming flour tortillas.

"A bit presumptuous, no?"

"I mean no disrespect." Bennett lifted his hands from the bar to show me his palms. "But here we'd be working together for the rest of the summer with this monkey on our backs."

I turned from Bennett, watched a waiter bend at the knee, transferring a tray from his shoulder to the wooden stand he'd shaken open beside the table. I swear, if it weren't for smells and songs, our memories would all be detached and anesthetized.

"So, no, Angeline, I wouldn't sleep with you."

"What if I seduced you?"

"I don't need anyone doing the seducing. I know what to do."

For the past two weeks, I had smelled nothing but fat-camp food. Textured vegetable protein instead of beef. Fat-free cheese that didn't know how to melt. Sugar-free Jell-O. Sugar-free peanut butter. Frozen mini bagels, thawed, not toasted. And now. Suddenly. One whiff of those fajitas and I was hurdled back to the hole-in-the-wall Mexican restaurant where my parents and I used to have brunch some Sunday afternoons—the cold, all-you-can-eat buffet of peel-'em-and-eat-'em shrimp, questionable oysters, flan, tortilla chips, every kind of salsa. Each time, my father ordered fajitas off the menu. As a child, I was afraid of them—their steaming and sizzling and popping. I thought of what Spider had said about the earwigs. I was always afraid of the wrong things.

"You hungry?" Bennett asked.

"I'm fine."

"You're staring at their food."

"No, I'm not."

"Then what are you looking at?"

"That woman . . . just looks like someone I know."

The woman was huge, dressed in denim overalls with a pocket on the front the size of a door. She was depositing a heaping forkful of rice and sour cream into her mouth.

It was possible to watch mouths eating and infer the bodies attached to them. You could have shown me slides of mouths, and the forks about to enter them, and I could have analyzed the ratio of food on fork to empty fork space to inches between open lips, and told you, with a negligible margin of error, who was fat and who was thin.

"We can get you something if you're hungry."

"I'm really not hungry," I said. I wanted to leap off my bar stool, scald my fingers on the sautéed peppers, bury my tongue in the sour cream and pico de gallo. I wanted to stuff my cheeks like pouches of marbles.

It surprised me, feeling hungry so close to Bennett. But this was a nostalgic hunger, like one last look in the rearview mirror. I thought of the day I'd left my father in the diner and vowed to change my life.

The bartender set a basket of tortilla chips in front of us. A white bowl of red salsa. "On the house," she said. She winked at Bennett. Her nails were long and sharp.

"Here." Bennett pushed the basket toward me.

I curled my fingers around my thumbs, imagining the crunch between my teeth, the salt on my tongue, the cool spiciness of the salsa. I salivated so intensely, my eyes burned. If I looked too long, I would touch them. If I touched them, I would never stop. Within three seconds, the napkin lining the wicker basket would be naked except for a grease stain or two.

"You didn't mean what you said, Bennett. When you said I'd break your heart. You meant you'd break *my* heart."

"Crazy talk."

"Aren't I right? If I sleep with you, you'll be through with me? Isn't that how men are?"

"So let's not. That's all I'm saying. We'll just be friends."

"Fine."

"I'm not out to hurt anyone, Angeline." Bennett cracked his knuckles one at a time.

I thought of my father tipping his head back, shaking the dust from the bottom of a bag of Cheetos into his open mouth. I thought of myself walking through the East Village, stopping in Dunkin' Donuts, in Moishe's Bake Shop, in the place that sold hot French fries in paper cones. I thought of my campers, the expanses of their bodies spreading as they sat on the edge of the pool. I thought of Mikey. I did think of Mikey. I thought of Mikey laughing. "When are you going to learn, Gray? Men don't want to be your friends." I thought of Azalea Bellham, of my father's lips on her mousy throat. I stared hard at Bennett until my hunger subsided. Then I took his clean-shaven face in my hands. I pulled it toward me and kissed him.

TWENTY-TWO

I drove drunk back to camp from Falling Rock, Bennett beside me in my father's car, his left hand on my thigh, his right hand tweaking the radio dial. The static of classic rock and the certainty of sex crackled in the dark, in the Blue Ridge Mountains, in the throbbing of the swollen moon. We spiraled down that drain of a road. I asked, "You still won't sleep with me?"

"Okay, fine, I'll sleep with you."

"I can't sleep with you."

"Whatever you say, Angeline."

At camp, I pulled my car up to the side of the boys' dorm, killed the engine, unbuckled my seat belt.

"Wait here," Bennett said, getting out.

I leaned my head back and closed my eyes. The dark spun and dipped and pulsed. When I heard Bennett open my door, I let my eyelids crack apart. He slid one arm under my legs and the other around my back. When he lifted me without so much as a change in his breathing, I was lighter than the bones of a goldfish. He carried me inside, and when he tossed me onto his bed, I bounced. He yanked my legs until my feet touched the floor. He unbuttoned my jeans and unzipped them.

"Do you have a condom?" My voice sounded as thick as cake batter.

"I'll pull out."

"That feels symbolic."

"Shh."

"You're protecting yourself."

"You're full of drunk talk."

"You won't let go inside me."

"Are you too drunk? Should we stop?"

"We should not," I said.

"Not what?"

"Not stop."

Then I was thinking of nothing. I didn't think of Mikey. I forgot the fajitas. I forgot Azalea. I forgot what my father had done to my mother and what I had done to my father. When Bennett touched my bare thighs, my legs were perfect and slim. When he pressed his lips to my ribs, to each of my hipbones, to my belly button, the weight of him kept me from floating away. I didn't need Eden! All I needed was this!

So finally, two weeks into the summer, on the 388th day I'd spent on the planet without my father, I willingly, gratefully, without restraint, flung my arms wide and surrendered.

TWENTY-THREE

The first time I kept a secret from Mikey, I didn't understand that he wouldn't find out. Before that, I could smile with my back turned and he would ask, "What are you smiling about?" I could scratch my chin in a certain way and he would tell me to stop being critical. We shared all the same opinions on every comic in the circuit. He knew every story I'd ever told. Back when we were falling in love, the first time he showed me his childhood photo albums, I sobbed into his pillow, sad that I'd missed so much.

"It's okay," he told me then, stroking my hair. "I'll catch you up on everything."

We were together for nearly four years before I kept my first secret. I waited. I watched his face while he drank coffee, wrote jokes in his notebook, clipped his fingernails into the trash can. I stayed awake while he slept, knowing that at any second he would open his eyes, turn to me, laugh at me: "Gray. Come on! Of course I know you killed your father!" I waited. I waited. I waited for him to show me that our brains were as fused as I'd thought.

Nothing happened.

TWENTY-FOUR

Still drunk, I ran back to the girls' dorm under a pink smudge of sky, my stomach roiling, my skull straining against my scalp. My cell phone, charging on the windowsill where I'd left it, showed six missed calls from Mikey. It was 5:16 A.M. I unplugged the phone, switched it off, crawled into bed, closed my eyes, and tried to add up the alcohol calories I'd consumed, but nausea kept distracting me, so I turned onto my side and imagined Bennett curled up at my back, his top arm draped over my hip or shoulder, but not my middle where the worst of me was.

Having fallen asleep for an hour or two in Bennett's bed, having woken to the sound of his snoring beside me, I hadn't wondered where I was, hadn't had to reassemble the night like a torn-up love letter. I'd known, immediately, exactly what I'd done.

Now I pulled the blanket over my shoulder and thoughts of Mikey crept in—Mikey on a stage, calling a girl in the front row "sweetie"; Mikey in our bed in the East Village, asleep in striped boxer shorts, huge limbs hanging over the mattress edges; the two of us a few years earlier on his first road gig, lying head-to-toe in a motel bathtub, where he'd lifted my foot from the water and sung "Crazy Love" into my sole.

Out my window, the birds were getting started and the sun was gaining strength. I would tell Sheena I was sick and take the morning off. Maybe Bennett would worry. Maybe he would spend the day remembering being inside me. Maybe he would stare at the girls' dorm, wondering which window was mine. I looked at my dresser and realized that I hated all of my clothes. They were fat clothes—the XXL tank tops I'd bought at Old Navy that spring after a particularly bad binge, shorts with elastic waistbands, unflattering yoga pants that folded over at the top and stopped at mid-calf. When I recovered from this hangover, I would have to find a mall. It soothed me to rest my thoughts on the easy comfort of commerce. I did not want to think of Mikey. I did not want to think of my father. But I remembered the night my father died, when I checked Mikey's body for cancerous moles. He'd taken a taxi to his parents' house in Brooklyn, borrowed their car, and made the four-hour drive to Boston.

Is it trite to say that I felt numb? Do I sound like a person who has never known grief, like one of those men who murders his wife, hides her body, and gives a tearful, televised eulogy? Do I sound like an ashamed virgin who compares a vagina to a blooming flower?

Perhaps I had no right, but I grieved. I will always grieve my father.

When Mikey hugged me on the threshold of the house I'd grown up in, I felt encased in thick plastic. An astronaut suit. I couldn't even feel the pressure of his touch, the weight of his body. I let him hold me. I must have hugged him back. It was midnight. I could hear the muffled inflections of my mother's voice from the living room as she spoke on the phone with a friend. I led Mikey up to my childhood bedroom and inspected him.

"You have got to start wearing sunscreen," I said. "You'll be thirty in a few years. And one day, forty."

"Okay," Mikey said, helping me part his hair, holding his ear open so I could peer inside. "You're right," he said, "I'll start."

My father hadn't died of cancer. And Mikey's dark Sicilian complexion wouldn't have lent itself easily to melanoma. I was scared not so much by mortality, but by the thing that had always scared me—the mind's disconnection from the body. There were women who made the news now and then, who had delivered babies, shocked they were pregnant. "I just felt something strange in my stomach," they would say, bottle-feeding an infant in a hospital bed, "and out it came."

My first summer as a comedy club booker, I was so preoccupied, so sleep-deprived, so driven, I'd unwittingly let my armpit hair grow out until Mikey had intervened. "You're regressing, Gray," he'd told me. "You're becoming early man."

And there was a news segment I'd seen on obesity—a six-hundred-pound woman rushed to the hospital with a fever. Weeks before, she'd stuck a hamburger under one of her breasts, saving it for later. Forgotten, it had molded, causing a nearly lethal infection.

And then there was my father, eating a slice of pizza in two bites; smoking cigars; drinking scotch; letting sweat roll down his face, unnoticed, while he sat watching television in the wintertime.

"We can get so out of touch," I told Mikey, running my fingertips over the birthmarks on his naked back. I knew every single one of those birthmarks—all the possible constellations. "It scares me," I said. "Don't you find that scary?"

We were sitting on my childhood bed, beside my stuffed stegosaurus that was missing an eye. As a child, I'd shoved that thing under my shirt and pretended to nurse it at my nipple. "Your baby looks just like you," my father used to say.

Mikey turned around and took me in his arms. I felt him this time—the blazing warmth of life just under his skin, his heart beating inside his chest, pounding down walls to reach me. I worried that he would make a joke. I thought I could hold myself together forever if he didn't make a fucking joke. He squeezed me until it hurt to breathe and said, "Gray, I won't let anything happen to you."

TWENTY-FIVE

I snapped awake to the sound of my door swinging hard on its hinges. When I opened my eyes, Sheena was sitting on my feet. "Well, *someone's* red-eyed and bushy-tongued. Girl, you told me you had the flu!" She was grinning, distractedly fingering the white scars beneath her lower lip, her cheeks splotched pink. "Bennett looks like hell." She bounced up and down on the bed and the springs squeaked absurdly. "Were you two doing the jiggery-pokery?"

"My feet, Sheena."

She got up and crossed the room to the full-length mirror that stood propped against the wall, and then gripped the frame to angle it so she could see her whole body. "You're so short," she said, smoothing her T-shirt over her hips, which had visibly narrowed. She spun around a few times and then leaned an elbow on my dresser, stretching her thick ponytail to one side to inspect the ends. Sheena was the first person I'd met in twenty years who owned and used a crimping iron. "He's not bad for an old man. Built like a brick shithouse."

I closed my eyes. "You have it wrong."

"Hmm."

"We drank too much last night. We're practically the only people here who can drink legally. That's all."

"The girls today! Spider's like one of those scratch-and-sniff stickers. She scratches herself raw. And sucks that EpiPen necklace. Eden hasn't stopped talking all morning. All. Morning. I could kick her. You know what your lying around in bed means? It means I have to listen to Spider and Eden. Come back from the dead, Lazarus!"

I opened my eyes. "What's for lunch?"

"Tacos. With textured vegetable protein."

Nausea slithered up through my chest.

"Can we just agree that you get Spider and Eden and I get Whitney and Miss?"

"What do you mean 'get'?"

"Whitney and Miss are my campers, and Spider and Eden are yours. And Harriet can be her own smelly island. Deal?"

"I have to sleep just a little more." I wanted to stay in the cocoon of my bed, remembering each muscle of Bennett's back, the clipped wings of his shoulder blades. I closed my eyes again, pulling the blanket over my face. "Please, Sheena. I'm sorry. Tomorrow I'll cover for you during my free period. Then you'll have two free periods. Okay?"

"Did you and Bennett do it? You know I'll find out."

Under the blanket, I opened my eyes, and the weight of Bennett's body, his hipbones on my hipbones, filled my head, threatening to spill out of my mouth. I had slept with a man! We weren't even in love! We had just gotten drunk and *done it*, and he was handsome! A brick shithouse. I wanted to feel the shape of those words in the air, to watch Sheena's face switch on like a lamp.

"Okay, fine, we had a little sex."

Sheena yanked the blanket down to my chin. Her eyes glistened. She was a dog awaiting a treat.

"Sheena," I said. "You can't tell a soul."

"Is he hung?"

"Is he *what*? I don't know."

"How can you not know?"

I rubbed my fists into my eyes. "Sure, he's *hung*."

"You're a cheater!" Sheena said, her tone light with dark edges.

I stopped rubbing my eyes. As my vision cleared, her face came into sharp focus—the lacing of white scars underlining her mouth, her eyes like black scopes. It occurred to me with some discomfort that Sheena was a stranger.

"Sheena, it wasn't anything," I said. "Really. Nothing has changed."

TWENTY-SIX

Lunch passed without me, and then rest hour, and then, finally, I rose on wobbly legs like a colt and checked my voice-mail messages.

Mikey.

"I'm worried about you. I dreamt that you were eating ham. And then I woke up and thought, *Something's wrong if Gray's eating ham. Even if it's just in my dream.* Is that what you're doing down there? All these Christmases you wouldn't touch my mother's ham . . . Does it sound like I'm coming on to you? 'Touch my mother's ham.' Maybe I should fly down there." I heard static. And then, "You'd better not be eating pork without me."

I deleted the message, my limbs so heavy I had to sit on the edge of the bed. I sent him a text message: "I'm fine! Just busy. No ham. Love you."

Then I put on sunglasses first, clothes second, and walked with my campers to the soccer field. The oldest boys were there with Bennett, who was wearing a faded tie-dye T-shirt and setting up orange cones as goal posts.

When he saw us coming, he yelled, "Ladies, you want to play boys against girls or mixed?"

I wanted to run into his arms. I wanted him to lift me off the ground so my feet dangled, so the grass blades had to reach for my toes.

"Mixed!" Whitney yelled back. "But put me and Miss on the same team." To Miss, she said, "I'm so sick of females."

"Girls can do anything boys can do," Spider said.

I tugged Spider's bushy ponytail. "You would have been a great feminist fifteen years ago."

"I was just being born," she said. "But know what? I was named after Emily Davidson. She was killed by the king's horse while trying to attach a suffragette flag to it."

"Your real name is Emily?"

"No, it's Davidson."

"Really?"

"No. It's Emily." Spider bumped her hip against mine. "You're so *serious*, Gray. You're like a soldier."

Harriet, dressed in yesterday's black outfit, grumbled, "It's too hot for soccer." I was beginning to think she slept in her clothes. She always looked like something thrown away. "I'll faint," she said.

I, too, felt deliciously faint. I hadn't eaten in twenty-one hours. My head still ached, but the throbbing was muted. Watching Bennett, I felt scooped out like a seashell. I saw him see me, and through his eyes, I saw a thin girl, a girl whose bracelets would fall off her wrists.

But when we reached the field, he said, "Gray, why don't you split the teams up?" and although he was wearing sunglasses, I could tell he was looking past my shoulder.

"Since when do you call me Gray?"

Above us, a fat cloud passed over the sun. Bennett kicked a soccer ball into the air and bounced it off the front of his head.

"Count off by twos," I told the kids weakly, and then nausea pushed me to the bleachers to sit. There was a wet-washcloth heat in the air, the rain ready to be wrung out. I touched my stomach and counted two rolls. If I sat up straight, they unfurled partway, but no position my body could take would make them disappear.

The kids played soccer, fell down, cried theatrically, limped away, rested on laurels, drank water, missed goals. I watched from the sidelines. Bennett blew his whistle, pumped his fist, yelled "Man on!" and "Breakaway!" He patted tops of heads, clapped his hands, pantomimed outside curve kicks. I thought of Mikey lying on top of me, pressing into me, his forehead against my forehead, his palms cupping my face. Over and over, I remembered slurring to Bennett, "What if I seduced you . . . seduced you . . . seduced you?"

I caught sight of Eden hanging back, off to the side, eyeing the soccer ball as it flitted from person to person, sneaker to sneaker, and suddenly I missed my father so much, the missing shook my vision fuzzy. Not the man who had tried to crush Mikey to dust, but the man who used to touch my nose and tell me, "When you're asking for something, make eye contact," the man who shuttled me around not on his shoulders like the other fathers did, but perched on just one shoulder, my legs draped down his chest. "This is the *dangerous* shoulder ride," he would say in his monster voice, and I would cling with all my fingers to the top of his warm head.

Once, my father and I drove all over the North Shore of Massachusetts in search of the perfect clam chowder.

Once, he shielded my eyes when we walked by a church.

"Read Maimonides," he told me. "We aren't supposed to look at crosses."

Then, some rainy Sunday, he took me to a Baptist church in Mattapan just for the music. Afterward, we ate lunch at a soul food restaurant, where he sighed, his mouth full of croquettes, and then swallowed and said, "We should have been born Southern Baptist."

My father—barefoot behind the barbecue, enormous in American flag swim trunks and a floppy white chef hat, saying, "Come here, Gray, I'll show you how to make a burger do a double back flip."

My father—smoking cigars with my uncles, making them laugh until they turned weak; making me, again and again, refill the peanut bowl and crack them new beers.

My father—tossing my mother into the air like confetti, yelling, "Gray, catch!"

My father—singing "I Can't Quit You Baby"—holding his arm out to me for a dance.

Bennett blew his whistle, and our night together, the distraction of it, felt ridiculous—the ponchos decorating the restaurant walls, the dorm room sex, the drunk driving.

I stood and cupped my hands around my mouth. "Get in there, Eden!"

She spun around to face me, her nostrils flared, her lips cinched up like the knot of a balloon. "What the hell do you *want* from me?" she cried, accomplishing, in the space of a second, the thing I'd thought only my father could accomplish. Who but immediate family could load words with deadly bullets? My breath caught in my chest. I lowered myself back onto the bleachers.

Eden threw her arms up and stomped off the field, and I felt a loosening inside me, as if something tight was unfurling, rolling dangerously out of my reach.

TWENTY-SEVEN

Fine, I'll admit that there were precedents. My father's death did not mark the first time I lost control. There was the time in college when I fell down the stairs and spent a month and a half on crutches. There was the first argument I ever had with Mikey, when we didn't talk for eight days. There were other binges, too, some without identifiable catalysts. Why enumerate them? Why wax nostalgic for them? They happened and then they stopped.

Each binge began without consulting me. It was outside, like a fly I distractedly swatted away. I had nothing to do with the hands paying the delivery guy, with the teeth coming together and separating, coming together and separating, with the exhaustion in the jaw, with the fingertips pushing open the front door of the bakery.

I'll admit there was something relaxing in it—relaxing the way ugly, loose-fitting clothes are relaxing, the way the certainty of one's own death is relaxing. As long as a binge lasted, I rarely answered my phone. I blew through deadlines. I attended no parties. I was busy. I was sick. I was consumed and consuming and unfit for public consumption. The things that normally moved me—love, money, a yearning to be remembered, a fear of exposing my self-absorption—were muted by the deafening call of ice cream and stuffed wantons and Cracker Jacks. The world would have to wait, or else trample me like a panicked crowd.

I knew better than to complain. Why be the rich person whining about wanting, the famous person jealous of the more famous person? Why be the toothache patient crying to the cancer patient? So I never said it aloud, but I understood what it was to be fat. As I ate and ate and stared at the wall, I knew what it meant to disown one's body, to survey it with disgust.

So after my father's death, I started telling almost-truths, frequently sidling up to the truth, but stopping short of getting behind it and shoving it into the spotlight. I told people, "I don't know why I'm so depressed."

"This is a rough year," they would say, squeezing my hand. "You lost a parent. Give yourself time."

Sometimes I could almost believe that I'd heal if I just gave it time.

Sometimes I told Mikey, "I'm scared I'm drinking too much."

"Then stop drinking too much," he would say. "And while you're at it, stop banging your head against the wall."

I began to tell everyone I was drinking too much. People thought I was confiding in them. They told me, "I always tell everyone I'm fine. I envy your frankness. It must be therapeutic."

Look, I *was* drinking. At Little Mermaid, I took shot after shot with the customers. If my shift ended early, I sat on the other side of the bar with a martini and spoke to the patron beside me. "I drink way too much."

"Tell me about it," strangers would sigh, raising their glasses to toast me. Or they would say, "It's New York. Everyone's drinking too much." Or they would say, "If you figure out a better way to pass the time, let me know."

There were many ways to explain my appetite. Maybe I was just hungry because I spent so many days dieting. Maybe my willpower simply suffered lapses. I read books about bingeing, learned names like Binge Eating Disorder, Food Addict, and Compulsive Overeating—big, fat, capitalized labels, none of which seemed quite applicable.

Other people who couldn't stop eating claimed to know the source ("I felt so angry, I just wanted to crunch!"), or they cited physiological factors, like mutated metabolisms and gluten allergies. They cut out carbohydrates. They cut out anything processed and packaged. They weighed their lima beans. They kept their chins up, kept online food journals, went to meetings, got walking partners, bought new sneakers, and planted vegetable gardens. They talked about their feelings until talking felt better than eating.

I didn't understand these people. They weren't like me at all.

TWENTY-EIGHT

That night, when Bennett finally approached me, I was sitting alone on the cafeteria steps, holding a pointless flashlight, playing Head O.D. He appeared below me, cast in shadows. When he climbed a couple of steps and came into the light, he asked, "All good out here, Angeline?" and gave me a double thumbs-up.

What was it with men? How could they treat sex like a decadent meal—a pleasant memory with no connection to the heart? Why couldn't I be so practical? Bennett and I didn't know each other. So what if we had mashed our bodies together? He wasn't the point of anything.

But my heart started going in my ears. "I'm thinking of leaving," I said.

"You are?"

No. "Yes."

I thought of my father saying, "Here comes Brenda Preston," which he always said when I was being theatrical, because

Brenda Preston was our neighbor who once, after fighting with her husband, walked out onto her front lawn and threw a heavy flowerpot at her own forehead, fainting while the neighborhood watched.

Bennett climbed the steps and sat beside me. "Because of last night?"

I looked away. This was a lie I wasn't sure how to draw out. I wanted to say, "New subject!" but instead I chewed my lip and stayed quiet.

"This was what I was worried about—that we'd sleep together and you'd hate me."

I looked at Bennett's blank blue eyes. "I barely know you," I said, but my words felt false. Camp days were like dog years. Each day was a month. In a way, already, the social circle I'd left behind in New York seemed like a group of people with whom I'd lost touch. Even my memory of my apartment was vague and shadowy, like a memory of the womb.

"I've never had much luck with women."

"I find that hard to believe."

"I don't understand the heart of a woman. Does that sound stupid to you? It probably sounds stupid."

"I mean, it's not very original."

Bennett tapped his leg to mine a few times. My thigh jiggled. I held it rigid. "What do you want from me?"

"Why does everyone keep asking me that?"

"Well, today I woke up and I wasn't sure what I was supposed to do. Was I supposed to act like your boyfriend?"

"I have a boyfriend."

"So you've said."

I looked at Bennett. He was so strong and sure, pinned to the earth, paperweighted by the muscles of his legs, his college-athlete confidence, the bold tattoo on his arm. I encircled his wrist with my fingers and hung on. He was a Band-Aid on my hunger. What I wanted from him, I had.

"Did you . . . like it?" I asked. "The sex?"

Bennett curled his fist and flexed the muscles of his free arm. "I'm a man," he said in an extra-deep voice. "A red-blooded American." He knocked his arm against mine. "You were terrific."

"I was pretty drunk."

"Crocked and cockeyed."

"I don't think I did much. I was more like a blow-up doll than a person."

"Seemed all right to me, Angeline."

"Just all right?"

"No. Terrific. I told you terrific."

"Terrific," I said like an echo.

"But let's not get ahead of ourselves."

We sat quietly for a few seconds, our hips touching, my hips shrinking. Then I said, "Maybe we can just have fun?"

Right. *Go ahead, make use of my body. I'll affect stoicism.* What was fun about that? When I was in new love with Mikey, I could have fun with the men in the street who bought my comedy club tickets. I could have fun with the other comedians. I could flirt and laugh and watch their pupils dilate like spots of watercolor.

But when my father died, when Mikey and I began to deteriorate, I could no longer talk with a man at a party without either imagining us old in matching rocking chairs, or feeling repulsed by the crumbs between his teeth, his bad posture, the burp he'd tried to hide by puffing out his cheeks.

I could see that Bennett would keep me busy. I would spend the rest of the summer scheming.

"I'm all for fun, Angeline," Bennett said.

I stuck out my hand for him to shake. "Then here's to a summer of fun."

TWENTY-NINE

Bennett's room was an apartment of sorts, twice the size of the campers' dorm rooms, attached to the boys' dorm. To get to him, I had to walk across camp, one-half of the loop. I never made the trip by daylight when campers would have seen me. Nights were tricky, too, because unless we were on duty—either as Head O.D. or on dorm patrol—all counselors had a midnight curfew. With the exceptions of our one free period a day, the few free hours we got every other night, and the long Sunday mornings when we could do as we pleased, we were supposed to be watching the campers.

Although the cafeteria was locked at night, if Sheena and I were absent from our dorm rooms, untold disasters could have transpired: unsupervised late night skinny-dipping in the swimming pool, a dash to the gas station convenience store for sugary snacks with unspeakable shelf lives, a date behind the gym for unauthorized, perilous sex. We were told to be on guard.

And so I had to sneak out.

I knew it wasn't right. But lots of things at Camp Carolina weren't right. For example, I taught water aerobics, even though I wasn't a lifeguard, had never done water aerobics, and knew nothing about CPR. It wasn't right that the personal trainer, the nurse, and the nutritionist weren't certified in their fields. It wasn't right that Lewis played therapist and wrote the menus, ignoring Mia's advice.

"Where the hell is the fiber?" she often complained to me. "The salad bar, fine. But that's not enough. The kids just pick at their salads anyway. And what about protein? There's all this sugar-free crap, white-flour tortillas . . . these kids are learning some ugly habits. What the hell did he make me the nutritionist for? A once-a-week nutrition lesson? That isn't anything," she said. "That isn't enough."

Sure, the kids were losing weight, but that was simple math: For the first time in their lives, they were expending more calories than they were consuming. But what about nutrients and vitamins? Even the vegetables in the salad bar looked old and bleached and sad.

What about roping in the parents, who hid their own fat in fat-people fabrics and said "Taste this, taste that," and asked "Is it good?" and "Does it need more sugar?" while smoothing the hair back from their children's foreheads.

Why should I have taken my job seriously? Camp Carolina was not a serious place.

Was I rationalizing? Yes. I was an expert at dispelling my psychological discomfort.

Each night, I waited until the kids were in bed, and then ran, under the Light Bright board of North Carolina sky, stars puncturing black, to Bennett's apartment. Each time I touched his door and found it unlocked, I wanted to fall to my knees in gratitude.

Within days, a whole year vanished (although "vanished" might be misleading; it was more like a nasty stain on the rug was now covered by a giant couch). Where had I been since my father's death, while my body grew softer and wider and pastier? Where had I been while my leg hair grew long and the hair on my head grew a permanent indent from the elastic that secured my bun?

Where had Mikey been? How could Mikey have watched as I ate and cried, as I moved away from myself as if from a foul odor?

Here is what he should have said: "You've let yourself go."

No, I know, he wasn't allowed. The feminists would have lined up in a row and barked at him like a Red Rover chain. "Send Mikey right over!" they would have cackled, their tight fists awaiting his gut. But couldn't he at least have shaken my shoulders and shouted, "We've hardly had sex in months"? Sex had become tangential to me—skin-to-skin contact, perfunctory orgasms. It seemed like a game for hyperactive children, not a pastime for thinking adults.

But now, with Bennett, I remembered—how beautiful it was, how vital it was, to keep in touch with the flesh.

By the fourth week of camp, I was barely eating. My heartbeat was a constant vibration, my mouth as dry as a gravel pit. At mealtime, I would have preferred to scream than to eat—to jump up on top of the picnic table, beat my chest, and scream.

Nurse told me, "You can't just stop eating. You have to set an example. You have to eat and take healthy shits."

"I what?"

"Doll baby, you know me. Always plain talkin'." She swatted my shoulder with the back of her hand. "People are so squeamish. But there's nothing more beautiful on God's emerald earth than the functions of the body."

"I just haven't been feeling well," I said, but that was a lie! A lie! A lie! I was glowing and quaking with life.

"You're losing too much," she said, and I almost laughed. Was I supposed to believe that Nurse was some expert on loss? Besides, what did I care what Nurse thought? Bennett loved my shrinking body. He encircled my waist with his fingers and said, "Look at you, thin as a pole."

I spent my free periods doing important things: folding Crest Whitestrips over my teeth, rubbing self-tanner into my breasts, trying on my jeans that were now too big, rolling the waistband down to admire the jut of my hipbones. I shaved my legs daily with scented hair conditioner. Now and then I drove to the mall in Melrose and bought smaller bras from the Victoria's Secret clearance bin, or size zero denim miniskirts from stores with pubescent names like Rave. I pored over my campers' discarded magazines, magazines I hadn't read since high school. The August issue of *Cosmo* had a special insert: "100 New Sex Positions."

Angry Butterfly.

London Bridge.

The Dictator.

Reverse Tornado.

I carefully tore the pages out and slid them into my pillowcase.

At night, Bennett touched my ribs, kissed my wrists, ran his tongue from my ankle up the inside of my leg. He liked to tell me in his southern drawl, "You are the most gorgeous creature I've ever seen."

And I was! I was the most gorgeous creature *I'd* ever seen! I would stand in front of my full-length mirror, comb my hair until it twinkled, and think, *You are so lucky to be gorgeous.*

These were, to be clear, exceptional delusions, and likely the product of sleep deprivation. In Bennett's bed, the sleeping I did was more like napping—active, athletic sleep that followed sex for which we could have won medals.

When I did sleep, I dreamt of eating—dipping a long spoon into an ice cream sundae, pouring syrup on a stack of waffles. I dreamt of the nearly forgotten sensation of filling my stomach to bursting. On waking, I would exhale long spools of relief, touching my stomach and finding it flat. Then I would roll over onto Bennett's sleeping body and whisper, "Once more before I go."

How had I forgotten the sheer ecstasy of fucking? All those years with Mikey, how had I survived without this bodies-only, mind-blowing fucking?

Bennett's body fat was 8 percent. "Unpinchable," he said of his skin. He pinched his stomach to prove it, a bit of skin the size of an eyelid. I would straddle him, kneeling, holding the handles of his ears. Or I would lean all the way back, my spine arched, my hair spreading over his feet. Or I would lie supine as he knelt above me, his legs as sturdy as Corinthian columns, my head hanging off the edge of the bed, a heel on each of his shoulders.

"Do they teach you this stuff up north?" Bennett asked.

"Who's 'they'?"

"Where did you learn to fuck like this?"

"*Cosmo.*"

And though during the day I was cheering for my campers if they ran a quarter mile, if they lost two pounds, if they fit into shorts that were size sixteen, at night, with Bennett, the fat disappeared, the fake injuries and tears and sad volleyball games disappeared. Nothing was wrong! Life was flawless! Nothing could ever harm us or our beautiful, thin, lean bodies.

Holy *God*, we were in good shape!

Every morning, I popped out of bed at five A.M., jogged back to my dorm while the world was unconscious, changed into workout clothes that hung loose on my bones, and ran six laps around the loop. And then I would shower and admire my figure, how it seemed to have shrunk in my sleep.

And then I woke up the girls.

"What is wrong with you?" Harriet grumbled one morning while I did jumping jacks in the hallway.

"Nothing!" I cheered.

"How can you possibly have energy?"

I stopped jumping and thought about it. "I wake up with electricity coursing through my veins."

Yes, my veins were electric cords. Live wires. I couldn't exercise enough. It didn't matter that we exercised all day. My body kept shrieking, "Work me! Work me!"

I started running during my daily free period. Sometimes Bennett ran with me, usually backward. "What do you think this is?" he would yell. "A stroll around a pond? Faster, girl! Dig, dig, dig!" I would run until I thought I'd throw up. But what could I have thrown up? Sometimes I dry-heaved into the bushes and Bennett rubbed my back. Then I would stand and stagger, dizzy and grinning.

"I can't wait to fuck you later," Bennett would whisper, slapping my ass like a coach.

Even when we weren't together, I could have pointed to him at any second—his face tucked into sunglasses, his hair coarse and sun-kissed and cut close to his head. I never let him too far out of my sight.

Mia and I spent most rest hours in the gym feasting on stomach crunches, cherry pickers, push-ups, and isolations. I would lie on my back on the dusty gym floor while she stood behind me, her feet at my head. Holding her ankles for support, I would tighten my stomach to lift my legs. Once my feet reached her, she would push them down. I would lift them again and she would push them back down. Lift, push, lift, push. How I grunted with glee and exertion.

O Sisyphus! They were wrong about you! Your fate was an homage to the body!

THIRTY

When I finally got caught, it was Eden who caught me, Eden who was awake at five in the morning, having left her room to sprawl on the hallway floor in an odd, splayed shape, like a body that had fallen from a window.

"What are you doing?" we asked in unison.

"Going for a run," I said, which, though true, made no sense because for one thing, I was coming in from outside, and for another thing, I was wearing a dress. "Do you . . . want to come?"

"Running at five in the morning?" Eden snorted. She was sucking on her Jewish star, the gold chain making an arrow over her chin to point to some place inside her.

"Why are you lying on the floor?" I asked, glancing nervously at all the closed doors. "Here, come into my room. You can lie in my bed while I'm out running."

"Why would I lie in your bed?"

"Changing beds might help you sleep."

"I don't want to sleep."

"You'll feel better," I said.

"If I sleep, I'll have to wake up. And if I wake up, I'll have to have another day. And I'm sick of the days here. I'm sick of life. No way I'm staying here the rest of the summer."

I skimmed over her words, rejecting their gravity, the way I skimmed over bombs in foreign countries when I read the morning news.

Eden sat up, then stood. She was wearing a long T-shirt that said APPLE-BOBBING FOR A CURE! Two leaves surrounded an apple's stem. It was an image of an apple that the world had agreed on, though it looked different from an actual apple.

She followed me into my room, where I changed quickly into running clothes. Eden flopped onto my bed and crossed her arms over her face.

"You've lost a lot," I pointed out. "What, twelve pounds?"

"Fourteen and a half."

"So that's really fantastic."

"Whatever."

"You can't leave while you're on such a roll!"

"I thought you're *supposed* to quit while you're ahead." Eden uncovered her eyes and looked at me, and I wished I could call my mother and tell her: I was looking at my father's eyes.

"Gray?"

"Eden?"

"Did you have sex with Bennett in the arts and crafts building?"

"What?" I stood, crossed the room to the window, and opened it, exposing a sky that was starting to lighten—a strangled, shamed pink. I turned on the window fan.

"It's what everyone's saying. That you guys are having sex. But isn't he, like, forty-something? And aren't you, like, twenty-something?"

I sat on the windowsill, letting the air hit my back. "In any closed environment, you're going to hear a lot of rumors," I said. "I used to work with comedians, and you wouldn't have believed the rumors. Really vicious, life-destroying rumors. I guess it was because they were all in competition, but it was also because they were together so much. Every night, they're all hanging out at the same clubs, trying to get onstage. They're spending all this time together. They can't get away from one another. So they become overly interested in one another's lives. It's this really amazing phenomenon that—"

"So you didn't have sex with Bennett in the arts and crafts building?"

I splayed my fingers in front of me and inspected the mess of my nails, the tiny crescents of dirt beneath the white, the fringes of peeling cuticles.

"Because I think it's poisonous to get that close to spilled paint and all that other stuff. You shouldn't be naked around spilled paint."

I curled my fingernails into my fists. "You don't have to be naked to have sex."

"I *know*. But—"

"Just kidding," I said. I bit my lip. "I have a boyfriend back home. He's a comedian."

"Is he funny?"

"He's funny. Anyway, that's how I started working with comedians. We've been together for years."

"Okay."

"Rumors are terrible." I saw myself on a picket line, with a sign on a stick that read RUMORS ARE TERRIBLE. "People like to judge when they don't know the whole story. It's a good thing to remember—not to judge when you don't know the whole story."

"You sound like a Sunday school teacher."

"You sound like my mother! You're interrogating me like I missed curfew."

Eden smiled. I had come to love her smile, how it swallowed up her eyes, consumed her whole face. "My mother made me come to camp," she said.

I stood.

"I told her, fine, I'd go, just not to one in Virginia because if anyone ever found out, I would die. And now . . . I hate Kimmy."

"What's she going to do, tell your whole high school?"

"Yes."

"Then they'll know she was here, too."

"So? Kimmy doesn't care. She probably had a going-away party. Bon voyage, fatty! A theme party. That's so Kimmy. Or at least, it's something Lily would do. Their family's, like, rich. Lily gets professional massages. And facials. And she has one of those dads who brings her chocolates on Valentine's Day."

"My dad banned Valentine's Day," I said. I waited. Eden said nothing. I waited until it became difficult to draw a breath. I added, "Because it's a saint's holiday."

"And nothing embarrasses the Jackson girls," Eden said, as if I hadn't spoken. "Everyone was probably like, 'That's so adorable that Kimmy's going to fat camp!' I'm sure Lily's told everyone in our whole grade that I'm here. It's fine if Kimmy goes to fat camp. But me? Not so much. Now everyone will call me fat, which they probably already do. And they'll call me a liar because I said I was going to my grandmother's for the summer."

"Your grandmother?"

My father's parents were long dead. His mother had died of ovarian cancer when I was a child. Many years before that, when my father was only six years old, his father, having suffered all his life from depression, wrote a letter to his wife and sons, and then swan-dove two hundred feet off a suspension bridge. (At my lowest point that winter, I'd thought of him, of the freedom of his demise. Oh, to be airborne, weightless, then gone!)

"Is your grandmother your mother's mother?"

"It was a lie, Gray," Eden said. "I told you, I made it up. Anyway, they'll also call me all the other really nice stuff they've been calling me all year."

"What have they been calling you?"

Eden pulled her eyelashes and turned her eyelids momentarily inside out. She looked dead.

"Did you ask Kimmy not to tell anyone that you're here?"

She blinked her eyes back to normal. "Gray. That's really dumb. If you tell someone not to say something, then they'll know you're hiding things."

"True, true, sorry."

"And then they're more likely to tell the whole universe." Eden crossed her arms over her face again. "Too late anyway. She told. God, I did something so stupid last year. Stupidest thing I've ever done in my life. And everyone found out about it. I mean, part of why it was so stupid was that everyone was obviously going to find out."

"What was it?"

"I can't wait until I'm a chef. I can't wait to get out of Bridger and go to culinary arts school." Eden sat up. "No one asked me why I did it."

"Why did you do it?"

"Are you seriously going running?"

"Planning on it."

"You're crazy." Eden leaned back against the wall, pulling her knees up to her chin and her T-shirt over her knees, the silk-screened apple stretching and growing like something important. "We were wasted," she said. "We were drinking forties. Do you know what forties are? I barely even remember anything," she said, closing her eyes and resting her cheek on her knees.

I thought of my father telling me when I was much younger than Eden, "Boys think about nothing but sex."

I had contemplated his claim for days. I had watched the boys in my class—carving drawings into their desks, eating lunch from orange trays, running wind sprints in shin guards—and I had decided that my father couldn't possibly be correct, that boys could not live the lives of boys with the array of activities that entailed, and all the while be solely focused on a thing they'd never done.

"If boys only think about sex," I'd finally said to him, "then why don't they just have sex all the time?"

My father threw his head back and laughed—I was always waiting for that laugh—his mouth flung open, his fillings gleaming, the laugh that seemed to come from somewhere deep inside him, his digestive system maybe, making his belly shake inside his shirt, the laugh I still hear in crowds and in laugh tracks. He suspended my chin on the tips of his fingers, as if my head were a thing for display. "If you remember nothing else in life, remember this: If you give boys what they want, they'll never give you what you want."

Had I gotten through high school without doling out blow jobs only because of my father's love? Or was it because I hadn't been fat, hadn't felt compelled to provide sexual favors in exchange for male attention?

"Eden," I said. "Just so you know, everyone makes mistakes."

"Sunday school teacher!"

"But listen. I mean this. Sometimes, you'll think one event is the most important thing that could possibly happen in your whole life. But it never is."

"Something has to be."

"But you won't know what it is until the very end of your life. Do you understand what I'm saying?"

"You're saying I can do anything I want and it won't matter."

"Kind of." I bit my thumbnail and thought of my father choosing my college major, and then of his fingers flipping through his record collection, extracting a cardboard square with a sigh. "No. That's not what I'm saying."

"Where were you coming from just now?" Eden asked.

The skin around her eyes was puffy, her irises as brown as puddles; I would have liked to splash around in them.

But I had time. I did. I had more than half the summer.

I sighed. "Do I have to tell you?"

Eden shrugged inside the bubble of her T-shirt. "Now I know your secret and you know mine."

THIRTY-ONE

After Lights Out a few nights later, I sat across from Sheena on her bed as she dragged the bristles of a nail polish brush across my big toenail. "When is he going to stop pretending this is a real camp?"

She meant Lewis, who wanted us to choose a camper to win an award. "'Kindest Camper Award,'" he had told the counselors after dinner, "which is better than 'Most Improved' or 'Most Valuable' because it highlights what's truly important. Tomorrow we will have Awards Night. And then a slideshow. Pudge and I have been working on a soundtrack, and we've come up with the perfect songs. They're both carefree and wistful. Everything from hip-hop to the Eagles. It's sure to make everyone cry. Or at least the girls. They'll tell their parents about the lifelong bonds they're forming at my camp, and then their parents will want to send them back here next summer. And the next. It's all about retention. I'm a businessman. But what sets me apart is that I also care about the kids."

"Real camps are at camps," Sheena said, "not at boarding schools. Real camps have lakes." She scraped stray polish from my cuticle.

I kept glancing at Sheena's window. The branches of a tree outside ticked gently against the pane. And through the branches, the seductive smile of the moon. I could see Bennett's face on it, like a president on a coin. As a child, I'd seen my father's. He'd once told me he was the man in there.

"Let's give Eden an award," I said.

"I'd like to give Eden a muzzle." Sheena grabbed my knees. "Can you tell I've lost weight?"

I looked at her. She looked freshly showered. At Camp Carolina, at all times, everyone was either freshly showered or unspeakably filthy. We showered three times a day. We watched our hair go dry and brittle from sun and too many showers. Our flip-flops made squishing sounds when we walked. We twisted towels over our heads like soft ice cream.

Sheena's thick wet hair was caught up in a high copper bun. She wore a strapless pink terry-cloth dress with a Velcro fastening near her armpit. Some of the fat had vanished from her wide white arms.

"I keep telling you," I said. "You look fantastic."

She had tucked a towel under my feet and was wiping the excess polish on it.

"How much?"

"Twenty-one pounds. I want to lose forty more. At least."

"Wow. Twenty-one pounds. Everyone will notice."

"He'll notice." Sheena waved her hand over my right foot, then filled her lungs with air and blew on the wet polish.

"Who, your ex?"

Sheena's walls were covered in glossy photographs, solo shots of Sheena—Sheena in a polka-dot teddy, Sheena posed like a baseball player at bat (but with no bat), Sheena on a worn couch, Sheena fully clothed on the closed lid of a toilet, Sheena wearing a cowboy hat and holding a bag of groceries.

"Yeah. He'll probably still be in jail."

"Jail?"

"Soon as he gets out, though, I'll find him. By then, I'll have lost everything." She bit her lower lip, her teeth fitting neatly into the grooves of her scar. "Can we give Miss the award?"

"She's not kind. She just has good hair. I think she put those bugs in Eden's bed."

"Nah."

"I do."

"Eden had those bugs coming to her." Sheena looked at the bristles of the wand, stuck her tongue out, and licked the polish off. She swallowed. "I've always wanted to know what that tastes like."

"What did it taste like?"

"Earwax." Sheena began polishing the big toenail on my left foot. "I get so hungry here, I want to eat nail polish. Sticks. Rocks. Dirt."

"Why is your ex-boyfriend in jail?"

"Because he's a fuckup."

"The abusive guy?"

"Yeah."

"Is that why he's in jail?"

Sheena looked up at me and smiled. Then her smile faded like a Polaroid in reverse. "You're staring at my scar," she said, touching it.

"No, I'm not."

"People have been staring at it all my life. You think I don't notice?"

"I didn't mean to."

"If you must know, my biological father almost killed me. I've had twelve surgeries. It's still not perfect. And it gave me a lisp."

"You don't lisp."

"I sort of do," she lisped. She tasted the nail polish again, and then bunched her fingers together at her mouth, kissing her fingertips like an Italian chef. *"Magnifique!"* she said. "Try it sometime. When you recover from your anorexia."

"When I *what*?"

Sheena scaled my arm with her eyes. "It's delicious to eat something that's not supposed to be food." She paused, and then said, "He poured boiling water over my head."

"Good God. Your boyfriend?"

"My dad. My biological father."

My chest compressed like an accordion. Why had I been so angry with my father? He'd never burned me, or scarred me, or raised me to be a person who taste-tested cosmetics.

"Do you . . . remember it?"

Sheena elongated her tongue to touch the tip of her nose, then retracted it in a wet pink flash. "People have stared at me since I was a kid. So I stared back. Now I see everything. There's hardly anything I don't notice." She scraped more polish from under one of my toenails, scratching the skin so hard, I gasped.

The room was stuffy, practically airless. I gathered my hair into my hands and pulled it into a ponytail. "Why don't we give an award to Spider?"

"Spider?"

"She's got those allergies. I just feel bad for her."

"Spider is gross."

"You don't think she's funny?"

"How about Whitney? Whitney's kind. Whitney gave Miss her Jell-O today at lunch."

"That's against the rules," I said.

"She broke the rules in order to be kind. That's true kindness."

I thought of Bennett in his bed, the hard lines of his body. "Whatever you want," I said. "I really don't care."

Sheena used tweezers to pluck a hair from my toe.

"Ow."

"How's Mikey?"

"Fine," I said. "Same as always."

When I called Mikey, I pumped him with questions that made him talk and talk; steroid questions that infused his talking with energy, and then I'd end the call so fast ("Shit! Gotta run!"), he had no chance to come down from the high and tell me that he loved me. Now I pictured our apartment, and then pictured it empty of furniture—the standing Kmart lamp with the three-piece stem, the chest of drawers that was missing a drawer, the full-length mirror with the Big Apple Comedy Club sticker. Gone, gone, and gone.

"So no more Bennett?"

I touched the place on my toe where the hair had been. It felt hot with loss.

"You know," Sheena said. "I lied to you about something." She polished my last toenail and blew on it. "When we first met. Me and you shouldn't lie to each other, since we're friends. Right?"

I pressed my toe harder.

"I didn't leave my boyfriend because he was abusive," Sheena said. "I helped the cops bust him for drugs."

I searched Sheena's eyes for her pupils. They were invisible, seamlessly incorporated into her irises.

"So he's in jail. And now he's like, 'Fuck you,' 'Never speak to me again,' 'Everyone's against me,' blah blah blah. That man has a temper like a red-tail boa."

The stubble on my legs rose to attention. Sheena yanked the towel from under my feet.

"He wasn't dealing or anything, but they thought he was. He was just a pothead. They made an example of him."

"And . . . you helped?"

"Sure. I made a hundred bucks." Sheena waved her hand over my toes and glanced at me.

My heart was chopping in my chest, a bonus cardio workout. I looked at my toenails. The red was darker than it looked in the bottle. It looked like blood. Why had I told Sheena about Bennett? Didn't I know this about secrets: that to give them away was to relinquish control to the person who received them? What had I been thinking, granting Sheena power? This summer was far too crucial to wreck by giving up power.

But I was in good company. Everyone told Sheena everything. She was the lenient gatekeeper of all camp gossip. We liked to hand her secrets like jewels, then kneel at her feet while she donned them and basked in their sparkle.

"I did love him," Sheena said. "I've never loved anyone like that. And I know I never will again."

I stood, keeping my toes spread as I pressed my feet into my flip-flops.

When I turned toward the door, Sheena grabbed my wrist. "Here." She was holding the nail polish bottle out to me, her fingers wrapped so tightly around me, I could feel my flustered pulse. "Taste it. It's good."

"I'm pretty sure it's toxic."

Sheena studied the bottle. "Are you saying you just let me poison myself?"

I yanked my arm away from her and backed toward her door. "You didn't eat much of it," I said. "Not enough to do damage. You know . . . I really don't care who gets the award. You can pick."

"Figured."

"I trust you," I said, slipping out into the hallway, closing her door, running from Sheena who knew one of my secrets, who charged one hundred dollars for her betrayal services. I ran into the night and the moon followed.

When I got to Bennett's, I burst in without knocking and found his room dark and filled with music, his body a bump under his top sheet.

"What's up, Angeline?" His voice was sleepy and far away.

I crawled on top of him.

"Hey," he said, chuckling in slow motion.

"Bennett." I wanted to unzip my skin and let my insides fall out. It made no sense. He was not a proper receptacle for my refuse. He would jump out of the way, let it all splash to the floor at his feet. And yet. This was the man I kept choosing.

I pulled my shorts off, my underwear, my shirt.

"Give me a minute," Bennett said. "I gotta wake up. Slow down."

"Please just . . ."

"What?" he said.

I slid my arms around his arms, under his body. I hugged him with all of my muscles. He was a floating log in the sea. I clung even as he warped. "Tell me something," I whispered into his ear.

"Like what?"

"Something that will make me feel better."

"But I don't know why you're feeling bad." He tapped my arm, signaling me to move. I clung more tightly, wrapping my legs around his legs. "You want some vodka? I picked up some of those red plastic Solo cups from Walmart. Those things remind me of college keg parties."

I stayed as still as I could, fusing our heartbeats until I couldn't distinguish them.

"Come on, Angeline. You trying to kill me?" He loosened my arms and lifted me off him, cast me aside, and stood.

"You're trying to kill me," I said.

"Now why would you say something like that?" he said, but he wasn't really asking. His voice was far away. He turned on the lamp by the bed. "You know this song?" He was naked and perfect in lamp light. He was an Olympian.

"Everyone knows this song."

It was Fleetwood Mac. Bennett sang along. He extracted vodka and a bag of ice from the freezer of his mini fridge and then banged the bag on his leg. The ice fell apart against the rocks of his thigh.

"Do you know that Stevie Nicks used to work as a waitress so Lindsey Buckingham could play music?" I propped myself on one elbow.

"God, I was in love with Stevie Nicks back in the day."

I covered my body with the top sheet. "She hated waitressing, but she loved to picture him lying on his floor, playing his guitar, getting more and more brilliant. She just wanted him to be as brilliant as possible."

Bennett brought two cups to bed and slid in next to me, handing me one, sucking condensation off his knuckle. "That right?"

The crowd cheered. Stevie Nicks thanked them in her sexy, raspy voice.

I took a long drink. The vodka was bitter and cheap-tasting and cold. The summer was half gone. "I don't want to go home," I said.

"You don't have to leave for another month."

"A month is nothing."

"Why are you thinking about it?" Bennett leaned his head back against the wall, resting his cup on the plane of his abdominal muscles. "You think too damn much."

"I think between twelve thousand and fifty thousand thoughts a day. Same as everyone."

Bennett laughed.

"Spider told me that."

I took another sip and began to feel better. The summer wouldn't end without my consent. Bennett and I would continue our routine. Eden and I would merge in an elegant, organic fashion. Sheena would keep on being Sheena, eating nail polish, teaching the same yoga postures day after day.

"Just tell me something good," I said, leaning my head on Bennett's shoulder and closing my eyes.

I love you. I tried to send him the message, to make him think that he'd thought of it, the words looping from my brain to his brain, from his mouth to my brain, and so on, forever. *Let me take you out of your life and insert you into mine.* I was so close to his tattoo, the red heart, another woman's name.

Bennett yawned. "It's *all* good, Angeline. Stop worrying about nothing all the time."

THIRTY-TWO

By the fourth weigh-in, Eden had lost sixteen pounds. Harriet had lost thirty-two. Pudge, who had deserted his wheelchair, evolving on fast-forward into a bipedal human, had lost thirty-six. I had lost seventeen. Every week, every single person at camp had lost at least one pound. Until now. Whitney had gained back two. Miss had gained back three.

"Someone must have smuggled candy in," Lewis said when he pulled me aside at Sunday brunch. "Have you been monitoring your campers?"

"Monitoring them?"

"How closely have you been watching?"

"I watch them!" I said, glancing away from Lewis, toward Bennett at the table on the stage—he was stretching his arm, pulling it across his chest. I glanced toward my group's table where Spider was singing a Japanese song, her arm slung around Harriet's neck. Harriet sat as straight and still as a stake. "But I can't catch everything. Maybe someone sent a care package?"

"We open every package."

"Maybe a parent cut the head off a teddy bear, stuffed candy inside, and sewed the head back on."

"This is a nightmare," Lewis said. "I can't have campers gaining weight. Staying the same from one week to the next, okay. People plateau. It happens. But gaining? What a mess. If they tell their parents . . ." He pulled his glasses off by one stem and massaged his forehead with the pads of his fingers.

"What?" I said, my heart speeding up. "What would happen if they told their parents?"

I knew the answer. The parents would enter by force, severing the summer with a guillotine blade, rescuing their children from the weight-loss camp that served candy and had no lifeguard and lacked a certified therapist.

"I go to great lengths to help these children," Lewis said, "and look how they repay me."

Lewis looked fatter every day, his hips expanding as if invisible forces were pulling them in either direction. Whenever I caught sight of his tray during mealtime, it was filled not with what everyone else was eating, but with four or five plastic cups of sugar-free Jell-O. No way he was subsisting on sugar-free Jell-O alone and gaining as much weight as I was sure he was gaining. I had difficulty looking at him for more than a few seconds at a time. He seemed so foolishly proud of his body, as if it were a foreign language of which he feigned knowledge. I thought of my three-year-old cousin turning pages of her books, pretending to read, making up her own stories, in which she starred as a beautiful princess.

Lewis walked up to the stage, clinked a spoon against a water glass as if to toast a bride and groom, waited for silence (which fell only after he hollered "Listen up!" at least six times, while continuously rapping the glass), and then yelled, "If anyone tries to give you food that's not part of my program, that person is not your friend!" He paced the stage, wagging his finger. "That person is trying to poison you! That person is your enemy."

Someone giggled.

Lewis stopped pacing and faced his audience, his hands on his hips. "It's not *funny!*" he shouted so hard, his body shouted with him, bending briefly at the middle.

And then he told a story about a pudding-eating contest he had won as a teenager. His manner relaxed as he reminisced—the self-satisfied tone of a man recounting the loss of his virginity—but toward the end, it seemed to occur to him that the story had no point, so he shifted gears and made it a parable, the moral of which was "Eating is probably not your only talent."

The campers sat quietly, blinking.

"You have got to surrender to my program!" he said, shaking his fist in the air like a revolutionary. "You might think you can eat one onion ring, or one York Peppermint Patty. But you can't! Food outside my program can lead to a binge. And you never know if it's going to be a one-hour binge or a sixty-day binge, a two-pound binge or a forty-pound binge."

"What's a forty-pound binge?" someone asked.

"What's his program?" someone else whispered.

Lewis looked around as if he'd been woken from a dream. Then he said, "If anyone is giving you poisonous food, you'd better tell me. I'll send that person home so fast, he'll . . . he'll . . . his *head* will spin." He pointed to his head. "And you won't get in trouble. But if you don't tell me, and I find out you ate poisonous food, you *will* go home. I'm not afraid to send anyone home! I don't care if I'm at this camp all by myself!"

When he finished, he sat down to his Jell-O, shaking open

a white paper napkin, making a bib of it over his T-shirt. It took a few seconds for the campers to cautiously resume their meals and conversations.

"Poisonous food?" Miss finally said, and she and Whitney laughed so hard, they had to lean together and brace each other from falling off the bench.

I looked at Eden, who was wearing a very new-looking baseball cap sideways, her black hair falling over the white sleeves of her T-shirt, and watching Whitney with a face that looked ready to eat contraband food, if only Whitney would invite her.

"Gray?"

I turned.

Spider was clutching her stomach, her tray pushed back, her face the white of Twinkie filling. "Talk about poisonous food!" she said. "I must have eaten . . ." She burped robustly, and then swung her legs over the bench and stood. She started toward the door. "I ate something . . . I might need to go to the—" Then, while we watched, before anyone could spring to action, Spider dropped to the floor, yanked her EpiPen necklace off her neck, and jabbed the needle into her own thigh.

The room emitted a collective gasp. Spider closed her eyes and sighed like a junkie, and then pulled the syringe out and let it clatter to the floor. Before anyone could reach her, she started gagging like a sick cat, covered her mouth with her palms, and vomited through the cracks of her fingers.

THIRTY-THREE

"She's just gotta puke it up," Nurse said, as we stood together outside the closed bathroom door in her "office," a large room on the first floor of the girls' dorm, while Spider let loose loud, belching, splashing heaves. "See? That was a good one. She's getting it out." Nurse plucked at the front of her T-shirt, rearranging it over her belly.

"Do you have more of that stuff?" I asked Nurse. "Whatever's in the EpiPen?"

Nurse shook her head. "Truth be told, I don't have much of anything."

"So what should we do if she doesn't stop throwing up?"

"Let's not worry about that just yet."

"What could she have eaten?"

Nurse turned up her palms. "There's no doctor back in the kitchen. It's just those ladies who snap their gum and say ugly things about everyone. Something needs to be done about that.

I'm going to make sure something gets done about that." She dropped onto the couch, the cushion rising on either side of her like a victory V, but when she leaned her head back, her stringy bangs parted, revealing tired lines on her white forehead. "They call Spider PITA."

"Why?"

"Stands for 'pain in the ass.' I told Lewis . . . this is a kid with serious allergies. I told him someone should be monitoring her food. Someone who really understands. Some kind of food allergy expert."

"What about you?"

Nurse closed her eyes and pushed her fingers through her thin silver hair. "But you can't tell Lewis anything."

"Spider's parents could sue."

"That's right," Nurse said. "Better believe *I* would."

My stomach swam at the thought of all the failures, of camp being whisked away like a dirty dish from a table.

"But then what?" I asked.

"Then Lewis will be in a heap of shit, that's what."

"But where would we all go?"

Nurse opened her eyes and gave me a tired smile. "Home?"

I looked at the cold, blank face of the bathroom door, the sharp angles of it in its frame.

"That wouldn't be the worst thing in the world, would it?" Nurse said.

Spider gagged violently, and I clutched my stomach.

When I heard a knock behind me, I knew without turning that it was Bennett. I could always feel Bennett.

"Anyone home?" He wedged into the office. "She okay?"

"She will be," Nurse said.

I could smell him—his summertime cologne and the soap we'd slid over each other's skin that morning. Because it was

Lazy Sunday, I hadn't bothered racing back to my dorm at dawn; instead, we'd lounged in bed, then ran twelve laps around the loop together, and then, against his wall before moving to the shower, engaged in sweaty, primal sex reminiscent of swinging from vines.

I was still half-hiding the fact of us, but the other half of me wanted the world to do back handsprings, have a light show, and close off the streets for our lust parade.

When I stepped a little closer to him so the backs of our hands could brush together, unnoticed, the bathroom door opened a crack.

"Nurse?" Spider's voice rose from the floor where she must have been sitting. She sounded like she was holding a tennis ball between her teeth.

"I'm right here, baby girl."

Spider let out a choking cough. "My tongue," she said. "It's filling up my mouth."

In the backseat of Bennett's car, I held the lump of Spider's hand, watching the pink puffs of her eyelids, telling her stories I'd learned from my father, tales of Eastern European Jews in tall black hats, gathering cobblestones from the streambeds to pave the streets, meeting ghosts who taught them lessons.

This was the day Lewis fired the kitchen ladies.

This was the first casualty.

This was the day I remembered the vending-machine smell of the ER waiting room, remembered how I had once, just over a year before, in a different ER waiting room, waited for the truth I already knew to become official; how I'd watched the plastic-guarded face of the clock and thought how different a clock looked, how different a chair felt, how differently my breath moved in and out of my lungs, now that my father was gone.

Sitting beside Bennett, I watched a nearby family pray, clutching one another's hands.

"Why are you crying, Angeline?"

"I'm not."

Mikey would have stopped asking and gripped my hand more tightly, but Bennett slid out of his seat and knelt on the floor, held my knees, and said, "You're sad."

I wiped beneath my eyes with the heels of my hands. I thought, *Maybe he's falling in love with me.*

"I can't stand to see a pretty girl cry," he said. He sounded confident like a congressman. I became glaringly aware of his hands on my body, the fat on my legs just past his fingertips. "Spider will be fine," Bennett said.

"Of course she will. Spider thinks she's a Japanese super-hero."

"Are you missing your dad?"

"I don't want my dad here. My dad would not like you touching my legs." I looked away from Bennett, toward two drunk-looking teenagers slumped in chairs, hats pulled low over their faces. "I miss you," I said, studying the teenagers. They wore matching shoes that looked made for basketball, the laces dirty and undone.

"That so?"

"I do," I said.

"I'm right here," Bennett said, but he drew away from me.

I wanted to move my knees back into the cups of his palms, but I did not want to be the girl I'd been, who would drench Mikey's chest hair in tears, responding with sobs when he asked, again and again, "What's wrong?" and then finally replying, "I don't know. I just feel sad," instead of saying, "I don't think I can love you anymore, after all that's happened." I didn't want to be the girl who hid the truth in her stomach, pressing it down to keep it from swimming up to her heart.

Bennett rose and sat beside me. I lifted my thighs slightly to slim them, listening to the prayers of a whole family of people who believed the same things.

"What if . . ." I said.

"Enough of that," Bennett said. "Let's just wait and see."

THIRTY-FOUR

Spider's father must have gotten dressed in a hurry because the buttons on his short-sleeved shirt were askew, creating a bunching of the plaid, a gaping hole at his chest that showcased a storm of coarse black hair. Apparently, he and his wife lived nearby; they'd arrived so quickly, like paramedics.

"What the hell is this?" he shouted. "I leave my child in your hands for four weeks! Just *four weeks*. A camp full of nutrition experts." He made quotation marks with his fingers to show what he thought of us being nutrition experts.

The nearby praying people looked up. They had stopped praying aloud, but remained huddled together, as if God might appear inside their circle and dance a solo.

"Russ," Spider's mother hissed, yanking her husband's elbow. She was a few steps behind him, sweating through the armpits of her appliqué T-shirt. The appliqué spelled STOWE. Beside the letters, a solitary snowflake.

Bennett rose and moved toward Russ. "Spider's going to be fine," he said. "We got her here quickly."

Russ's belly was a watermelon, suspended inside his shirt. He was shorter than Bennett, not much taller than I, and could have been described, kindly, as stocky. Now his eyes narrowed and his fists curled. He expanded like a peacock. Then he wound up, and with a peculiar foot shuffle and grunt, he launched his fist up toward Bennett's face.

"Russ!" his wife shrieked, covering her eyes with her hands.

Bennett stepped back, out of the fist's path. "Just a minute," he said. "Just a minute now."

"Help!" I yelled as Russ's fist sliced through the empty air a second time.

He wound up once more, and Bennett ducked, drilled his head into Russ's chest, and threw his arms around Russ's torso, the side of his face pressed to the uneven buttons. He hooked his heel around the back of Russ's leg, causing Russ's knee to buckle. Together, they tumbled to the cold floor.

"Are you going to calm down now?" Bennett shouted.

I sat beside Spider's mother, who had sunk into a chair and begun to sob soundlessly, her shoulders shaking.

"Are you calm?" Bennett asked, his voice lower this time.

Russ grunted.

I had never been so close to violence. Or if I had—in a comedy club, at Little Mermaid—the lights had been down, the men anonymous. I was surprised to see how embarrassing it was. For a second, it had almost looked loving, like two friends locked in an embrace.

"Are you okay?" I asked Spider's mother.

"I'm okay if my daughter's okay."

"Spider will be fine."

"She sure will." She touched the inner corners of her eyes,

and then fished an actual handkerchief edged in lavender embroidery from her purse. "Spider's our little fighter."

We watched the men. Russ, on his back, an insect pinned to a cork board, struggled and squirmed under Bennett's knee. Finally, he gave up and lay still.

"She's done really well at camp," I said.

Spider's mother blew her nose.

"She's so upbeat," I said.

"That's Spider."

"She's funny, too."

"Well, we sure think so."

By now, an orderly and two waiting-room laymen, chests filled with air, had gathered around Bennett and Russ. Bennett was saying, "We're all right. Just got a little emotional over here." He was helping Russ to his feet, his biceps ballooning when he took Russ's hands. Russ stood, bull-breathing through his nostrils, wiping the seat of his shorts, looking everywhere but at Bennett.

Spider's mother lowered her voice. "Russ didn't want to send her to camp. You know how fathers are."

I felt something contract inside my chest. "What did he want her to do instead?"

"Stay home." She spread her handkerchief on her lap and folded it into careful quarters. "She's our only child, and she's got those allergies. He likes to keep her close."

Russ crossed the room to the receptionist. Bennett locked eyes with me and pointed to the restroom, then headed toward it.

"I don't know what happened today," I said. "Everyone's been careful about her allergies. Spider most of all. She only eats her special meals."

"Russ is going to say, 'You see? I told you we shouldn't have trusted them.'"

"Someone made a mistake. Things happen."

She seemed not to hear me. "And I'll have to say, 'You know what, Russ? You were right.'" She blew her nose again, and then wound the handkerchief around her hand. "'You were right, Russ,'" she said softly.

The anger that rose inside me then was unexpected, filling my stomach like lava. It was true that we weren't trustworthy. We were a cast of charlatans. But had it been such a bad thing for Spider to get away for a summer, to taste independence? What did Russ know about what she needed? He was her father, but he wasn't Spider.

"Maybe he's got us wrong," I said.

Spider's mother examined me. "You're not a parent, are you?"

"No."

She tucked her handkerchief back into her purse and chuckled to herself.

"So?" I said.

"There are just things you wouldn't understand then. I hate to tell you."

"My father used to say that to me. Parents love that line. 'You have no idea what it's like for us.' Do I have such a limited imagination that I couldn't possibly conceive of your life?"

"You'll see when you're a parent."

"Maybe. But in the meantime, I don't walk around telling everyone, 'You have no idea what it's like to be me.'" I looked at Spider's mother, whose eyes were on Russ, and I felt my face get warm. "Sorry." I touched her arm. "You hit a nerve," I said. "I didn't mean to be rude."

Spider's mother surprised me then. She took my hand and squeezed it. "I have no idea what it's like to be you, honey." She looked like Spider when she smiled. "And I wouldn't dream of pretending to."

Russ approached us then, grabbed his wife's hand and pulled her out of the chair. "Come on," he said, towing her away.

She followed her husband. She didn't look back.

I watched them speak with the receptionist, Russ holding his arms away from his body as if his muscles were so big they required that space.

When Bennett returned, he glanced at Spider's parents, lifting his cap off to wipe his forehead with his arm.

"Are you okay?" I asked, standing.

"Sure. Are you?"

"I think I'm in shock."

But I wasn't in shock. In shock, I had zeroed in on trivial details: the color of the sky as the sun melted into it, the sound of a car that wouldn't start, a strand of hair stuck to my lip. In this moment, I saw the important things: the muscles in Bennett's forearms, the bulge of his Adam's apple. I went to him, lined the tips of my toes up with his.

"Let's get out of here," Bennett said. "Everyone's looking."

I touched his chest. His heart ticked rapidly. It was trite, really, feeling aroused by a man who had won a fight. But to me, this animal attraction felt novel. At one time, I'd been aroused by Mikey clutching his microphone, quieting a heckler, dominating an audience with his clever crowd work, with his swaggering ripostes.

How exhausting it was to love like that, to receive love from a man like that. How exhausting it was to be loved with a man's whole brain, to be loved despite gaining fifteen pounds, to be loved by a man who didn't notice that his girlfriend had gained fifteen pounds.

I leaned my face on Bennett's chest. In his arms, behind my closed eyelids, I saw Camp Carolina, the green of the grass and the trees, the sparkling turquoise blue of the swimming pool; I could almost feel the cool breeze from my window fan. I told Bennett, "Let's go home."

THIRTY-FIVE

Bennett drove us back to camp in his banged-up Explorer, his fingers crawling up the hem of my shorts, the Eagles on the radio, our windows down so my ponytail blew free like a flag in the wind.

When we exited the highway onto the road that snaked through pastures, past a solitary church that looked closed for business, I said, "Pull over." I pressed my thumb to the buckle of my seat belt and the strap zipped away.

He parked in the shade of the woods. The sound of wind still screamed in my ears, even as the heat of stillness seeped in. I pulled off my shorts, climbed onto Bennett, and unbound him from his seat belt. He slipped his arms around my neck, forked his fingers up the back of my scalp, and kissed my bottom lip, my top lip, each of my earlobes, fitting my neck into his mouth. My body felt full of him—my organs, my skin, my muscles, my stomach. I couldn't remember anything ever making me feel so full.

When we pulled into the campus, the kids were lounging on the cafeteria steps eating sugar-free Popsicles. Seeing them, I exhaled for what felt like the first time that day.

Everyone wanted to know about Spider. Now that she was absent, they loved her. They wanted to protect her. Their eyebrows came together like roofs at the centers of their foreheads. The people outside of camp, the hungry, thoughtless masses who dined in shopping mall food courts, who ate popcorn from large tubs in movie theaters, were not allowed to take her from us. Spider had to be returned.

"She'll be fine," Bennett said. "Probably back tonight."

Whitney and Miss were huddled around Sheena, each weaving an orange braid like pilot fish grooming a shark. Eden, who would have otherwise been angling for a third of Sheena's hair, was standing with Alex, the weird kid with glue-white skin, who wore tinted glasses and slip-on sneakers over tube socks, and whose pale calves were as thick as his thighs. I had seen him staring at Eden all summer and once offer her one of his iPod buds so they could listen to a song together.

Alex had a secret, too. Everyone knew it because he told everyone, prefacing it each time with, "This is a secret. You're the only person I'm telling": His high school classmates had built a website, the home page of which said, *Alex Hartson Should Kill Himself* in Times New Roman 48. They e-mailed him the link. Once he perused the site, clicking on tabs labeled *How to Effectively Cut One's Wrist* and *Top Ten Reasons Why We Hate Alex Hartson*, he swallowed every pill in his house: Tums, Tylenol, vitamin C, capsules that curtailed his stepfather's prostate. Half an hour later, he walked downstairs to the kitchen, told his mother the story, and vomited on the linoleum.

Now, while he spent the summer at camp, Alex's mother and stepfather were filling boxes, taping them closed, donating things they wished to forget to the Salvation Army, and heading to California, in pursuit of scraps of gold. "In California," his mother e-mailed to tell him, "you'll be the most popular boy in school."

Eden was wearing Alex's shoes—walking across the cafeteria steps in his black-and-white-checkered slip-on sneakers. "They're so big!" she said.

This was the first time I'd seen Alex smile. He sat in colossal white socks, his lips turning red from his Popsicle. "They fit me fine," he said, and his face blushed the color of pink carnations, of sunsets in Santorini, of valentines.

"I guess I'm just small," Eden said, and her smile stretched until her eyes vanished into her cheeks.

THIRTY-SIX

At dinnertime, Lewis ushered Sheena and me outside.

"Spider is not coming back to camp," he said.

"Is she okay?" I asked.

He looked at me with eyes like barbs. "Of course she's okay." He pinched the wire stems of his glasses. "She was always okay. Her parents probably gave her those allergies. Put them in her head. Parents will do that. I know those types of parents. I've been working at camps since the eighties. Those types of parents . . . they're not doing their kids any favors feeding them from silver spoons. Spider's parents would throw a sheet over her and keep her in a closet all her life if they could. Want to know how I raise my kids? I tell them, 'You're fine.' I tell them, 'It's just a scratch.' Right? 'Buck up.'"

"And who names a kid Spider?" Sheena said.

"Exactly my point," Lewis said, even though it wasn't.

"It's a nickname," I said. "Spiders don't die of natural causes.

They can live forever if they're kept safe. In China, there are three-thousand-year-old spiders. Preserved. She's been in the hospital twenty-five times. She's tough. Like a spider."

Sheena and Lewis drew closer to each other.

"Her real name is Emily," I said.

"Emily, Spider, whatever. That girl is high-maintenance," Sheena said.

I laughed. "Spider? High-maintenance? You give her a Japanese comic book and she's happy for hours."

"She's always scratching all over everyone," Sheena said. She shuddered. "Skin flakes. Everywhere."

Lewis said, "Kids throw up sometimes. It's nothing to run to the judge about."

"Sorry," I said, "but if that was my kid, I'd be pissed off, too. You promised to serve her food she could eat. At every meal. For the whole summer. You knew she had allergies."

"Things happen," Lewis said, his voice climbing. "You can plan for everything, and still things go wrong."

"You can't cater to someone every second of the day," Sheena said.

"But you should," I said. "If it's a matter of life or death. And if her parents are paying you to cater to her food allergies. And if you promised that you *would* cater to her food allergies." It was not lost on me that I was contradicting myself, repeating Spider's parents' argument, blaming Lewis for what had likely been an honest mistake. A vein did push-ups in Lewis's forehead. But I couldn't stop: "What if you lose the camp?"

"I guess you'll be happy to know that her parents are suing me, Gray."

I felt a stabbing in my gut. "When?"

"I could lose everything."

DIANA SPECHLER

"Will they wait until the end of the summer?" I pulled my collar away from my neck and fanned my skin.

"This is my livelihood. My wife and kids are counting on me. And what do I get? I get nothing from the people I help. I was helping Spider. Spider had low self-esteem when she got here. She wouldn't even uncross her arms from her chest. Now she's down sixteen pounds and she walks around in a bikini—that anime bikini."

"That is one god-awful bikini," Sheena said.

"Then she gets a little sick one day and suddenly I'm the bad guy? I'm the villain?" Lewis scratched the top of his head. "I always say that this is not a weight-loss camp. Don't I always say that?"

"I've never heard you say that," I said.

"It's a self-esteem-building camp. Every kid will leave here with high self-esteem. Happy and changed. They'll be new kids because of me." He released a deep sigh that withered him, and looked toward the girls' dorm, where the maintenance man, a scrawny guy in jeans and no shirt, was riding his tractor over the grass.

"Yee-haw!" the maintenance man cried, waving a bandanna over his head like a lasso.

"It's the givers who always get taken advantage of," Lewis said. "It's so hard to be a giver." His shoulders were slumped as if he were carrying a sack of presents. He reached between his legs and heaved his balls from one side to the other. "I've been one all my life."

THIRTY-SEVEN

This was Bennett: Sometimes he disappeared. When Mikey disappeared, he wanted company. He wanted to lie beside me in bed, a pillow covering his eyes. He wanted to turn off his phone and hold my leg to make sure I stayed put. From under his pillow blindfold, he would mutter, "I hate comedians," or, "I must be some kind of masochist, telling jokes on all these stages."

Whenever Bennett disappeared—missing a lunch, or cals, or an evening activity—the air he left behind pulsed with his absence. Curtains fluttered in open windows. Vases fell from sills and shattered. Once, I found one of his whistles, strung onto a Panthers shoelace, abandoned on the soccer field. I knelt beside it, and then stuffed it into my pocket, and when I stood, I glanced around furtively before lowering my sunglasses over my eyes.

Whenever Bennett disappeared, I believed I would never see him again. My skin would feel feverish, and I would shiver, wishing for our bodies to come together, facing one direction, curved into matching shapes. I would sneak to his apartment and touch the white vinyl siding. I would put my fingertips on his dark window. I would twist the doorknob and find it locked.

When I saw him next, I would tell him, "Just warn me. Please. Just tell me you're going to sleep through fifth period. Tell me you're running to Walmart instead of coming to evening activity."

"Angeline," he would say, tapping his knuckle against my forehead. "What goes on in that imagination of yours? Where would I go? Where could I possibly go?" He would crook an arm around my neck and pull me into his chest, and I would breathe in his clean T-shirt smell and feel Camille's name pumping blood by my ear.

All of this was new to me. For the past year, living with Mikey had meant waiting, constantly, for him to leave, to give me a few hours of privacy. "Space," I'd called it. "I need my space." By which I'd meant, *Let me eat in peace.*

But now I remembered food like a former lover whose cruelty had excited, then alienated me—remembered not the way it knelt repentantly at my feet, kissing the caps of my knees, but the time it grabbed my arm in anger, the night it kicked the wall so hard, our neighbor kicked it back. Whenever I dreamt of returning to it, I woke to a sigh of relief.

So when I couldn't locate Bennett, my legs grew weak, my stomach rumbled, my head felt loose on its axis.

And then he disappeared for three days.

Partway through the first day, Lewis told me that Bennett was sick.

"With what?"

"Maybe he's sex-starved!" he stage-whispered, jabbing an elbow into my rib cage.

"What are you talking about?"

"You think I don't know everything? This is my camp. I know everything. Look, I'm glad you two are having healthy, aerobic sex. Maybe he just needs more of it."

"Um."

"I used to do that instead of exercise," he said. "You know, back before I was married."

"Is he really sick? Stuck in bed?"

"Down for the count."

"He didn't warn me," I said, and I turned away from Lewis, remembering a time, two years earlier, when I ate bad tuna and couldn't stop vomiting. Too sick to reach the bathroom, I lay writhing in bed, and Mikey brought me the biggest pot we owned, the one we'd used a few times to cook excessive amounts of chili. I threw up over and over, and Mikey stroked my hair, emptying the pot when it needed emptying.

Mikey's eyes were big and brown like a deer from a cartoon. He rarely touched people, but when he did, it was because he was feeling their feelings, making contact to share their pain— his fingers lightly cupping an elbow or steadying the space between two shoulder blades.

Mikey would never disappear from me. Maybe Bennett was a bad person. That leap of logic soothed me the way it did the wolf in that fable—the grapes were not out of reach, but sour. I could convince myself of this! Maybe Camille had left Bennett because he was bad. Poor Camille! Perhaps she'd had to escape him.

How I wished to believe this invented scenario, to disregard these truths of human nature—that good people didn't leave bad people, that bad people were only bad when spoiled by love, and that good people were only good while they loved disproportionately.

Then, in the next relationship, the bad person became the good person, touching the bone of his new lover's cheek, mesmerized by the curve of it. And she, having just been left by a man who had gambled her savings and worn a scuffed leather jacket, relished her newfound power, punctuated by flashes of guilt ("You're such a good person," she would say wistfully, watching his eyes go foggy with love). Around and around it went. Mikey loved me and I'd replaced him with Bennett, who loved Camille, who probably loved some guy who still loved someone else. After loving my father, Azalea must have treated the next man like a paper napkin—making a mess of him, crumpling him up, tossing him away.

During the three-day illness, the outgoing message on Bennett's voice mail sound-tracked my mounting panic. *Hi, you've reached . . . Hi, you've reached . . . Hi, you've reached . . . Hi, you've . . .*

By day three, I couldn't move from my bed. I was weak, as if I were starving. I wondered if I'd caught Bennett's illness. I wanted Bennett's illness. I wanted to breathe him in, to make us feel all the same things. It became a matter of survival: I had to get to Bennett.

I got out of bed and hobbled to the cafeteria. I took Bennett's place leading stretches on the steps, looking down at the cluster of campers who wore clothes that were now too big for them, the girls with sleepy ponytails on the tops of their heads, the boys shrunken in huge sneakers. They were fidgety children and slouching teenagers.

"Reach your arms for the sky," I told them, my voice worn out like a stretch of bad road.

They reached, T-shirts rising to expose stomachs, wrists rotating over their heads. I thought of them in their school cafeterias, fatter than everyone, sitting alone, eating baked potatoes from tinfoil. Something popped inside my chest. I watched the sea of hopeful hands, reaching, grasping, empty.

Breakfast was silver-dollar pancakes, two per person, with sugar-free syrup. I cut a bite from my pancake, imagined how dry it would feel in my mouth, how it would expand like foam rubber as I chewed. I left it on my plate, my fork stabbed through it.

And then, it was this easy: I rose from my seat, walked to the door, left the cafeteria, and crossed the campus to the boys' dorm. No one called out to me or followed, as if I had dieted down to invisible.

Because no one was near, I didn't mind banging on Bennett's door as hard as I could. The weakness I'd felt upon waking vanished. I used both fists, pummeling that door like a punching bag. I could feel the blood pumping through my arms, the outer edges of my hands bruising, but the ache only made me bang harder.

And then the door opened and Bennett caught my elbows. He was wearing green mesh shorts and no shirt, squinting in the sunlight. "What in . . . Angeline. What are you doing?"

"Hi," I said. My hands tingled, the sides of them flecked with white paint chips. I put my arms around Bennett's neck and pressed into his body.

He held my waist in his hands, only partway joining the hug. I pulled him closer. He was warm and solid, a body I wished would absorb me.

"What's going on?"

"You disappeared," I told his neck.

"I've been sick."

"You could have called."

"Angeline . . ."

His thumbs pressed my stomach, pushing me away. I hugged harder, remembering how it felt to yank a Barbie doll's arm through a tiny sleeve, how my father had told me, "Don't force it. It will break if you force it."

"Can I come in?"

"Well. Okay."

I followed him into his apartment. It smelled stuffy like sickness. The shades were drawn. Three fans were going, blowing Bennett like helicopter propellers. He lay back on his bed, inside the windstorm, and covered his eyes with the top sheet. "Everyone at breakfast?"

"Yeah." I sat on the foot of his bed, my muscles tight, my mouth dry. "Bennett?"

"Mm?"

"Are you really sick?"

Bennett pulled the sheet off his face and looked at me. "I just needed a break," he said. "You ever get that feeling? Like you just want a break?"

"Never."

"No?"

"I'm kidding. Sure, I've had that feeling."

"It's a normal thing. Needing a break."

No, I thought. *No, I wouldn't need a break from you, Bennett, any more than I would need time off from breathing.*

"A break from me?" I asked.

"Not from you. Not exactly."

Lying beside a man who inexactly needed a break from me, I rested my hands on my stomach, willing it flat, willing it never to grow, never to change. *Stay down*, I thought. I closed my eyes. I would not touch him. I would wait for him to fill the space between us.

He didn't move. For several minutes, he didn't move.

I rolled over to lie on top of him.

THIRTY-EIGHT

"I need to get laid," Sheena said on Monday afternoon. We were sitting on the edge of the pool in our bikinis. I watched our feet that hung in the water, white-blue, annexed from our bodies. Our campers should have been swimming. We had been yelling at them all day to run, move, crunch, and kick. Now we were sick of it. We let them languish.

Miss was alone in the deep end, floating on a kickboard. Harriet and Eden were closest to us, tossing a rubber ball back and forth. (I heard my father's voice: "How did I wind up with a daughter who throws like a quadriplegic?") Since Spider's departure, Harriet and Eden seemed engaged in a lukewarm affectation of friendship.

Whitney, in shorts and a sports bra, had spread a red towel over the cement between the chain-link fence and the water. She was doing sit-ups, the brown rolls of her stomach contracting and expanding.

All summer, Whitney had avoided the pool. She was having her "monthly visitor," she said every day, her "redheaded cousin from Dixieland," and her tone implied, *What? Should I prove it?* She walked laps in the heat every afternoon while the rest of the girls swam. (Even Harriet swam! In full clothing, but she swam.) Sometimes I glanced up from teaching water aerobics to see Whitney walking the outer perimeter of the fenced-in pool, the sun glistening off her hair, her brown skin slick with sweat, and I thought of hurricane images I'd seen on the news: people wading through rivers that had once been streets, holding babies and stereos aloft.

"I might visit Duane in jail," Sheena said.

"Your ex?"

"Nah. This other guy."

"You know a lot of people in jail."

"I'd say I know a lot of people who are down on their luck. Not everyone's got a charmed life, you know."

"Sheena, I do know that."

"Sometimes I'm not sure about you."

"I think you think I'm wealthy or something."

Sheena pushed her lips together and examined me. "Do you have two parents?"

"No."

"Why not?"

"My dad died."

"When?"

"Last summer."

"So until then, you had two parents? You grew up with two parents?"

"I did."

"And your dad had a job?"

"Of course."

Sheena leaned forward and splashed water onto her thighs. "Then you're spoiled."

"How so? Before I got here, I was bartending. At a fish place. I constantly smelled like fish."

"Bartenders have rich parents. Bartenders are trying to be movie stars. You don't see bartenders in jail. Kids in group homes don't grow up to be bartenders. If you were really poor, you'd work for the city. You'd work for minimum wage. Like Duane. Duane couldn't catch a break. Now he's been in jail for a year. Year and a half. He writes me letters with a pen. On lined paper. He wants me to send him pictures of me in my underwear."

"Oh! Be careful, Sheena."

"Gray, you're such a prude," Sheena said, pulling her Jackie O sunglasses from the top of her head to cover her eyes. I tried to think of people I knew in jail. Having no friends in jail made me feel provincial.

"I'm taking a day off tomorrow," Sheena said. "Lewis told me I could. Since I work so hard on the evening activities."

Sheena had come up with most of the evening activities: the Cross-Dresser Beauty Pageant, Casino Night, Carnival Night, the night we piled into a bus to go to the movie theater in Melrose, each camper armed with a small ziplock bag of air-popped popcorn. Lewis had named Sheena the director of activities and begun paying her an extra two hundred dollars a week.

"Sheena and I have business plans," I'd heard him say, slinging an arm around her shoulder.

Sheena had recently told me, "When summer's over, me and Lewis are going to start a Meals-on-Wheels type of program for foster families. That's my dream. I grew up in two foster families. Why are you looking at me like that? Not everyone's royalty, Gray. Not everyone lives in New York City. Not everyone gets to go to cocktail parties in the Empire State Building. Not everyone gets to climb the Statue of Liberty and kiss her torch, or whatever y'all do up there. I grew up eating the kind of food you give people if you want them to gain ten pounds a day. That's how I got fat. Me and Lewis are going to have this healthy food delivery service. For foster families, so that the kids don't have to eat like shit just because their foster families are poor and fat."

"That's a brilliant idea."

"We're going to call it Mealz for Realz. With two Zs. Lewis has cash," she'd said, rubbing her thumb against the pads of her fingers.

Now she said, "I can go see Duane. Bang him at the jail. That's kind of hot."

"It is?"

"It's that or pick up some stranger at Walmart. Some Melrose dude. And they don't have teeth. They have diseased gums."

More than half of the summer now eaten away, no one wanted to think about food anymore. Camp food was not worth discussing. We were resigned to it. Home wasn't worth discussing, either. Home was somewhere we had lived long ago. All that was worth acknowledging was that we were blessedly diminished. Layers of us had shed. So when a breeze came, when someone accidentally bumped into us, when a person's hand reached out, it was closer to us, to our genitals, to our hearts, than any contact or almost-contact had been in a very long time.

"Whitney and Pudge are fucking," Sheena whispered.

"Lewis told me that fat men can't get it up."

Sheena tapped her sunglasses down her nose to scrutinize me. "*Lewis* can't get it up. Lewis is, like, old. Pudge is eighteen."

"No, the point of his story was that he, against all odds, has always been virile."

"I met his wife. She was here the other day. She's deaf."

"What do you mean?"

"What do you mean what do I mean? She's deaf. You'd have to be, to marry Lewis. But she reads lips. I tried talking really fast and she still understood me. Spider would have loved it. She would have finally had a reason to speak sign language." Sheena looked at me. "He shouldn't have told you that . . . about how he's so . . . what was the word you used?"

"Virile?"

"About how virile he is." Sheena leaned back on her elbows and lifted her face to the sun. The sun shifted to accommodate her. "Considering what people are saying about him."

"What are people saying?"

"You don't know?"

"No."

"Seriously?"

"Sheena, no one tells me anything."

She sat up again and drew an imaginary zipper across her lips. She rubbed her elbow, then bent forward and dipped her arms into the water. "The pavement's hot." She scooted off the lip of the pool with a splash and swam past Eden and Harriet. I watched Eden's eyes follow as Sheena swam the length underwater, then emerged like a breaching dolphin to join Miss, who immediately offered her the kickboard.

THIRTY-NINE

Mikey was pulling the magic trick of men with cheating girlfriends—shifting suddenly from clueless to clairvoyant. This was a man who never remembered our anniversary; never guessed when I wanted to be left alone, strewn with confetti, or admired from a distance. He never guessed when I wanted him to say, "Please tell me what I can do for you." Once, he thrust a bouquet of roses at me and said, "They're yesterday's roses! Bodega guy gave 'em to me cheap as hell."

But now that my eyes were locked on Bennett, Mikey could see me perfectly through the six hundred miles between us.

"I'll come for the weekend," he told me on the phone. "I'll get a hotel room. I'll see you at night. Whatever it takes. I'm sick of you being gone. Something about this feels really . . ."

"There's no time," I told him. "I get a couple of hours to myself every other night. It's not worth it. I'll see you when I get back. It won't be long."

"I'll borrow my parents' car. I'll drive down, give you a kiss, and turn right back around. I just need to see your face. I just want to touch you. This is unnatural. This life I'm living. Telling jokes to strangers, coming home to an empty apartment. Too much alone time. This is how men become creepy. Soon I'll be one of those guys who plays that computer game. You know that computer game?"

"Which one?"

"Where you pretend to have a second life?"

I was sitting on my bed, trying to decide what to wear to dinner—my jeans that folded down twice over my hips or my faded pink sundress that now fit me like a sack. "I do know it."

Mikey sighed static into the phone. "I miss you, baby."

Bennett liked me in dresses. I would wear the sack sundress with nothing underneath, and tell him so.

"The summer will be over soon," I told Mikey.

"I would even watch you sleep. Can't I drive down and watch you sleep?"

"Wow," I said, laughing. "You *are* getting creepy." But Mikey had always liked to watch me sleep. Sometimes I woke up to the sight of his face above me, his eyes misty, his hair tousled. Bennett would never have watched me sleep. He was barely interested in watching me when I was awake.

"Gray, I just . . ."

"What?"

"I just love you."

"Mikey," I said, "I love you, too." But the words felt stale in my mouth, like old crackers.

FORTY

Sometime during the fifth week of camp, I adjusted to camp life as if to a scorching hot tub. Now I couldn't imagine climbing out, could only imagine remaining inside it, weightless and torpid. Until the weigh-in. Whitney showed a nine-pound weight loss. Miss had dropped seven pounds. So had Kimmy, who had lost only half a pound at the fourth-week weigh-in.

"Something is off," I heard Lewis tell Nurse. "Something is weird." But he was rocking on his heels, his spine straighter than usual, as if he'd been carrying the girls' extra pounds around all summer.

"This makes me uncomfortable," I told Lewis.

"What?"

"It seems like a thing to pay attention to."

"What are you saying?"

"So much loss."

"Thank the Lord I'm not married to you," Lewis said.

"What does that have to do with anything?"

"You with all your hang-ups. Your *feelings* about things. Who-ever marries you has his work cut out."

"Thanks."

"Can't you just go with the flow? Quit rocking the canoe? Bend like a reed?"

"No. I guess I can't."

"Don't worry," Lewis said. "I won't tell Bennett."

At the end of brunch, I was sitting across from Eden, the rest of the girls having finished and disbanded. My eyes were fastened to the thick black braid draped over Eden's shoulder, and to her face that looked, every day, more and more like our father's, as if her weight loss were chiseling away the other half of her DNA.

She was pushing her turkey sausage links and salad around with her fork, making the links mushy with fat-free Italian dressing. "Everyone except me is losing, like, millions of pounds," she said.

"You've lost a lot," I said.

She looked up at me and squinted one eye, the way my father had whenever he thought I was being illogical, my arguments marked by emotional rhetoric, exaggerations, and convenient guesses. "Think things through," he always told me, tapping his forehead with the knuckle of his index finger. "Don't just speak because you feel like it. Don't let your emotions rule you. Don't ever give men reason to discredit you."

"At least I'm not puking to lose weight," Eden said.

I cocked my head at her. "What are you talking about?"

"Nothing." She pushed her tray away and looked out the window. The cafeteria was nearly empty, except for a couple of the younger girls who were standing in front of the television on the Dance Dance Revolution mats, shoes kicked off, watching the screen to follow the footwork prompts.

Holy hell, did we all love Dance Dance Revolution. The whole camp. Even Nurse. Even the new kitchen ladies (who were more or less replicas of the old kitchen ladies). We loved to dance the way the kids did in 1980s movies after they broke free from the confines of one institution or another.

"The whole world thinks I like Alex," Eden said, "and I so don't. He's a dork."

"Alex? He's . . . nice."

I'd once seen Alex smiling at me from across the cafeteria, and then mouthing something to me, so I had smiled back and cupped a hand around my ear, only to realize he was talking to himself.

"Do you know what happened to him at his school?" Eden asked.

"The website thing?"

"See?" she said. "Dork."

"That doesn't mean he's a dork. He was a victim."

"But if he was cool, that wouldn't have happened. That's not the kind of thing that happens to cool kids."

She looked out the window. I followed her gaze. Whitney and Kimmy were teaching one of the younger girls how to do a cartwheel. The girl kept throwing herself forward so her hands hit the grass, but she couldn't get her legs up in the air.

"Why would anyone think I like him?" Eden said. "Not that I care. I don't care what anyone thinks of me."

"Good."

Eden swung her legs over the bench one at a time. She stood and lifted her tray from the table. "I'm just saying," she said. "Some people care so much, they puke up everything they eat. They think if they eat, they'll never be skinny, and that if they're not skinny, people won't like them."

"Are you trying to tell me something?"

"Like what? I would never puke up my food on purpose! I don't even want to be skinny. Boys don't like skinny girls. Boys like thick girls. Girls with ass." Eden looked around. No one was watching us. She lowered her voice anyway. "I hate Sheena."

For a moment, I felt as if Eden had set a crown on my head. I beamed at her. And then I made myself stop. "Sheena's just insecure."

"She's a counselor!"

"Counselors can be insecure."

"An insecure *grown-up*?"

I laughed.

"Why are you *laughing*?"

"Sorry. She's only nineteen, you know."

"But she's supposed to be in charge! The other day during kickball, she got mad at me and scratched me."

My skin grew cold. "What do you mean?"

"I mean she grabbed me and dug her nails into my arm." Eden looked down at her T-shirt sleeve.

"On purpose?"

"Yup."

"Eden, if that's true, I have to . . ."

"What?" Eden lifted her eyes to the ceiling. "What are you going to do? She would just be like, 'No, I didn't,' and that would be the end of it. No offense, Gray, but she's kind of more popular than you."

"I don't care about popular."

"And by the way, she's not insecure. She thinks she's perfect."

"Everyone's insecure."

"Except Sheena. And me. I'm not."

"Okay. So you're not."

"Sheena was the one who put those bugs in my bed. She was the one who poisoned Spider's food. She thought it was funny.

She switched up Spider's bread when Spider was in the bathroom. Ask Harriet. Harriet cried about it for, like, two days."

My stomach churned the way it had when Saul told me about Azalea. What was it about bad news? Why did it register as information I'd somehow already known? "Are you sure about all this?"

"Gray. You are so clueless."

"Are you making yourself throw up?"

Eden shook her hair out of her face. "The way I see it, if someone throws up the food someone made . . . that's the same as taking an artist's painting and tossing it in a fire."

"The kitchen ladies aren't exactly artists."

Eden looked out the window again. I looked, too. The girl who had been attempting cartwheels was lying sprawled on the ground, snow-angeled. One of the other little girls was sprinkling grass on her face. It was starting to feel as though there was nothing left to do here. We'd done everything. Every day. Now people were engaging in the pastimes of the understimulated—grass sprinkling, cartwheeling, taking turns sitting in Pudge's wheelchair and rolling down a hill.

When Eden spoke a minute later, I couldn't tell whether she was still addressing me. "I don't care if people like me or not. I'm a free spirit. That's what everyone back home calls me. A free spirit. I hate people," she said. She stomped off toward the trash cans to scrape away her uneaten food.

FORTY-ONE

Evening activity was a scavenger hunt of Sheena's design. I stood with Lewis on the loop while the kids ran around, seeking clues. I told him, "Sheena was violent with Eden."

He was watching the kids. One of the younger boys was standing on Alex's shoulders to get a view of the library roof. Lewis chuckled and pointed. "They're loving this," he said. "They'll all call home and tell their parents how much fun they're having here."

I doubted it. I had heard my campers on the phone with their parents. "Get me *out* of here," they said. "Can't you just come get me for a day?" Most of the kids had not been forced to come to camp. They'd wanted to come. They were sick of being fat kids. They fantasized about returning to school in the fall, miraculously transformed. But that didn't keep them from complaining.

Lewis said, "The parents will tell their friends, 'My kid's having so much fun at camp, he doesn't even *notice* he's dieting.'"

"I'm worried about this thing," I told Lewis. "She scratched her."

"You and your melodrama."

"She dug her fingernails into Eden's arm. Why would Eden lie? What if she tells her mother?"

"What do you care about her mother?"

"I don't care about her mother."

"Worry about Eden."

"Lewis! I *am* worried about Eden. What if another kid calls home about it? What if the lawsuits start piling up? You could lose the camp."

He looked at me. "Kids exaggerate, Gray. You haven't figured that out yet? I've been working at camps since the eighties. Sheena wouldn't do something like that. Look at her." Lewis pointed toward the library again, toward a cluster of kids on their hands and knees in the grass, crawling, searching. Sheena was carrying one of the youngest girls on her back. Another one was holding Sheena's hand, looking up at her adoringly. "The kids are in love with her. She really connects with them. Aside from me, she's the one they turn to. I'm like a father type of figure to them. But Sheena's like an aunt. She's like this aunt I used to have who always had butterscotch candies in her purse. Every time I saw her, I would paw through her purse for those candies. Auntie Bee. I loved my auntie Bee."

"That's how people win the affection of dogs," I said. "They stuff treats in their pockets."

"Well, she was more than just a lady with candy. She had a Ph.D."

"Lewis. Please—"

"Eden's got problems. Eden's troubled. She's one of the troubled kids. I can pick out the troubled ones from ten miles away." He nudged his glasses up his nose. "Twenty."

"All these kids have problems! Everyone in the world has problems! You don't have problems?"

"You know what my problem is?" Lewis picked something imaginary off the shoulder of his T-shirt. "My problem is I'm too nice."

As if she sensed that we were talking about her, Sheena bent to let the kid off her back, loosened her hand from the other girl's grip, turned toward us, and hurried up the hill.

"Lewis," she said when she reached us, panting. She wore a white-and-red-striped tube top. Her hair was separated into two thick orange pigtails that bounced cheerily against the soft pale spread of her shoulders. "My camera's busted."

"Bennett's got mine," Lewis said. "We'll find him."

"He's in the gym," I said.

They looked at me.

"I think."

"Come here, Sheena." Lewis held his arm out so he could put it around her naked shoulders. He pulled her close and they faced me together like stern parents.

My vision became very clear for a second, honed to a point. "No!"

"Sheena?" Lewis said. "Did you—"

"Lewis!" I grabbed his wrist.

Sheena looked at Lewis. "What?"

"Did you dig your fingernails into one of your campers' arms?"

"Huh?"

"Gray here seems to think you had a problem with Eden."

"No!" I said. "Lewis, I just—"

Lewis pulled free of my grasp and held up a palm to silence me. "I'm trying to clear up the confusion."

Sheena looked at me, each pupil bleeding into an iris abyss. Then she crooked her fingers and considered them. The nails were bitten down, the cuticles shredded around the messy remnants of black polish. "I don't even have fingernails."

"You see, Gray?" Lewis said. "Kids get hysterical sometimes. You need a better bullshit detector. You need a better filter. You can't get hysterical every time a kid gets hysterical. You know what you need? A game face."

"You do," Sheena agreed.

How odd red hair looked without blue eyes and freckles. It was a rare mutation, like fangs—smooth skin, dark eyes, red hair.

"A game face," Sheena said. "Work on that."

FORTY-TWO

Later that night, a few minutes before Lights Out, as I was making my way back from Nurse's office, where I'd gone to get calamine lotion for my mosquito-mauled campers, I saw two bodies, intertwined, standing between two bushes at the side of the girls' dorm. When I got closer, I recognized Alex's hands on Eden's hips, Eden's arms linked around his shoulders. They were kissing the way kids do when they don't know what comes next— hands and bodies motionless, heads barely moving, wet kissing noises, erratic breathing.

If I'd wanted to do my job responsibly, I would have told Eden to get inside and sent Alex back to his dorm. But I stood still and watched them, silver in the moonlight.

Alex pulled back and said, "You're the prettiest girl at camp."

"Whitney is really pretty."

"She's ugly."

Eden giggled.

"She's fat," Alex said.

"Everyone's fat."

"But she's mean and fat."

"I'm fat."

"You're beautiful."

"What's beautiful about me?"

Alex shifted on his feet. I held my breath. The cicadas paused.

"You have really big boobs."

"I know. They hurt my back."

"And you kind of look like this girl I know who's, like, *really* hot."

"Okay," Eden said.

When they began kissing again, under a moon so full that it sagged in the sky, I backed away quietly and rerouted to the side door of the dorm.

FORTY-THREE

Everything began to unravel when a blood vessel burst in Miss's left eye. I noticed it when I gathered my group in the hallway one morning before breakfast and saw Miss in her red Coca-Cola T-shirt, her hair unfurled in golden swells down her back. All that red and yellow made her damaged eye conspicuous. Almost half of the white was marred by a purple welt.

"Are your contacts dirty or something?" Harriet asked Miss.

"I don't wear contacts," Miss snapped, linking arms with Whitney.

Harriet looked at the floor and began to sniffle.

During breakfast, Nurse came to our table and stood over Miss in her leggings and tent of a T-shirt.

"I *thought* I saw something peculiar on your pretty face," she said.

Miss set her fork down and looked up at Nurse, the most loved person at camp. It was impossible not to like Nurse. She was coarse and affectionate, like a well-trained pit bull. Nurse and Dance Dance Revolution were the glue that held the whole operation together.

"Well, I don't like the looks of that one bit." Nurse bent closer to Miss, holding Miss's chin in her fingers, rotating her face from side to side. "Happened to me once when I farted, but not like that. It was just a little red."

Harriet covered her mouth and laughed hysterically into her palms.

"It'll go away. Just be careful," Nurse said, standing up straight. "Those blue eyes of yours are too pretty to mess with." She patted Miss's head and walked away.

I saw Miss glance at Whitney, and then at Sheena.

"What are you looking at, Gray?" Sheena asked. She was smiling. Or rather, her teeth were bared. "You're always looking at everyone."

"I was looking at Miss's eye," I said.

"Look at yourself for once."

"Miss's purple eye is my responsibility. In a sense. So I'm looking at it."

"Well, *you're* the one with an eating disorder."

I squinted at Sheena. "Why do you keep saying that?"

"How much weight have you lost?"

"Please."

"I'm serious."

"I eat what everyone eats," I said. "I just lost weight quickly. Not my fault."

"You don't eat," Sheena said. "You never eat. We all see you not eating."

I caught my smile before it spread open, and then looked

down at my lap. My thighs barely expanded on the bench any-more. My stomach felt flat and light. I looked up at Sheena again and said, "I'm not going to speak with you about this in front of the campers."

"First of all, they're not babies. Second of all, can't you take a joke? I'm playing with you!" Sheena reached across the table to smack my arm.

I felt the burn of her fingers on my skin long after she turned away.

FORTY-FOUR

Something was up. And Eden seemed to know it (she would barely look at me). And Sheena and Whitney and Miss seemed to know it—the knot of them was tighter than ever. And Kimmy seemed to know it, too: Every time I saw her, she was frantically sucking her thumb or holding Whitney's hand. I wanted to ignore it all. So I did. Until I couldn't. Because the next morning, the secret came out.

It happened at breakfast when Whitney went to the bathroom for twenty minutes, and then returned, resuming her place on the end of the bench next to Harriet, smelling unmistakably of vomit. I caught a whiff from across the table.

"That is gross!" Harriet said, pushing away her bowl of partially eaten oatmeal, her untouched half of a grapefruit.

I looked at Whitney's glazed expression, at Miss's purple eye, at Sheena, who was staring at the window. I looked at Eden, who was looking at Whitney the way she often looked at Whitney—

ready with a smile, just in case Whitney glanced at her, the way I used to gaze at my father when he was a nucleus in a crowd, using his whole body to tell a story.

I stood abruptly. "Whitney, Miss," I said. "Outside. Now."

Everyone looked up. I barely spoke around my campers, especially when everyone was together, and if I did speak, I certainly didn't make demands.

"Now," I said. I didn't look at Sheena, but at the edges of my vision, I saw her head turn from the window.

On the cafeteria steps, I told Whitney and Miss, "Obviously, you two are making yourselves throw up."

They had their arms folded over their chests and were standing so close to each other, their T-shirt sleeves were touching.

"You're just saying that because you hate us," Miss said, squinting her purple eye at me.

"I don't hate you. I'm concerned."

"Everyone knows you hate us because we're close with Sheena."

"Yeah," Whitney said. "You're all up in Eden's shit and you hate us."

I paused to consider the accusation. It was true that I wasn't crazy about Miss, but once I'd watched her pick a scab off her elbow and inexplicably wanted to cry. And it was impossible to hate Whitney. She gave feverish, nonsensical sermons, and everyone paused to listen. No, I was angry, I realized, the way I felt angry with adults who had been born into limitless wealth. Why should things be so easy for them? Why should Miss and Whitney get to enjoy all the food they wanted, and then flush the calories down the toilet?

Plenty of times in the past year, I'd wanted to purge. Plenty of times, I'd even hoped that a binge would make me sick. But I'd always stopped myself from forcing it. I'd been afraid to do it, afraid that it would hurt, afraid that if I did it once—ate all I wanted, then vomited—I would spend the rest of my life doing nothing but eating and vomiting.

"How many other girls are doing it?" I asked.

"Doing *what*?" Miss whined.

"I'm sick," Whitney said. "I think I have the flu."

Miss glanced at her.

"Whitney," I said. "I'm not an idiot."

"I didn't say you were. Did I say that? Miss, did I?"

"No."

"Thank you."

"Look," I told them, "I'm not mad. I want to know what's going on. I want you both to talk with Nurse. I want to know who else needs to talk with Nurse."

They stepped closer together, the outer edges of their sneakers touching. They were fused like paper dolls.

"We're not equipped for these kinds of problems here," I said. "That's what's upsetting to me. Nurse isn't even a nurse. If anyone is sick—bulimic or whatever . . ."

"We're not bulimic!" they shouted like cheerleaders.

"Then what? Should I go get Lewis? Should he call your parents?"

"What would y'all say to our parents?" Whitney asked. "That we have eating disorders?" She took Miss's hand and raised their arms between them, showcasing their bodies. Whitney had narrowed all over. Her hips had moved inward. Her legs had more shape. But still. She was not thin. Nowhere near. And Miss was larger than Whitney. "Do we look like we have eating disorders?"

"Whitney, you smell like barf," I said. "Sorry. But you do.

And you lost nine pounds this week. You didn't even lose that much the first week."

"Even if I was throwing up," Whitney said, "which I'm not, that's my choice. Females have choices in this decade."

Miss hit Whitney's arm.

"What? I'm just saying. I'm not throwing up on purpose, but I could if I wanted to. It's my body."

"Wait here," I said. "Don't move."

I turned and went back inside, straight to the stage where Lewis sat at his kingly table, eating green Jell-O for breakfast. "I need you," I said. I kept my eyes away from Bennett, who moved his knee to brush against mine. Goose bumps rose on my skin. In the mornings, leaving the warmth of Bennett's body was becoming an increasing struggle. I had forgone my 5 A.M. run a few times now for an extra half hour in his arms. This was week six, and next week would be week seven, and then it would be week eight. And then.

I wondered if in this moment I looked different to him, since my attention, for once, was focused elsewhere.

Back on the cafeteria steps, I told Lewis, "Miss burst a blood vessel in her eye. Whitney just came back to the table smelling of vomit. The weigh-ins have been strange the past couple of weeks. Can we all agree these girls are making themselves throw up?"

Lewis looked at them. "Girls? You wouldn't do that, would you?" He was smirking a little, as if to say, *I'm on your side*, implying that he was as sure as they were that I was acting hysterical.

"No!" they shouted.

"You know that's not a healthy way to lose weight, right?"

"Obviously!"

The door opened and Sheena appeared, her fiery hair wrapped into Princess Leia buns. Kimmy followed, her thumb plugging her mouth.

Sheena gripped my arm. "You've got to cut this shit out."

I yanked my arm away, stepping backward. "If there's a problem," I said, "then it needs to be addressed."

"*You* have problems." She poked at my chest with her fingertips. "You, you, *you*."

"Wait a minute," Lewis said. "Everyone calm down. Whitney? Why do you smell like vomit?"

"Because I threw up. I don't feel well."

"Then please go see Nurse. Miss, what happened to your eye?"

Miss covered her eye with one hand. "How should I know?"

"Kimmy?" Lewis said. "Do you have something to say?"

Kimmy removed her thumb from her mouth, pulling out a string of saliva. "I don't know." She reinserted her thumb.

Lewis looked at me. "And that's how you mediate a problem," he said, tugging at his drooping shorts.

Sheena smirked at me. "Nothing like a good shit storm, right, Gray?" She turned to Lewis. "Have you noticed yet that Gray *loves* to stir shit up? This is what spoiled brats do. They make drama because they're bored with their lives." She looked at me again. "If you had real problems, you wouldn't have to create fake ones."

"You don't know anything about me," I told Sheena.

"The thing is," she said, smiling, "I do."

"I've been working at camps for two decades," Lewis told me. "There's nothing that could shock me. Nothing I don't know how to handle." He patted Kimmy on the top of her head and turned to go back inside.

FORTY-FIVE

That night, at a sports bar in Melrose, Bennett and I drank light beer from the taps as half a dozen televisions flickered around us and the occasional *tock* of cue to pool ball punctuated the din. We sat turned toward each other on our bar stools, Bennett's hand on my knee, my knee and thigh bare below the hem of the black minidress I'd recently bought at the mall. But for the first time, I wasn't leaning into him, trying to hook his eyes to mine.

"Feeling better, Angeline?" Bennett asked as I drained my second beer and ordered a third.

"The lack of professionalism is disturbing," I said. "Lewis is a joke. I can't even do my job because there's no support."

"I support you."

"How so?"

"Hey now. That's not nice."

"Well? You didn't even come outside today. You stayed in the cafeteria. You didn't say a word. I think the whole camp knows what Whitney and Miss are up to, and no one's going to do anything about it. I think Nurse even knows. But everyone's afraid of those girls. And of Sheena."

"Sheena's okay. She's just a kid."

"Why is a 'kid' my co-counselor?"

"Because this is summer camp."

"You should fire her."

"No one's getting fired. For what?"

"I don't know exactly what's going on, but I loathe her. She's up to something with those girls."

"That won't fly. 'Sheena, go home. Angeline *loathes* you.'"

"No one will fire her. No one wants to do the right thing," I said, and then I cringed. Who was I to talk about right and wrong? I wanted to get rid of Sheena not because of her unprofessional behavior, but because I had disclosed too much to her, and I worried that she was ruthless.

"If you think about it," Bennett said, "in the grand scheme of things, none of this really matters all that much. You ever think about that when you're upset? How compared to something really bad, it's nothing?"

I stared at Bennett. His eyes were wide and blue. In a lineup, I would have easily identified Bennett's arms, but his eyes looked like many people's eyes. They were mass-produced eyes. Flyover state eyes. The largest demographic eyes.

"Did you come up with that all by yourself?" I asked.

"What?"

"That philosophy." I slid off my bar stool, teetering on high heels.

"What philosophy? Where are you going?" Bennett grabbed my hand.

I looked at the rows of bottles behind the bartender. I looked to the pool table, to the exit sign, to the jukebox in the corner, to the TV screens boxing me in. There was nowhere I wanted to go. I wanted to jump out of myself and run.

"Bathroom."

"Are you hungry? I could order some cheese sticks or something."

"Fried food? Are you serious?"

"Out in the real world," Bennett said, chuckling, "people eat cheese sticks now and then. Remember?"

I pressed my palm to my stomach. "Stop offering me food. That won't make anything better."

Bennett raised his hands as if I might shoot. "I never—"

"Just. Stop." I snapped my purse up off the bar and stomped to the bathroom.

The lights inside were fluorescent, merciless. The full-length mirror was incongruously, glaringly clean. There I was. A girl with a suntan. A girl who needed a haircut. A girl in a desperate dress. I set my purse on the tile floor and smoothed the dress in the front. I was embarrassed to see how visible my panty lines were through the spandex.

God, I wasn't even that thin. I wasn't as skinny as I'd been believing I was. How I had been relishing the delusion of regressing, of becoming new, of reversing time. I'd been walking around believing that my arms were bony, that my clavicles were standing at attention, that my legs were skeletal, my ass nonexistent.

I turned sideways. My ass existed. How shameful that I'd been imagining myself skinny, acting skinny, when in fact I was only skinny compared to fat people. The Camp Carolina population had become my point of reference. When Nurse told me that I needed to eat more, I lapped up her concern instead of looking at the facts.

Fact number one: Nurse was obese.

Fact number two: Nurse was surrounded by obese people.

But. But! It was true that there was less of me. It was true that I was smaller than I'd ever been in my adult life. I imagined Mikey grabbing a handful of my ass, the way he often did. "This ass of yours," he always said. I imagined him seeing me in a couple of weeks and wondering, *Where is the rest of you? Where is the part that you used to let me love?*

When I got back to Bennett, when I sat on the stool and heard it squish beneath my weight, I was seeing my body, *really seeing* my body: There was still a roll in my stomach—diminished, yes, but there. I drank my beer and felt the roll swell.

"Please tell me what I did," Bennett said with a sigh. He inspected his thumbnail, then tore off the cuticle with his teeth.

"Nothing. Don't worry about a thing."

"Don't be like that."

"Why should I have to explain everything?"

"I would gladly stick up for you. How can you say I wouldn't?"

"Well, you didn't today."

"I wasn't even involved. How could I have? I wasn't even *with* y'all."

"You could have come outside."

"I didn't know what was going on. What are you so angry about?"

"Stop asking me that. I'm telling you what I'm angry about."

Funny how all lovers' quarrels resemble one another, how the fight I was having with Bennett felt like the fights I had with Mikey, how I watched myself run for the same arsenal, watched myself select the weapons I hadn't seen in months, brush off the dust, and take aim like a pro. Funny how Bennett sounded to me like Mikey with a different accent, a different vocabulary.

Until he reminded me that he wasn't Mikey. He wasn't the man who had been loving me for years, who believed in an airbrushed version of me.

"I've had it," he said, rising abruptly from his stool and fishing his wallet from his back pocket. "I try to treat you right, but you know what, Gray?"

I set my beer down and looked up at him. "Gray" sounded harsh coming from his lips, like chewing-tobacco spit. "What?" I said. "Tell me. Tell me about how you've had it with me. Don't you think I've had it with *you*?"

"I haven't *done* anything."

"Exactly."

"I don't make demands of you. I don't expect things from you."

"We're fucking!" I said too loudly. "We're allowed to expect things from each other."

"God, you're foulmouthed sometimes. It's that Yankee upbringing."

"Don't start on my upbringing. You know nothing about it. You're being racist." I sounded like Whitney.

"You're going to run back to your life in New York in a couple of weeks," Bennett said. "I'll just be some redneck you had some fling with some summer. You think I don't know that?"

"You're *making* this a fling. You create distance between us on purpose."

Bennett threw cash on the bar and stuffed his wallet back into his pocket. "I don't have to fight with you. I don't have to listen to you bitch at me, and I don't have to defend myself. You're not my wife. Don't sit there and tell me I owe you things."

He picked up his glass and drained his beer. He was gorgeous. He was a man with blue eyes and a perfect body in flip-flops and cargo shorts, in a crisp white button-down shirt and a Hurricanes cap. I looked at the lines in his face and I loved them. I loved the memories in those lines that I would never be a part of—the best soccer game of his life, the day he fell for Camille, the first time he saw his baby's toes.

Bennett pulled his keys out of his pocket, gave them a quick toss, and caught them effortlessly in his palm. Then he turned from me without another glance and walked right out of the bar.

I watched the door for a few moments. When it finally opened, two women walked in wearing shirts that displayed their bellies. They were thinner than I was. They had fake tans. Their skin looked toasted.

A man beside me said, "Not too bright, that guy. Leaving a beautiful woman like that." I looked at him. He was two hundred years old. He spoke into his scotch. His head was bald; his spine so hunched, his body was a comma. The sight of him, the reminder of what eventually happened to every living thing, even the most beautiful living things, made me so depressed, I wanted to run outside and jump in front of a speeding car. Bennett would kneel over my body—lifeless, still imperfect. He would be grief-stricken. He would weep and hyperventilate.

I touched the backs of the man's fingers. "Thank you for calling me beautiful," I said.

What a dumb daydream—getting hit by a car. I didn't mean it. Not really. Months had passed since I'd longed for death. Besides, if I died, Bennett wouldn't care for me any more than he already did. Or maybe he would for a few weeks, but in time I'd become a distant memory—a weird thing that once happened to Bennett. In the end, no one would sob, "If only Bennett had given her enough love, she would still be alive." Instead they would say, "Wow, she must have been really fucked up."

I stood and crossed the bar. I opened the door and stepped outside. The night was hot. I could never get used to summer nights. I was always expecting them to disappoint me, to suddenly turn cold.

Bennett was sitting in the driver's seat of his car. His window was down. I stood at the door and held the base of the window frame. Bennett's keys were stabbed into the ignition, but the engine was silent. Keeping his eyes straight ahead, he said, "You know I would never have left you here. Right?"

"Of course you wouldn't have. Southern gentlemen don't leave their ladies at sports bars."

He almost smiled. Then he said, "Sometimes I feel like I'm taking care of someone else's car. I'm watching your boyfriend's car for the summer so it doesn't get scratched up."

"You've scratched me up pretty good," I said. I touched his face. I took his earlobe between my thumb and forefinger, the perfect skin of it. A child's earlobe. I leaned in and kissed it. "I'm sorry," I said. "I picked that fight."

"Why do women pick fights?"

"To get to the other side."

Bennett turned to look at me. "Of what?"

I withdrew my hand. "Never mind."

"What happened to fun? Isn't this supposed to be fun?"

"It is fun."

"Is it? You're sort of crazy."

"What kind of crazy?"

"It's like you're . . . I don't know, in love with yourself."

"Self-absorption is different from self-love."

"I don't know what the hell that means."

"Self-absorption has more to do with self-loathing."

"Whatever you say, Angeline."

"Well," I said, "anyway. *Someone's* got to be in love with me!"

I saw myself with a microphone, onstage at a comedy club, saying, "*Someone's* got to be in love with me." I could practically hear the silence of the dark and restless crowd.

Bennett opened his car door and got out. He took me in his arms and pressed me up against the car. He pushed the hem of my dress to my hips. No one could have seen us. Or maybe they could have. It didn't matter. I wrapped my arms around Bennett's neck and smelled the summery scent of him. He lifted me off the ground. One of my shoes fell and plopped on the asphalt. I pushed the bare sole of my foot up his shin, into the leg of his shorts. I exhaled. It was still summer. The stars winked at us. The nearby traffic sighed for us. The temperature held its breath and promised to hold it as long as it could.

FORTY-SIX

Dear Fat People,

Don't judge me. Don't you dare judge me. If you were thin, you would make the same mistakes; you would have more room in your life, in your personal space, in your clothing, to make mistakes. You probably wouldn't even call them mistakes. You would be having so much fun shrinking, and so much fun making the things you used to call mistakes.

Mistakes are rationed. You use yours up on your daily food choices, your daily commitment to a sedentary life. If you lived healthily, if your step had a spring to it, if you picked daintily at your fruit salad instead of scarfing five pastries for breakfast, you could do things like sleep with a man who was wrong for you just because you felt like it. You could walk around his room naked while he lounged in bed and watched you. You could pretend you had no idea he was watching until he said, "Your body is a work of art." (He would not mean Rubens's art.)

You could half-smile and say, "Thank you," as if you heard this so often, it was predictable.

You could wear his pale blue button-down with nothing underneath.

You could stand naked in his giant shoes.

You would no longer have to settle for comfort over excitement; for contentment over beautiful, reckless unrest. Don't you want to live to the very edge of life? Don't you want to live the way everyone's afraid to? Don't you know, deep down, that when you are doing what the world calls stupid or selfish—hurting someone for the sake of your lust, loving someone who doesn't love you, loving with your whole self with no regard for consequences, generally ignoring the reality of consequences—you are actually alive?

Be honest with yourself for once. This is no way to live—backpacking through Europe one summer, and then holding a funeral for your youth. This is no way to live—surrounded by a fence, your refrigerator stuffed. This is no way to live—as if sex is something that other people do. This is no way to live—sitting in a comfortable chair, eating doughnuts beside some person who makes you feel big and numb.

FORTY-SEVEN

It was Kimmy who broke open like a piñata, who scattered her friends' secrets like hard candy. It happened on a rainy afternoon in the gym during an all-camp game of dodgeball. I was watching Pudge, who was wearing a baseball cap that said PHAT CAMP in red embroidery and white sneakers that Lewis had bought him, the leather so new it hadn't yet creased. Pudge wasn't exactly running, but he was throwing and catching, walking to half court, bending down to pick up balls. His wheelchair was a relic from another era.

Lewis often said, loudly, that Pudge was a charity case, that he lived in the ghetto, that he binged daily on Doritos and ice cream to soothe himself because he feared for his life, for his mother's life, when he heard gunshots out the window of his trailer. Were there trailer parks in the ghetto? The story sounded suspicious. But Pudge undoubtedly had survival skills—he knew that as long as he hailed Lewis as king, Lewis would treat him like a prince.

Whenever I spoke with Pudge, my tongue felt heavy and slow, in part because his southern accent was almost incomprehensibly thick, but also because his wide, sad eyes made me hope that he would like me, made me wish that I could save him. He could make a person feel that if she saved him, she would get to be on *60 Minutes* and also go to heaven. Lewis took him shopping. Nurse hosted him for long hours in her air-conditioned office. Together, Nurse and Pudge watched television long after Lights Out.

I saw him throw the ball that glanced off Kimmy's shoulder. It was just a red rubber ball, partially deflated, but when it hit her, she crumpled to the floor, curled up like a snail, covered her head with her arms, and began to moan.

It took everyone a few seconds to make sense of what was happening. Bennett blew his whistle and jogged across the gym to Kimmy, where the kids had begun to gather. KJ, who during fair weather stood sentinel at the pool, started waving his arms like a referee calling for a time-out. "Give her air!" he shouted uselessly. "Give her air!"

I hung back and watched Bennett crouch beside her. "What's the matter?" he asked. "Are you hurt?"

With her arms covering her head, she wailed, "I can't take this anymore!"

Bennett looked up at Nurse, who had made her way over with Lewis and was bent at the waist, peering at Kimmy, her hands on her thighs.

"Kimmy?" Lewis said. "Do you want to go to Nurse's office? Maybe you need an ice pack."

"I'm not hurt!" Kimmy shrieked.

"An aspirin? You might need a glass of water."

"I just . . . can't *take* this anymore!"

"Take what?" Bennett asked.

Sheena poked through the crowd. "Kimmy," she said, getting down on her knees. "Why don't you come with me? Come on. Let's go talk." She looked at Bennett, then up at Lewis and Nurse. "I think she's just a little homesick. She's been homesick lately. I can handle it."

"Just a sec," Nurse said. "Sheena, just hold your pretty horses. Kimmy? You've got to sit up and talk to us. No one can help you if you don't sit up and talk. Sit up. Let the blood circulate. Take deep breaths." She drew a deep breath to demonstrate.

"I'll talk to her," Sheena said. She pulled Kimmy's arm. "Get up, Kimmy. We're going for a walk now. Just the two of us. Okay? Get up. Come on, babe."

Kimmy pulled away from Sheena and sat up. Her freckles had expanded beneath her tears. "I have to talk to Lewis," she said, her bottom lip quivering. "Alone."

After Kimmy and Lewis left the gym, Bennett tried to keep the dodgeball game going, but no one was interested in pretend conflict, now that there was a real conflict. Sheena, Whitney, and Miss stood huddled together, whispering. Eden watched them for a while, and then started whispering to Harriet, who didn't know how to engage in friend-whispering, and kept stepping backward, as if the whispers were blowing her away. Some of the boys decided to play H-O-R-S-E, but no one wanted to shoot first. Finally, they started throwing balls at the wall and catching them.

A few minutes passed before Lewis returned to the gym and called Bennett and Nurse out. A few minutes after that, Nurse came back in and called Sheena, Whitney, and Miss out.

My group was reduced to Eden and Harriet. I suggested we

head back to the dorm. As we walked, Eden asked me, "Do you know what's going on?"

"Not really. Do you?"

Eden glanced at Harriet. Neither of them spoke. But for the first time, I didn't care to excavate Eden's secrets. After a month and a half of dieting, I was thinner than I'd ever been. "Have some self-confidence," I could hear my father saying. And now I did. It seemed absurd that I had ever eaten two packages of Chips Ahoy! cookies in one sitting. Who was that person?

She was a person who hadn't met Bennett. And a person who found comfort in the certainty of death, rather than in possible solutions to her problems.

I would tell Eden about our father, eventually, because it was the right thing to do, but not because my life depended on it.

Harriet turned to me and said, "I'm di—" but then she closed her mouth and kept walking.

"Dizzy?" I asked.

She didn't answer immediately. We walked on, gravel crunching under our shoes. "I was going to say that," she said. "That I was dizzy."

"But you're not."

"No," she said.

"I'm glad," I said.

At dinnertime, Lewis came to the cafeteria and asked to speak with me outside. We sat on the steps and he told me the story: Every night after Lights Out, Sheena had been herding Whitney, Miss, and Kimmy out of the dorm and into her car, and driving them to McDonald's in Melrose for a nightly fast-food binge. Once the weigh-ins showed that the girls had gained weight, Sheena had taught them how to make themselves vomit. Whitney and Miss had taken to it. Kimmy just wanted to go home, where perhaps she was fat, but at least no one was pressuring her to stick her head in a toilet and her finger down her throat.

"You had no idea?" Lewis studied my face. "Tell me you had no idea."

"I told you Whitney and Miss were making themselves throw up."

"No, no, you didn't. If you did, we wouldn't be in this mess."

"All right," I said. "Well. I had no idea they were going to McDonald's."

"Good. Because, Gray, I've always thought you and I were on the same side. Like a team. You remind me of women I knew in the seventies."

"I do?"

"Women who did drugs. Really fun, tremendous women. I think you and I will be friends for life. We're on the same wavelength." He poked my forehead with his finger. "I'm just sorry you didn't catch Sheena. But you were asleep. Doing what you were supposed to be doing."

I saw myself then, running through the dark to Bennett.

"I do so much for everyone," Lewis said. "It never ceases to amaze me, how willing people are to just screw you over when you're the nicest guy in the world. I told the girls, 'Lewis Teller is the nicest guy in the world. But when you take advantage of Lewis Teller, you'd better be prepared to pay the price.'"

We stared together at the drab smile of the loop, the green trees that swayed dreamily to silent music.

"I don't know why anyone would risk getting kicked out of camp," I said. "It's wonderful here."

"It is."

"I feel so clean here. Even though I'm sweating all the time. It's like I'm sweating my whole past out. I feel new."

"You are new. That's the thing about my camp."

"Are you going to send the girls home?"

"I should," Lewis said, rubbing his knees.

"Maybe Kimmy should stay? Since she's the one who spoke up?"

He didn't respond. "Sheena's out of here," he said. "She has until eight o'clock to pack her things and get the hell out. You think I care? I don't care. I'll fire anyone. I could run this whole place myself. You'll see major changes in Whitney, Miss, and Kimmy. Just watch. They were sobbing their eyes out when they thought I was going to send them home. For two hours I let them think they were done here. And then I told them, 'Okay, I'll give you a second chance.' I told them, 'But!'" He shook his finger. "'But,' I told them, 'no more of this little clique of yours. You have to start being real participants in the Camp Carolina community.' I told them, 'You're going to have to work your butts off the rest of the summer.' I told them I won't tolerate bad attitudes. They were practically kissing my feet." I looked at his feet. They were white with blue veins, hairy, housed in enormous imitation Tevas. "It was like I had just spared their lives." He chuckled. Then he grew serious again. "You know why I didn't send them home?"

I did know. Campers were worth eleven thousand dollars apiece. He didn't want to tell their parents that under his supervision, their children had eaten McDonald's and were now toying with new eating disorders. He didn't want to explain to them how loosely he had screened candidates during the hiring process. He didn't want to lose campers when, compared with other weight-loss camps, he already had so few. He didn't want to deal with angry parents asking for refunds or writing on weight-loss camp websites about how incompetent Lewis Teller was, how his brand-new revolutionary weight-loss camp for children was nothing but a joke.

"I didn't send them home because I believe in every child. Some just need more help than others."

"So they're going to get help? Are you bringing in a shrink or something?"

"There's nothing I can't handle."

"Aren't eating disorders . . . um . . . serious?"

"They don't have eating disorders."

"They eat and throw up their food."

"They'll stop now."

"How do you know?"

"I told them they better cut the shit."

"So you don't think—"

"Some kids just need more help with their self-esteem. That's what I'm here for. That's why my camp will succeed when all other camps have failed: I'm committed to the children. People will know me as Lewis Teller, the man who really cares about the kids."

FORTY-EIGHT

At Lewis's request, Bennett stood outside Sheena's room while she packed, to prevent her from pulling a gun from under her bed and moving through the dorms on a shooting rampage. Every female camper and counselor had gathered in our hall. Kimmy hung back on the edges of the crowd with one of her counselors, sucking her thumb, her puffy eyes wide. Among the Sheena supporters, several campers were weeping with their whole bodies, shouting that Sheena had been framed.

Eden was leaning against the closed door of her room, a solitary tear dribbling down her cheek ("Here comes Brenda Preston!" I could hear my father saying).

"It wasn't Sheena's fault!" Whitney shrieked. She had slid down the wall and was sitting on the floor, her knees tucked to her chin. "She's the best counselor in the whole camp!"

Whitney's words felt, not like a punch or a stab, nothing that drastic, but at least like a jostle—like someone had knocked into me in a crowd, not bothering to turn around and apologize. I wasn't delusional; I knew *I* wasn't the best counselor at Camp Carolina. But Sheena? Really? I looked around at the tear-streaked cheeks, the kids standing in supportive clusters, arms snaked around one another's shoulders, and I saw that it was true: Sheena had made an impact, forged a closeness with the kids, made camp more fun. What had I done? I had experimented with green eye shadow and glitter. I had meditated diligently on blow jobs. I had done Kegels. I had found an aesthetician in Melrose to wax my pubic hair into a heart.

"Nobody cares about us!" Whitney said. "Sheena's the only one who ever cared." She climbed to her feet. "We're all going to have to go back to being invisible now. We'll just be the fat kids everyone pretends not to see." She raised her arms and tipped her face toward the ceiling, as if to invoke lightning. "Sheena saw us!" she shouted.

Eden used the knuckle of each of her thumbs to wipe dramatically beneath her eyes. Miss, who was sitting and weeping at Whitney's feet, wailed, "This camp is gay!"

This was not the picture Lewis had painted of Whitney and Miss and their repentance. These were not girls who seemed sorry.

When Sheena finished packing, she stood on the threshold and looked out on the chaos. The crowd went quiet, as if she were controlling the volume with a dial.

"Let's go," Bennett said, slipping into her room. "Let's get your stuff to your car." He loaded his arms with her things.

Sheena ignored him. "Y'all," she said, "don't worry." She looked at me then, her face serene. "You'll see me again." And with that, she lifted a duffel bag in each hand, squared her shoulders, and strode toward the stairwell, Bennett trailing her.

We all followed, a crowd that should have been carrying votive candles and humming something sad and strong.

"We love you, Sheena!" the kids shrieked. "Don't leave us here!"

Even a couple of the counselors cried quietly, walking with their heads bowed, as if toward Sheena's crucifixion.

Lewis and Nurse were waiting in the parking lot by Sheena's silver Camry. The boys were clustered nearby, some of the young ones perched on the shoulders of their counselors. Sheena and Bennett loaded the trunk and the backseat. And then Sheena opened the driver's side door, bent into the car to start the ignition, and stood again to address the masses. She wore a flowing white sundress that fell to her ankles, delicate leather sandals adorned with turquoise beads. Her hair was crimped and loose and full of fire, a flame blowing in an unlikely wind. I had never seen her more beautiful. A cloud or a stage should have appeared beneath the soles of her shoes.

Everyone went quiet, awaiting a speech.

"Y'all know how to reach me," she said. She held her cell phone aloft like a sword. "I know how fucked up this place is. You know I do."

"That's enough," Lewis said, stepping toward her. "You're finished here."

Sheena looked at him, her eyes smoldering like cigarette burns in the smooth white plane of her face. She lowered her arm to her side. And then she smiled two smiles—with her lips and with her scar—and said something cryptic: "Child molester." She balled her fist, the cell phone inside it, wound up, and punched Lewis squarely in the gut. For a second, her hand disappeared up to the wrist.

The crowd sucked in a collective breath. Lewis whimpered in one warbling note and doubled over, his knee jerking up to his chest. When he righted himself and tried to speak, Sheena lifted her skirt above her ankles, picked up one leg, and launched a powerful kick at Lewis's crotch.

"Stop that!" Bennett said, reaching for her. "Sheena! What in—"

Sheena hopped into her car and backed it out of the parking lot with a screech. The tires crunched over gravel. The silver paint glistened and winked in the sunshine. She honked her horn twice. She straightened the car. And then she was gone.

The second casualty.

FORTY-NINE

Now that Kimmy—Judas, Brutus, Benedict Arnold—was on the outs with Whitney and Miss, she spent her time with the other thirteen-year-olds in the intermediate group. The wide-eyed anxiety left her face. She sucked her thumb with less urgency. Kimmy didn't care who was popular. She never had. That was what had made her popular in the first place. Kimmy just liked to be comfortable. If she'd grown up when I had, she would have favored beanbags and Laura Ashley bedroom sets. I expected that one day she would be a mother who wore the best, most expensive sweat suits and sipped hot tea from a meticulously chipped mug. With Sheena gone, Kimmy was comfortable. Ex-communicated and comfortable.

And so the meek inherited the earth: For the first time in her life, Eden was "in." It started with the tears she shed upon Sheena's departure. That night, she, Whitney, and Miss locked themselves in Miss's room for hours. At Lights Out, when they finally emerged, Eden's initiation was sealed. Her skin glowed. Her fingernails were painted red.

I slept in my own bed that night. Staring at the moonlight through the unfamiliar slits of my blinds, I called Bennett from my cell phone. "You're so close. I can't believe how close you are and I can't touch you."

"Blame Sheena."

"I do," I said.

"Why'd she pick McDonald's? McDonald's hasn't had a good special all summer."

I hugged my pillow to my body. "What the hell happened today?"

"Well, a nineteen-year-old girl kicked Lewis's ass."

I giggled. "But why did she call him a child molester?"

"I was wondering the same thing," Bennett said. "I was going to ask you."

Whitney, Eden, and Miss began writing WEM on the walls and on their clothing. They walked in an impenetrable, unsmiling line, elbows linked, heads up, potent in movie star sunglasses. They told everyone, "You can't touch WEM."

Eden promptly withdrew from me. Gone were the days when she would sulk on my bed, my window fan blowing her hair across her face. Around Whitney and Miss, she was cautious, but elated. I could practically see the static of excitement crackling on her skin. She stopped talking like she was black, but started trying to do her hair like Miss's, even though Miss's hair was gorgeous, thick, sparkly, and full of light, whereas Eden's was greasy and stringy and dark. Miss wore her hair in a high side ponytail, so Eden did, too. Sometimes the three of them wore matching outfits. Sometimes they suffered synchronized injuries. They frequently disappeared into one another's rooms and locked the door. If I walked by, I could hear their muffled laughter. Camp was quiet. Sheena's absence felt like a fragile calm, a crystal figurine teetering, seconds from shattering on hardwood.

While the campers walked solemnly around the loop the morning after Sheena's departure, I stayed with Lewis on the cafeteria steps.

"Can you handle your girls yourself?" he asked. He looked me up and down as if sizing me up for battle.

"Four campers? Sure. By the way, are you all right? She hit you pretty hard."

"I didn't even feel it. I used to wrestle in high school."

"Right, but—"

"I was always big. But I was the athletic kid. Everyone knew not to mess with Lewis Teller." He held his fists up in front of his face and jabbed at an imaginary enemy. "I could teach you how to fight," he said. He shuffled on his feet like a boxer. "Everyone should know how to fight."

"Sure," I said. "Maybe sometime."

Lewis stopped jabbing. He was out of breath. He set his hands on his massive hips. "Things are going to get better around here," he said. "I'm glad Sheena's gone. She was bringing everyone down." He squinted at me. "How much weight have you lost?"

I plucked my sunglasses from the neck of my T-shirt and put them on. "I stopped weighing in."

Twenty-two and three-tenths of a pound. I weighed myself every morning before the world was awake.

I looked at Lewis's body, from his sneakers and striped socks to his pleated gray shorts to his yellow Camp Carolina T-shirt. He looked bigger every day. Sometimes he looked bigger at dinner than he had at breakfast, as if he would eventually float into the atmosphere, farther and farther from Earth, finally becoming tiny.

"I knew when I met you that my camp would change your life. You didn't think so. I could see you didn't think so."

"My eating habits are totally different," I said. "I eat much smaller portions. I need so much less."

"You'll never be the same again," Lewis said.

I thought of Chinese Buffet, the gulping, greasy indulgence of it. "I hope you're right," I said.

"Gray. Don't you know me by now? Am I ever wrong?" He grabbed for my hand and twirled me, and then gracelessly dipped me. I stumbled to a lower step. He pointed down at me with an outstretched arm. "You, Gray Lachmann, are changed."

FIFTY

Dear Fat People,

I see you in motorized wheelchairs, in bus seats that don't ac-commodate you. I see you taking breaks when you walk, pretend-ing to admire the scenery. Good God, I am afraid. Not for your hearts and your joints and your arteries. No, I'm afraid for myself. I know that you're inside me—flesh flies laying your infinite eggs in my open, pus-slick wounds. Your young will hatch in my body and eat their way up through my skin.

Yes. I am being mean. So? You, of all people, should recognize my reasons for acting mean.

FIFTY-ONE

This was a summer of loss. We lost Sheena. We lost Spider. We lost weight. We lost our inhibitions. We lost socks when we sent the laundry out. We lost our minds when it rained too much. We lost track of time in the swimming pool. We lost our old reflections, the stretch of space we could claim on a bench, some cellulite, a roll or two, our salt cravings, our caffeine habits, our distaste for sugar-free Jell-O. And then I lost my hair.

With not even two weeks left of camp, I found that if I touched my hair—to make a ponytail, to scratch my head, to rake it back off my face—I'd wind up with a handful of it, as if it hadn't been stitched to my scalp. I began to wonder whether, if I gave the whole mass a good tug, it would come off in my fist like a wig. I didn't try. I didn't tell anyone. Instead, I just ignored it. If I ignored the problem, I knew, it would take the hint and go away.

•   •   •

"Angeline," Bennett said.

We were at Water Nation, land of the great, looping blue slides; of the fried dough and fat families and *E. coli* scares. My group—Whitney (who had begged, unsuccessfully, to stay behind at camp), Eden, Harriet, and Miss—had merged with Pudge and a couple of the other boys, and Brendan. Bennett and I were trailing behind them as they walked in a tight mass through the park. Brendan and Miss had their arms around each other's waists. It was becoming a familiar image, the two of them linked like Rockettes. They had the air of a genuine couple, people who had been in love for years, who looked at each other for long stretches and had conversations with their eyes. Even when Brendan was alone now, he looked confident, his body language less awkward, his smile easier.

Bennett touched the side of my head.

"What?"

"Nothing."

"*What?*"

"Your hair . . ."

I touched my hair. I had tied it into a messy knot.

Bennett pressed his thumb to the side of my head. "You have a bald spot. Maybe it's just the way your hair's done up, but . . ."

I combed my fingernails through the sides of my hair. "That better?"

"I can still see it."

"Then stop looking."

"You got it, Angeline. Whatever you say." Bennett hooked his arm around my neck in a brief headlock, then let go before anyone could see.

I should have recognized an omen. I should have known that the day Bennett pointed out a flaw on my body would mark some sort of ending. But I was oblivious. Willfully so. I wasn't fazed by the hot gray sky that looked ready to explode. Camp would end in just over a week. But I didn't think it would ever rain.

We walked in our bathing suits, in love with our bodies. We were a parade for our bodies. We were one thousand pounds lighter than we'd been when we'd met.

"I want to go on the Death Drop," Miss said. She hopped in the air like a thin person and took off running, Whitney just behind her, Eden in tow, toward the slide that started in the sky and dropped at a ninety-degree angle to earth.

Everyone followed. Of course we did. We had been following Miss and Whitney all summer. When we got to the base of the slide, I sat beside Bennett on a bench. Everyone else joined the line.

"I thought Harriet would for sure stay with us," I said. "And Whitney. And Pudge."

"How 'bout that," Bennett said. "Whitney on a water slide."

"Nah. She won't go through with it. Neither will Harriet. If they even let her on."

"You don't give anyone enough credit."

I leaned my head on his shoulder. "If we have kids one day," I said, "we should take them to this water park." I glanced at his face, surprised not to feel his muscles go tight. "Unless they're fat. Then we'll make them run wind sprints."

"You won't have fat kids," he said after a minute.

"Me. Right."

"What?"

"You said, 'You won't have fat kids' . . . Forget it."

"If I had my son with me all the time, no way he'd be overweight."

"You don't have that kind of control."

"No? When you have kids, you'll see, Angeline. If you keep

an eye on them, they'll have the best bodies in town. Besides their mama's."

"I'd feed them healthy food, but what if they're lazy? What if they eat desserts at their friends' houses? What if they're the types of kids who hide candy in their drawers? What if they hate to run around? What if they love video games?"

"Then you'll have to be the kind of mother who goes through her kids' drawers."

I thought about that. "You know? I think I *would* be that kind of mother. Maybe I'd be looking for candy. I would want to eat their candy." I laughed, but it came out sounding strange and choked.

Bennett shifted in his seat and his wooden cross grazed my face.

I imagined his home. Me inside it. Children who looked like him and would never know my father. I imagined waking up beside Bennett on a Sunday morning, zipping myself into a long floral dress, twisting my hair into a low bun, and affixing to my head a wide-brimmed, avocado-green straw hat adorned with a fat white ribbon. I imagined gathering my skirt into my fist to climb into Bennett's car, and letting him drive me to church, a brood of children in the backseat eating MoonPies and lunch meats from plastic wrappers. My mother visiting us in the winter, standing in Bennett's living room, tiny beside a towering Christmas tree; sipping eggnog from one of Bennett's mugs that said WORLD'S GREATEST DAD, watching as I moved through my home in a Christmas sweater, a Christmas vest, pleated pants, a wreath pin that lit up and flashed red and green.

To be clear, Bennett had never told me that he lived this way, never indicated to me that his life was some deranged homage to Christmas. Nor had he given me any indication that he hoped I would bear his children. And yet.

"I won't always be in my best shape," I said.

"You'll always be hot."

"One day I'll be forty."

"First you'll be twenty-eight."

"Forty. Then fifty. Then sixty. If I live to sixty. My father didn't make it to sixty."

"I'm in the best shape of my life at forty-one. You just have to work at it all the time. You just have to commit to never letting go of it."

"Everyone lets go eventually."

"Think positive."

"One day I'll be lumpy. One day I'll be shriveled. One day I'll be pregnant. One day I'll be pregnant and craving Nutella. I'll eat ten jars of it."

"You wouldn't."

I laughed. "You don't know me."

"I don't think that's true at all."

"I'd eat twenty jars."

"Hogwash."

"You know nothing about my genetic makeup."

"Your what?"

"And you don't seem to understand that there's more to life than bodies."

"Hey. Thanks a lot."

"I feel like my body has to be perfect for you."

"Are you picking one of your fights?"

"I'm not my body," I said, but even as I said it, I knew that it was nonsense—meaningless jargon. Like when people talked about toxins. Or vibes. Or bad things happening in threes. What the hell did any of it mean? We *absolutely* were our bodies. To deny that was to court disaster: to wind up in labor, cluelessly pregnant; to become infected by a forgotten, moldy hamburger.

"You want to test me?" Bennett said. "Go ahead. Get fat. I'd still throw you up against the wall and have my way with you. Go eat a cheesecake."

"Gladly."

"And a loaf of bread."

"With butter."

"I'll roll you through the streets. I'll tell everyone, 'This is my girl. She's fatter than Albert, but she's a top-shelf lay.'" He whispered, "That'll be us," and he pointed to a couple walking by. They were both covered scalp to toenails in tattoos. The man, in lace-up board shorts, was scrawny and couldn't have been more than five feet tall. The woman towered over him in a purple tankini; she must have weighed at least three hundred pounds. They held hands, soaking wet, wearing inflated inner tubes around their waists like misplaced halos, leaving water droplets in their wake.

I sat up. "I don't want to talk about this anymore."

"You and your mood swings."

"It's just that you don't mean it."

"I was just playing. I thought we were playing. Don't be like that, Angeline."

I crossed one leg over the other, making myself small, re-membering taking the N train deep into Brooklyn with Mikey every year for all-day Easter dinner at his parents' house, where his uncles called us "yous guys," and his father called me Yellow or Purple or Pink, and his mother leaned out the bathroom window, pinning laundry to a clothesline, and his aunts smoked Virginia Slims while they glazed the ham with paintbrushes and fought over which knife to use to cut fresh mozzarella for the antipasti. I remembered the time Mikey bought me a car air freshener even though I didn't have a car, just because the word "sexy" was printed on it in block letters.

I remembered when we first started dating and he asked if he could wash my hair. ("It's just so pretty. I just want to *do* something for it.")

My fingers moved to my scalp, searching out my bald spot. I pulled my hair out of its elastic and tried for a new ponytail, one that covered all the naked parts of my head. I squinted in the flat light at clouds the color of harbor water.

"You know," Bennett said, "if you loved your boyfriend, you'd be with him now. You wouldn't have left him for two months. It's not my business, but I can see he doesn't make you happy."

"Sometimes we're happy."

"Anyway, you don't have kids with him. What do you owe the guy?"

"Please don't call him 'the guy.' We've been through a lot together. I love him," I said, remembering that day in the diner, when I'd said those words to my father. Back then, they'd meant something so different—that I was starry-eyed about some aspiring comedian I'd met on some West Village street.

At that moment, Eden came barreling down the Death Drop, her body like a corpse in a coffin—her ankles crossed, her forearms folded into an X on her chest. She cried out as she dropped through the air, momentarily weightless, and I pictured Mikey thoughtlessly eating chips from the bag, getting crumbs on his shirt while he watched television. The image created an unbearable stretching inside my chest. I did love Mikey. I did. Now that I was thin, maybe I could return to New York, healthy, and we could start from scratch. Maybe we could go back to being the kids we'd been when we met.

Pudge came down the Death Drop next, screaming, his arms and legs coming uncrossed and splaying wide open. When he hit the pool, the splash was a geyser.

"I guess we'll see, won't we?" Bennett sighed. "I guess we'll see what happens in a week. I hope for your sake that you do what's right for you."

"Nine days."

"Huh?"

"We still have nine days. Why are you trying to speed the summer up?"

"Nine days. I just hope you find happiness, Angeline. I mean that."

Brendan came shooting down the Death Drop.

I knew what Bennett was saying: that he wished me all the best, and that he wasn't going to know me.

Miss came down the slide next, shrieking unmistakably for her mommy before splashing into the pool. And then Harriet's body filled the platform in the sky. She walked to the edge, then turned and walked away, walked to the edge, then walked away.

"No way," I said, making a visor with my hand. "Harriet? No way."

"She fits," Bennett said. "She's lost a lot of weight." He squinted. "She's smaller now. It's really noticeable."

"And she showers on occasion."

"She ran part of the loop yesterday."

"She hasn't told me she hates me in a while. At least a week."

And down she came. A streak of black like a cannonball. A sound from deep inside her like a dying, braying donkey.

Then the rain began, as if the crash of Harriet's body had jolted it out of the sky. I held my palm up to the drizzle.

"I *told* Lewis it was going to rain all day. We're supposed to get thunderstorms." Bennett looked up. "I guess this means we'll go back to camp and watch *Bugsy Malone*."

"What is it with Lewis and that movie?"

"I can try to veto it, but . . ."

"We should watch a *real* classic. Like *Dirty Dancing*."

"The little kids can't watch *Dirty Dancing*."

"Why not? He's shown *Bugsy Malone* three times. *Dirty Dancing* is beautiful. It's an important film. I think I was eight when I first saw it."

"Eight!"

"Nine?"

"This *has* to be a Yankee thing."

The rain began to gather strength. And when I looked up, I saw Whitney. If I hadn't looked at precisely that second, I would have missed it—she didn't make a sound. Her body landed with hardly a splash, drilling cleanly, gracefully, through the surface, as if, just as she'd suspected, the water had been waiting to swallow her.

The campers had assembled near our bench, dripping puddles from their bathing suits onto the pavement.

"Was that Whitney?" Brendan said. He turned to Miss, who was holding his elbow. "I can't believe it! Whitney in the water!"

Bennett and I stood at the first crash of thunder. We would have to find Lewis and receive instructions.

A few minutes later, when Whitney made her way back to the group, soaked, baptized, stunned, she stood before us with a blankness in her eyes as if she'd had a revelation.

Miss momentarily separated from Brendan to hug her.

We all looked at Whitney. She was wearing a black one-piece bathing suit. It was pilled and sagging, a few sizes too big. Her hips looked whittled down. It occurred to me that she hadn't necessarily been suffering from fear of water, from post-traumatic stress, but from the agony of how she looked in a bathing suit, the fear of wearing a bathing suit in front of members of the opposite sex. I understood: It was less mortifying to be naked than it was to wear a bathing suit, that relentless antagonist of the imperfect body.

I wished I had known. I would have told her it wasn't so bad. She looked better than Miss, better than Harriet. And who would have judged her anyway?

"I want to do the Death Drop again," she said.

And why not? When you've finally come through something, when everything's changed, the last thing you want is to get on a bus and ride back to where you were.

FIFTY-TWO

On the bus back to camp, Lewis sat beside me. "I've made a decision," he told me. "I've spoken with my wife about it. But I haven't told anyone else. Can you keep a secret?"

I'd been looking out the window, watching the rain. I turned to him. "That's one of my specialties."

"At the end of the summer, I'm going to save Pudge."

"Pudge?" I twisted in my seat and looked to the back of the bus, where Pudge and Whitney were kissing industriously, holding each other's faces, her leg slung over his. Across the aisle from them, Brendan sat massaging Miss's shoulders. Her eyes were closed in ecstasy. I turned back around.

"He and his mother are going to move in with me in Durham. Pudge has only finished ninth grade. Did you know that?"

"No."

"He's going to be eighteen in a few months. Eighteen with a

ninth-grade education. I'm going to enroll him at my kids' high school. I'm going to save him."

"For how long?"

"What?"

"For how long are you going to save him? Won't it get expensive?"

"His mother will have to get a job." He counted on his fingers. "Six months? I'll give her six months to find work. I'll support them until then. Like family. And then they'll have a new life. Where they live . . ." He whistled. "They could die out there. In that trailer. If Pudge keeps getting fatter and fatter, he'll die. He's been hospitalized a few times now. One time a priest came to his hospital bed and did last rites."

"Who told you that?"

"Pudge."

I looked at Lewis's face, where the skin sagged at his jawline, where the bags under his eyes were the color of bruises. I saw him, for just a second, the way he might have been as a child—the one whose clothes were too tight, the one who was either invisible or too visible, maybe the one who carried around an unwieldy black instrument case and a filthy backpack; or the one who once, while wearing sweatpants, got a hard-on in math class that everyone discussed for a year.

"That's really nice of you," I told him.

Lewis smacked his thighs. "Lewis Teller is the nicest guy in the world," he said. "If anyone needs help, I help them."

It was pouring when we drove through the entrance past the Carolina Academy sign. It wasn't even noon yet. The kids would need lunch. And then there would be rest hour. And then a movie, or a game of dodgeball in the gym. A day of laziness and bad hair. The campers filed out of the bus and ran, screaming, for the dorms, their arms wrapped uselessly over their heads.

"See you in a bit?" Bennett said before we hurried in opposite directions.

We touched hands briefly. And then I ran toward the rest of my life. Not that I knew that. How could I have known? But as I ran through that rain, I thought (really, I thought this; it's not rosy hindsight), *Rain is cool and magnificent.* I lifted my face to it. I also thought other things, like, *This sucks, I wanted to go for at least one more run today.* And, *I might really kill myself if I have to watch* Bugsy Malone. But I did enjoy those last few seconds. I did. I loved that rain.

I ran to the side door of the dorm because it was closest. But if I hadn't, if I'd gone through the front, what happened would have happened differently. I get hung up on that sometimes, even now: thinking about all the various ways in which many things could have been different.

Inside, at the base of the stairwell, in the dim light, on the gray linoleum, I saw him. He was sitting on a step. He was wearing a windbreaker I'd never seen. That was my first thought: *I've never seen that windbreaker.* It was black and blue, like something hurt.

"Mikey."

He stood. He reached for me. Looked hard at my face. Then he pulled his hand back like I'd bitten it. And then he started to cry.

FIFTY-THREE

Mikey was addressing me with his back. He kicked the wall. The sound echoed, and the sole of his sneaker made a little black streak on the plaster. When he turned around, he had stopped crying, but his eyes were wet, laced with red squiggles. I reached for him, wanting to hug him, not because I was glad he had come, but so that I could hide my face.

The hall where the youngest girls lived was filled with noise. From where I stood, I saw several of them dancing outside their rooms. Music was blaring: "My milkshake brings all the boys to the yard . . ."

I winced. "Is something wrong?" I tried to swallow, but my mouth was dry.

Mikey's lips turned up for a second, as if he might smile or grab my throat. He looked the same. He looked like Mikey. He needed a haircut. I could see whiskers on the spot under his chin that he often missed when he shaved. But he also looked different to me. Had he always had the posture of a dying flower? Had his face always been so ashen, his eyes so dull, as if he hadn't had a glass of water in months? I looked at his jeans, where they sagged in the back. Had he never had an ass? Had he always been so out of shape?

I knew he wasn't the one who had changed. But he just looked so unhealthy. He leaned on the banister now, as if even standing up straight were too much exercise.

"I thought I would see you and I would know right away that it wasn't true. I thought I would see you and you'd be so happy to see me, the way you used to be happy to see me."

"I'm happy to see you." My voice sounded like an automated recording, echoing in the stairwell.

For a moment, Mikey pinched the bridge of his nose with his thumb and index finger. Then he let go and locked his eyes onto mine. "I thought I'd see you and you would be the old Gray and I'd know it was all a lie."

"Know what was a lie?"

"But I saw you and I knew." He snapped his fingers. "Right away." He pushed his hands over his hair. "Jesus Christ. Of all the things. I thought this was the thing we would never do to each other. But it happens to every couple. Eventually. Right? No reason our relationship should be different. We're just like everyone, in the end."

"How . . ."

"How what? You thought I wouldn't find out?"

"Um. How did you get here?"

"This whole year I've been so patient with you. Yeah, your dad died. I get it. That's hard. And you have all your daddy issues. But a year with hardly any sex? What guy would put up with that? But I did." He flattened his hand over his chest. "I

DIANA SPECHLER

put up with it. I gave you your space. I didn't say anything. And when girls came up to me after shows, I didn't even flinch. I swear to God, I hardly ever even glanced at any of them. And then I'd go home to you, and you'd look right through me."

"Mikey."

"You never used to be so wrapped *up* in yourself. This whole year . . . I'd come home and maybe I'd have things I wanted to tell you, but you'd look right through me. You'd be reading that dumb, life-affirming crap. It was like everything that used to be cool about you was gone. And I was left with this person who read self-help books and didn't want me around. And then you'd go to sleep without even saying good night."

"I said good night."

Mikey stared at me. He stood up straight, towering over me. Outside, I could hear the rain subsiding. Nearby, I heard one of the little girls say, "I'm going to lie on my back and you should put pennies all over my face and then take a picture."

"Was this some kind of game for you?"

"Was what—"

"Was it fun? Telling everyone here about me. Telling them my name. Directing them to my website? While everyone here knows you're fucking someone else. Was I the joke? Everyone could laugh at your boyfriend back home while they watched you cheat with some douche bag personal trainer?"

I held my head in my hands. "What are you—"

"I thought it was some kind of joke. I was like, 'It's camp. The kids can't use the Internet at camp.'"

I held my stomach. "What kids?"

Mikey didn't understand that this wasn't a real camp. The kids, those who didn't have Internet access on their phones, used the computers in the library.

"Sheena? Wasn't Sheena the girl He-Man?"

"No, that's—" I sucked in air. It made a sharp sound. The rain grew louder outside—an exclamation point—and then slowed again.

"So you're fucking a personal trainer."

"*Sheena* told you that?"

"You fucked him in the arts and crafts building. I was like, 'What in God's name is an arts and crafts building?' I mean . . . you and I are not the kinds of people whose lives include arts and crafts buildings."

"I don't know what kind of person I am," I said. "I'm trying to figure it—"

"I do." Mikey shoved his hands into the pockets of his windbreaker. "You're selfish. Look. You helped me. You did a lot for my career. I'll always be grateful for that. But it wasn't because you loved me. It wasn't because you believed in me. It was because you had a score to settle with your dad. You think you were fooling anyone? You're selfish, Gray. And not because your dad died. It's just you. It's a character flaw. He died over a year ago—"

"What is it with the one-year cutoff? Everyone's like, 'The first year's so hard, but then you'll be perfect.' I get a pass for one year? And then I'm supposed to be over it? Says who?"

"You despised your dad."

"That's a shitty thing to say, Mikey."

"A year after the fact, you should be like, 'Well, the shock's worn off, and now I can enjoy life without that asshole in it.'"

I stuck my palms to my ears. "Stop it."

Mikey stepped close to me. He grabbed my wrists and yanked my arms back down to my sides. "You *hated* him."

"Don't."

"You wouldn't speak to the guy. And honestly? Why should

you have? You and your mom . . . the two of you pretended he was the king. But *God*. The way he would flirt with waitresses in restaurants, right in front of her? The way he would cut her off if she tried to speak? The way he would sip scotch and swish it between his teeth? What a schmuck. And here I was, a man who was good to that guy's daughter, and he hated me. He hated me because I made it harder for him to control you."

I felt sweat break out on my hairline. "Why are you saying these things? This is my family."

"Because it doesn't matter anymore."

I reached for his face. He jerked his head away. I started to cry.

"Don't bother with the tears. Look. I just wanted to come here to see. I wanted to see if it was true. I thought, *If I get there and she's happy to see me . . . if I see it in her face right away that she's not cheating . . . that the e-mail was some kind of prank . . .*" He watched me for a second. "I knew I'd be able to see it on your face. So I thought, *If it's not true, if she's the old Gray, I'll drop to my knees and make that girl marry me. It's been long enough.*"

"Mikey . . ."

"But it is true. And I'm not entirely unhappy to be free of you, Gray. I feel relieved. Already."

"How can you—"

"I feel lighter."

"Lighter?"

"Yes."

"You're just saying that."

"You used to be fun."

"I'm still fun."

"I feel sorry for that trainer dude. I do." He was looking past my head to the door.

"Where are you going?"

"Home. I'll break the lease tomorrow, find a studio, find a girl to bring home this weekend. Find another girl for next weekend. Respond to some of those e-mails I've gotten from girls after my shows."

"You're being disgusting."

"I'm an idiot. You took everything you owned out of our apartment. You knew exactly what you were doing."

"I didn't know. I still don't."

Mikey stepped past me and pushed the door open. Then he turned back to me, his feet on the threshold, his body backlit by the sun that was fighting to shine. "I know I'm a good person. That's why I'll be okay. You're the one who has to live with yourself. You'll always live with this. You'll always think, *I had a boyfriend who loved me so much. He understood me and he loved me anyway.* Deep down, you'll always know that you made all your choices according to what your dad would have wanted, or wouldn't have wanted. You used me to piss him off."

"You're being crazy, Mikey."

"And then he died and I became useless to you. You let your father rule our relationship. He's been standing between us the whole time."

I saw him then. I saw my father step in front of Mikey, facing me, concealing him. I saw him laughing, his hands on the swell of his belly.

"You wrecked everything," Mikey said from behind my father's body.

"Maybe it takes two. Maybe I'm not the only one who should be getting blamed."

"Right. You ruined us and I let you. I kept letting you."

"You're oversimplifying—"

"But it *is* simple! I would have done anything for you. I always told you I wanted to marry you. Down the line, you'll think about that. You'll remember all the times I told you I wanted to get married, all the times you made a bad joke to change the subject, and you'll be like, 'Why did I think I'd have a better offer one day?' You won't have a better offer."

"Are you cursing me or something?" I wiped my eyes with the heels of my hands.

"I'm just giving it to you straight. You were special to me because I loved you so much. But you're not special. You're just a person. Like everyone else." He pointed to me. "You have a bald spot, by the way."

My fingers moved to my temple.

"So you lost some weight this summer." He patted his palm with his fingers, golf-clapping for my weight loss. "You think that's some earth-moving development? You think you're so much hotter than you were a couple months ago? You think you can do better than me now? You think losing weight is going to change your life or something?"

My father faded into the air. Mikey pulled his hood over his head. Stepped outside. The door closed behind him. And that was the last I saw of Mikey Cosenza for a very long time.

FIFTY-FOUR

It is time I explain what I did to my father on my twenty-sixth birthday. From my parents' house, he drove me, in the car I'd grown up in, to Morgan Rye's Steak House. On the radio, Billie Holiday sang, and behind her, men played saxophones. I was wearing a long red sundress, hoping that it made me look happy.

I hadn't seen him in three years. He looked fatter than I remembered. His face was a deeper pink. His hair was grayer, and there was less of it. His breathing seemed labored, and sweat shone on his neck, minutes after his shower.

He asked, "You doing okay with money?"

"Fine," I said.

"Yeah? So you're still . . ."

"Yup. Same job. Same career. Comedy. Booking."

"Terrific. And . . . you like it?"

"Obviously. It was my idea."

"Right, right."

"I get to be with people. And they're funny. And it's challenging."

"And it pays the bills." He chuckled and signaled left, and the turn signal lulled me with its *click-click, click-click*, the way it had in my childhood. "So your old man doesn't have to worry."

I leaned my forehead on my window. *Don't say it*, I told myself. I told myself, *Gray, don't start.*

Inside the restaurant, chandeliers hung like costume jewelry, bartenders wore bow ties with matching vests, and the white tablecloths still held creases from when they'd been folded into smaller versions of themselves. We were the early birds. The scattering of diners were couples with canes and hearing aids, families with children who colored on paper place mats.

My father ordered us a bottle of Chianti. A creamed spinach appetizer. Extra bread. "And plenty of butter," he told the waitress. He laughed and grabbed her hand as if they were old friends, as if she were in on the joke, as if his ordering extra butter made this dinner a wild party.

The wine helped. It was a thing we could pass between us like a guitar at a campfire. But still we were stuck there together. We were sitting by a window. We both kept looking through it, gazing longingly at the trees, at the highway, at the parking lot where pigeons hunted scraps on weightless feet.

"Your mother and I haven't been here in years," my father said. "I like this place."

"It's good. I mean, I remember it being good."

"Yeah, it's good. It's really good. Consistently. Always gets ranked in that thing . . . What's that thing?" He snapped his fingers a few times.

"Oh, um . . ." I snapped my fingers, too. "Whatever," I said. "I know what you're talking about."

"Yeah. That thing. Whatever it's called." He laughed too loudly. He shoved his linen napkin into his collar.

When the waitress brought the appetizer, she refilled our wineglasses, and my father set to work smearing butter and creamed spinach on chunks of bread. I wasn't hungry. My stomach felt tight. I sipped my wine and looked out the window.

"So Mikey's good?"

I looked at my father, who was intent on his plate, pushing food into his mouth, his pink chins spilling over his napkin bib. Tears burned my eyes. I tried to focus on the birthday party I would have the next weekend, how my friends had reserved the back room at a little bar in Alphabet City, so we could sit too close around a too-small table, drunk on Belgian beer and the love that exists only among company one's chosen to keep.

I took a deep breath and released it. "Mikey's good."

"He's still . . . performing his comedy?"

"Performing his comedy? Yeah. He's a comedian, Dad. What else would he be doing?"

"I don't know." My father swallowed and brushed crumbs from his hands. "How should I know?"

"Right. I guess you wouldn't."

I often replay that part of the conversation in my mind. I want to know who started it. Which of us first let the venom in?

My father ordered a porterhouse. I ordered a rib eye purely because we were at a restaurant that served steak and I couldn't think of what else to do. I drank more wine. I sat stiffly in the silence.

"How's that wine? Good, right?"

"It's fine, Dad."

"I had it last time I was here. Can't believe it's still on the menu."

"Wow."

"I love Chianti."

"Yeah?"

"Sure. If I'm going to have wine? Chianti. Otherwise, scotch. But it's your birthday. Makes sense to celebrate with a bottle of wine. If you want champagne, just say the word."

I picked at my mashed potatoes, but I barely touched the steak. It was fatty and greasy and slimy. I felt hyperaware that it had once been alive. I poked it a couple of times with my fork, as if I might revive it.

"I'm thinking of becoming vegetarian," I told my father, even though I was not. "I'm starting to have a visceral reaction to the reality of what meat is." I set my fork down.

"The solution," my father said, taking a gulp of his wine, then smacking his lips together, "is to stop thinking about it. If you stop dwelling on it, on what that meat *was*, if you just enjoy it . . ."

"Impossible."

"You're choosing to make it impossible."

"Not everything is a choice. These poor animals. They don't get a choice in things."

"Choice is such an American concept, Gray. Specifically, it's a disease of your generation. You're so focused on your choices. You're overwhelmed by them, terrified of them, so you do things like become ski bums. Or you become glassblowers. Or you extend your youths so long, you forget to have children. You tell everyone you're following your hearts. But really, you're just not choosing. Not engaging in life. Or you're choosing the wrong things."

"Me?"

"Did I say you?"

"I'm asking."

"Trust me, Gray. If you just go with the flow, if you just do what you know you should do, and don't question it too much . . ."

"Like eat meat?"

"Sure. For example." He pointed to my plate. "If you don't question everything to death, you'll be content."

"Ha!" I said. "Quite a thing to raise me to be a critical thinker, and then tell me, now that I'm all grown up, to stop asking questions. I should close my eyes and accept everything at face value, and then I'll be content? Is that what you're telling me?"

"You're twisting my words." He smiled as if he pitied me. "Besides." He pointed at my steak with his knife. "You'd miss meat."

"Maybe I wouldn't. Maybe I'd think, *Wow, I should have given up meat a long time ago. I've never felt better in my life. I can't believe how many years I spent letting meat drag me down.* It does make you sluggish, you know."

"Just stop thinking about what it is. You can't bring this cow back to life, can you?"

I looked at what was left of his steak: a few bites in a pool of watery blood.

"So just enjoy it in its present form."

"Barbaric."

"It's called letting go. It's called letting bygones be bygones. The rabbi at the Cha—"

"La la la," I said, sticking my fingers in my ears.

"What?"

"No rabbi talk."

"I just wanted—"

"Not tonight. Please don't."

"All right," my father said, lifting his palms. "All right, all right, I won't. Since it's your birthday." He was quiet for a few minutes, eating. And then: "But one last thing: Do you want to come with me to the Chabad House tomorrow? There's this terrific class." He pulled the napkin out of his collar and tossed it on his plate.

"Dad!"

"Okay, okay." He refilled his wineglass. Swigged his water. "I know how you are. But you would like it. If you just opened your mind to it. Anyway, it's relevant to you. It's a class about interfaith relationships. It's a lecture that . . . explores them."

"You mean condemns them."

"You'd be surprised, Gray. You'd be surprised by how open this rabbi is. How clear-thinking. How brilliant."

"So with his brilliance he'll talk me into breaking up with my boyfriend. Yeah? Dad? Really? You had to bring this up?"

My father sighed. He plucked his napkin from his plate and patted his lips. Then he searched my face and his eyes looked old. "Gray, I don't want to fight with you," he said. "I love you. But you're—"

"No, no, no, no, no, don't *say* it."

"—making a mistake—"

"Dad . . ."

"—and I can't just sit here and watch." His speech picked up speed. "It's been agony sitting here and watching. Three years. For three years, I've been hoping you would come around."

"Around to *what*?"

"You don't seem to know what you're signing up for. How hard your life will be."

"What is it that you think I don't know? I'm a grown woman. I'm responsible. I haven't asked you for a dime since college. I pay my rent on time. I run a goddamn business."

"Please don't speak like that."

"You keep thinking I'll become like you. You think when I grow up, I'll become like you."

"It's not that."

"But I *am* grown up. You had your chance to instill your values. You've instilled many. Maybe too many. But now, the parenting part of your life is over. I'm an adult! I vote! I read the news!"

"That's beside the point."

"Are we seriously having this conversation?" I stared at his flushed cheeks and hands, and I thought (this is the hardest part to admit, but I thought), *He looks like a heart attack waiting to happen.*

And then I pushed my plate toward him.

"Have this," I said. "I don't want it."

"Gray, eat. Why don't we just—"

"No. Really."

So he ate. We didn't speak. He finished every last bite of my artery-clogging dinner. Even the buttery mashed potatoes.

And then?

And then the entire floor staff of Morgan Rye's Steak House gathered around our table in their black tuxedo pants and vests and sang "Happy Birthday."

"Christ," I said, as one of them set a dark chocolate soufflé between us. A blue candle flickered sadly in its center.

"Please don't say 'Christ,'" my father hissed.

"Make a wish!" our waitress said, straightening her bow tie.

I didn't. I was massaging my forehead with the tips of my fingers. I took a break from doing that just long enough to blow out the candle, to watch the thin wisp of smoke slither into the air.

My father ate the whole soufflé.

DIANA SPECHLER

•   •   •

In the parking lot, we were almost at the car when I stopped walking and stood still beneath the cottony pink dome of sky. My father stopped, too.

"I have to tell you something," I said.

He looked at me, wide-eyed, hopeful. We were standing inside two yellow lines that designated a parking space. We were too close.

I stepped outside the line, arranged my shoes so they didn't touch the paint. "Mikey and I are getting married."

The hopefulness faded from my father's face. Then he laughed.

"It's not a joke." I linked my hands behind my back in case he decided to check for a ring. "We got engaged last weekend."

He stopped laughing. Then he sighed.

I thought he sighed.

I suppose it was something else: the life being squeezed from his lungs, the sound one makes when one's heart explodes. He fell to his knees as if to pray. And then it was my turn to laugh.

That was our last exchange: He didn't believe me that I was breaking his heart. Then I didn't believe him that his heart was breaking.

His heart was literally breaking.

For at least half a minute, I didn't believe that he wasn't joking, even though faking a heart attack was not his kind of humor. He never cared for physical comedy, never delighted in the sole of a shoe skidding with a banana peel. For many years, we'd laughed together at the things he'd deemed funny—someone he disliked displaying foolish bravado, or the time my mother's cousin left her vibrator in our shower. So what I thought was,

We're going to go back to the way we were. We have agreed to spend our time laughing again. I thought this even when he toppled sideways, even when I saw the life leave his eyes; saw his lips, open, emitting no breath. And by the time I understood, it was too late. And that was when I screamed.

FIFTY-FIVE

Dear Fat People,
  Fuck you.

FIFTY-SIX

I sat on the steps and waited, not moving, counting silently. By twenty, Mikey would be back. Or by forty. Or one hundred. Mikey never stayed angry with me, never stayed away from me.

If he didn't come back, I could talk my way out of this. Mikey always let me talk my way out. I could tell him he had caught me off guard, hadn't given me a chance to give my side of the story. "I'm not cheating on you," I could say. I could even twist it around a little: "How dare you accuse me?"

Yes. I could call him on his cell phone. Maybe he'd driven all the way from Brooklyn in his parents' car, and now he had hours ahead on the road. Or maybe he was driving a rental car back to the airport. He was alone. He missed me. He was heartbroken. I could win him back.

I watched the door. The rain, slower now, ticked against the rectangular window. And then the rain stopped. And then the sun came. I heard one of the little girls say, "Can we go back to the water park now?"

Yes, please, I thought. *Let's go back.*

FIFTY-SEVEN

At lunch, I approached Lewis, who was standing by the salad bar making a cat's cradle out of the shoelace that held his whistle. I told him I needed the rest of the day off.

"But after rest hour, we're going to play dodgeball."

"I need to go to bed."

"But you love dodgeball."

"Since when do I love dodgeball?"

"Who's going to cover your campers?"

"I don't care," I said.

"*Excusez-moi?*" He let the cradle collapse and caught the whistle in his hand.

"I'm sick," I said, heading for the door. "I've never felt worse in my life."

Outside, the air was hot and moist. For the first time all summer, I hadn't bothered with sunglasses. I wanted the sun to burn my irises. I wanted to feel the weight of the heat like bags of sand behind my eyeballs.

Alex was sitting on the steps, his knees tucked, his arms wrapped around his pasty shins. I knew he was supposed to be inside eating lunch, but I couldn't imagine caring less about anything than I did about whether Alex ate lunch.

"If you're out here to make me go inside," he said, "you won't succeed." Tears streamed from behind his tinted glasses.

I'd been planning to head to the dorm, to lie on my miserable mattress and stare at my ceiling, but how could I ignore Alex? Moreover, how could I walk to the dorm, open the door to the stairwell where I'd found Mikey, climb the stairs to my room where I hardly lived, and let the window fan blow August at me and the humidity crawl on my skin?

Because then what? What would I do after that?

I remembered once, as a child, thinking hard about my breathing until I practically hyperventilated. Life felt like that now; a thing that had been involuntary had all at once become unmanageable. How would I swallow the next minute, and the one after that, and all the minutes that would comprise the rest of my life from this moment forward?

"I'm not out here to make anyone do anything," I told Alex. I touched the top of his head, wondering about the people who loved him. His parents. Perhaps a sibling or two. As he got older, less awkward, would his circle of love expand? Would he ever be a person who was surrounded and bolstered by love? And if he did become that person, if he became an adult whose friends affectionately called him a nerd, who adored him *because* of his terrible glasses and his inability to dance, would he ever be able to shake the fear that no one could be trusted?

I thought of Mikey speeding north in his parents' car, his window down, his elbow resting in that open space. I tried to conjure his expression. And I wondered not, *How will I ever earn his forgiveness?* but, *How can I trick him into thinking that I didn't do anything wrong?*

I sat a couple of steps below Alex. "What is it?" I asked. "Why are you crying?"

"Because everyone sucks." Alex wiped his nose with the back of his wrist and dropped his forehead onto his knees. His hair was greasy, stuck to the back of his neck. Some orangey wax was worming its way out of the hole of his ear. I wondered if he had a mother who would dampen a washcloth and wipe it away. "Eden's a jerk," he said. "She makes me pretend she's not my girlfriend because she's embarrassed of me. And then today before we got on the bus, she said, 'I can't talk to you at all anymore. Pretend for the rest of the summer that you don't know me.' She said, 'Don't even say hi to me ever again.' She's a turncoat!"

"How do you know that word?"

"From history class." Alex sniffled.

"Good word."

I thought of Eden's claim that Sheena had harmed her. I thought of Sheena's grand exit, and of the tear Eden had shed that sealed her popularity. I thought of Eden lying on my bed while I sat on the floor, and of the way she was now barely willing to glance at me. I wondered if she and Whitney and Miss knew about Sheena's e-mail to Mikey. I thought the answer to that question was probably yes.

I also remembered that Eden was only sixteen. And besides, I had taken her father from her. And planted myself in her path. And chosen to cheat on my boyfriend. Who was I to have opinions on loyalty, to pass judgment on Eden's allegiances?

"Do you know what this means?" Alex said. "It means that I'm more embarrassing than Pudge and Brendan. Those guys are way fatter than me, but Miss isn't embarrassed of Brendan, and Pudge and Whitney make out all over the place. I'm worse than Pudge and Brendan!" Alex lay back on the steps, his limbs splayed. "I could just lie here forever," he said. "I weigh a million pounds. No one would be able to lift me."

I watched Alex's chest rise and lower with his breath. Then I lay back beside him and closed my eyes. We were layers of sweat glands and hair follicles and fat cells, two bodies laden with million-pound losses.

FIFTY-EIGHT

Back in my dorm room, I slept like someone from a Disney movie. I slept for many years while the kingdom crumbled around me. I woke up every few centuries and there was sun on the window. Or rain. There were voices in the hall or no voices. And always, my mouth was dry, as if I'd chewed up the summer. But every time, I was too tired, too confused, to figure out how to get water.

It had been so long since I'd slept like I meant it.

"Wake up, babe."

I thought it was Mikey. I opened my eyes. The windows were black with night, but someone had flipped the light switch, and the naked bulb on the ceiling glared. I covered my face with my palms.

"Angeline."

I spread my fingers and saw Bennett through the cracks, standing on my threshold. When he saw me look at him, he slipped into my room and closed the door behind him.

"You're not going to believe what's going on."

"What?" My voice was full of sawdust.

"Lewis got arrested."

I sat up.

"Everyone's in the canteen."

"*What?*"

"No one knows yet. Except Nurse."

"What time is it?"

"It's almost Lights Out. We can't tell the kids tonight. It would be chaos."

"What are they doing in the canteen?"

"Watching *Bugsy Malone.*"

I rubbed my fists into my eyes. "I'm so confused."

"I'm confused, too." Bennett sat on the bed beside me. "The cops came. They handcuffed him, and then I saw them push his head down when he was getting into the car. Like in the movies."

"So . . ."

"So I'm in charge." He smacked his thighs. "I guess. This is the most doggone thing. Are you feeling better?" He took my hand.

I looked at him as my eyes adjusted. He looked old. There were lines all over his face. His forehead. Beneath his eyes. I thought—Why did I think this? What did it matter?—*I will never again be loved by a man who knew me at twenty-two.*

"I feel okay."

"Think you have a bug or something?"

I wondered if I should tell him about Mikey. But I was so much better at not telling.

"I think I'm just thirsty."

"Well, then let's get you some water." Bennett smoothed the hair back from my face. "I'll bring you some, and then I gotta run. You'll meet me in the canteen?" He kissed my forehead.

It felt like nothing. It felt like kisses I received from my parents' friends, who told me they'd known me when I was *this big*, whose names I could never remember.

While we were watching the end of *Bugsy Malone*, Bennett's cell phone rang. I watched him pull it out of his pocket, and then disappear from the canteen for the rest of the evening. When the movie ended, I herded my campers back to the dorm.

As we walked, Eden asked, "Can Miss and Whitney sleep in my room tonight?"

I looked at the three of them. I almost grabbed Miss by her gorgeous blond hair and yanked her to the ground.

"No," I said.

"Why not?" they all said together.

"Because."

"Because why?"

"If you ask me another question, we're going to have a problem," I said.

"This is so *unfair*," Miss whined.

"Miss," I said. "Life is—" I stopped myself before I could finish. "Tomorrow night," I said. "Maybe tomorrow you can all have a sleepover."

Half an hour later, Bennett was back in my room. It didn't matter anymore. Who would see us? Who cared if anyone saw us? He sat on the foot of my bed, his cell phone in his hand.

"Was that Lewis who called you?"

Bennett looked at his cell phone, and then shoved it into his pocket. "Nope. Some policeman. Real nice guy. Melrose PD, I guess. He sounded like he felt bad. Anyway, I guess Sheena called the cops and said that there were rumors all summer that Lewis was touching the kids."

"What?"

"I mean, messing with them. Like—"

"No. Right. I understand what 'touching the kids' means. I'm just . . ."

"She said she heard all kinds of stories all summer. She told him the campers always told her everything."

"Well, they did."

"She told the cops everything she'd heard. Or supposedly heard. He wouldn't give me details. I told him she's a disgruntled employee. That we fired her for taking the kids to McDonald's. Which made the cop about wet himself."

"Why?"

Bennett laughed. "It didn't sound strange to me either when I said it. We've been here too long. Our reality's all out of whack. It's actually funny, but I didn't even realize it."

"I don't think it's funny."

"Anyway, the cop said she might be telling tall tales, but they had to check it out. Lewis is going to have to answer some questions. And then they'll decide whether he's a pervert, I guess. I think tomorrow's going to get crazy. I think kids are going to get questioned. That kind of thing. I have a feeling tomorrow will be the last day of camp. Once the kids find out what's going on, they'll call home. And then . . ." He opened his palms on his lap.

"Don't say that."

"Which part?"

"That tomorrow will be the last day of camp. We still have nine days."

"I doubt that at this point."

"Nine days. The banquet. We'll have to have the banquet. It's all Lewis talks about. How we won't eat all day, and then we'll have eighteen hundred calories for dinner."

"Apparently, Sheena also ran her mouth about what happened with Spider."

"She's the one who *did* that to Spider. Eden saw her switch up Spider's food."

"And about how the kids swim in the pool every day with no lifeguard. Some other stuff, too. It's not good. We're probably going to get shut down."

"Where will everyone go?"

"What do you mean?"

"I mean if camp closes."

Bennett laughed. "Home."

"But . . ."

"That's not the problem. Everyone's got a home. Lewis is the one who's got a big problem on his hands."

I looked at my window and chewed my thumbnail.

"I doubt I'll be getting any sleep," Bennett said. "Nurse is waiting for me in her office. I have to fill her in. And you'd best stay here tonight with your kids."

"Right. And then tomorrow . . ."

"Let's just take things minute by minute."

I closed my eyes.

"Everything will be okay, Angeline."

I didn't answer.

"Won't you go home? To your boyfriend?"

I opened my eyes and shook my head.

Bennett took a long look at me, and then reached out and touched my bald spot. I flinched. "You never were going to, were you?"

I looked at the dark window again, at our reflections on it. I thought of my vacuum cleaner, my computer printer, my winter coat—all the bits of my life that I'd stuffed into my father's car. The past year, when I'd fantasized about breaking away from

Mikey, about leaving behind the life that reminded me of all that I'd tried to prove, I'd never imagined cheating and then returning. I'd always imagined starting over. Or, not just starting over, but becoming some other person. Thin and lithe with wind blowing my hair, laughing on a beach, running, holding my sarong like a flag in the breeze. Like a woman in a feminine hygiene commercial.

"You're right," I told Bennett. "I guess I never was."

I thought of the last winter in New York, Mikey crawling into bed late with cold skin. I'd pretended that I couldn't feel him. But the night before I left for camp, we'd been briefly happy again, eating dinner at a restaurant with an outdoor garden, getting into bed early and talking for hours, my head on his hairy stomach. I drifted to sleep that night, and then woke abruptly, saw the moon out the window, and felt Mikey tracing my hand with his finger, as if to memorize, before I left, the part of me that touched him.

I thought now of a friend who'd had to put her old, sick dog to sleep. When the vet administered the injection, the dog sprang to life, hopped off the table, and bounded around the room like a puppy. She'd teared up telling me about it. "I thought maybe he was going to be healthy again. I thought maybe he could be saved."

Bennett opened my door. "I have to go."

I stared at him. The muscles in my face wouldn't move. My voice wouldn't come. I wanted to beg him not to leave me. But what would my request have meant? Don't leave this room? Don't leave my life? Marry me? Never die?

Bennett closed the door and came back to me. He knelt on the floor and took my hands. "You're a crazy woman," he said. He kissed each of my knuckles. "But you're pretty cute."

Then he got to his feet and left.

FIFTY-NINE

At Lights Out, I knocked on Eden's door. When she yelled to come in, I found her sitting up in bed, brushing her hair, looking at a magazine that was spread open in her lap.

"They're not in here," she said. "So you can chill."

"I didn't think they were."

Her legs were folded into a loose knot under her top sheet. I felt as if I hadn't seen her in years. She was so much thinner, almost average-size. And she looked more confident, more grown-up, as if the light Whitney and Miss had cast on her had caused her to flourish. She set the hairbrush down and turned a page.

"I just wanted to say hi."

"Hi," she said, turning a page.

"Eden," I said. "Did you know what was going on?"

She looked up and knit her eyebrows, which desperately needed plucking. I imagined sitting with her, plucking her eyebrows, waxing her legs. In real life, did sisters do things like that?

"The whole thing with Sheena," I said. "That she was taking the girls to McDonald's. You were trying to tell me, weren't you? That day in the cafeteria?"

Eden shrugged one shoulder. "What does it matter now?"

"I guess it doesn't."

"Things are fine now," Eden said. "No one's bulimic or anything. That was just one dumb week. Maybe two. Bulimia needs to last longer than that to really be bulimia. Kimmy's got a big mouth. Didn't I tell you? Right from the beginning I told you Kimmy was the worst."

"She just didn't want to keep secrets."

"Sometimes you should keep secrets. It wasn't just her secret. She betrayed her friends. But anyway. It's all in the past."

"The past is tricky."

"Okay."

"You never know when it's going to pop back up."

"Whatever." Eden looked back down at her magazine, revealing a complicated, zigzagging part.

I had a sudden objective vision of myself: a woman standing in a teenager's doorway, speaking cryptically, studying her. But I had lost track of how to act. I felt, after today's events, like I'd been hit by a bus and survived against my will. The very air had a dreamy, wavering quality to it, as if I were living inside a mirage.

Watching Eden, I remembered the night five years before when Mikey and I had dinner with my parents at that seafood restaurant. I saw the four of us around the table with the white tablecloth. Then, in the picture in my mind, I saw my father's image fade and vanish. Beside him, Mikey's image faded, too. And then my mother and I looked across the table at each other and threw our linen napkins onto our plates. As if to say, *Game over.* As if to say, *Who were we ever, really, without the men in our lives?*

I was sick of waiting for my father to tell me what to do. I was through with all the secrets. It was time to tell Eden the truth.

"Do you want to go somewhere?"

Eden looked at me and laughed. "You and me?"

"Why not?"

"Now?"

"Yup."

"Where?"

I glanced over my shoulder into the hallway. It was empty and quiet. "McDonald's?"

Eden laughed again, but she wasn't smiling. She scratched her head. "You're . . . kidding?"

I saw us together in a shiny booth. I would buy her a Happy Meal. I wanted my sister to be happy.

But she didn't look unhappy. She looked puzzled, shrinking away from me.

How could I have spent the summer assuming that Eden would come to me? I had done nothing to win her affection. And now I expected her to jump out of bed and follow me out of camp? I had spent nearly four years working in sales, pushing comedy club tickets on strangers who had had no intention of buying comedy club tickets. After dismantling my business, after losing my taste for sales, I'd had to wonder if I'd wasted my time.

Now I saw that I hadn't. It was useful to know how to sell things.

"Forget it," I said. "It's late. I'm probably going to head into Falling Rock by myself."

"For what?"

"There's this new restaurant. I read a review of it today. Some hotshot young chef who turned down all these New York City restaurants to open some kind of comfort food joint in Falling Rock."

"Which chef?" Eden closed her magazine.

"I don't know. I skimmed the review. I never retain that kind of information. I don't know much about chefs. Wish I did, though."

"What do you want to know? I know a lot."

"It's supposed to be one of the best new restaurants in the country. Affordable comfort food with a southern flare."

Eden pulled her legs out from under the top sheet and swung them over the side of the bed. "You think it's still open?"

"I called earlier. It is."

"And . . . you'd take me?"

"You want to come?"

"Obviously."

"Hmm. All right. You've worked so hard all summer. Why not?"

"You could get fired," Eden said. "Like Sheena."

"Eden," I said. "I can think of nothing that worries me less."

I wondered if Eden would ask me about the seat belt extender. But she didn't, because what was truly distracting was the clutter—my life, which filled up the car.

"Is this, like, everything you own?"

"Pretty much."

"What about your furniture?"

"Our furniture is all crap from the Salvation Army and Craigslist. I could throw it away. It's not like it's really mine."

"Whose is it?"

"I just mean that nothing's really anyone's." I was stopped

at the end of the dirt road that led from camp to the highway, signaling right, waiting to merge.

"You're weird," Eden said.

I started up the highway toward Falling Rock. I had twenty minutes, at most, to say my piece. Twenty minutes before Eden would realize that the restaurant I'd told her about didn't exist.

"I like knowing I can fit everything I own into my car," I said.

Eden scooted closer to her door and leaned her head on her window. "Why?"

"I don't know. I like feeling . . . light."

"I feel light."

"Do you?"

"Lighter."

"You are lighter."

"Yeah, but the second I get home, I'm going to this bakery by my house where I worked last summer. They taught me how to bake all this stuff. Baklava. Cannolis. I got to use the pastry bag for filling. You know what I'm talking about? That plastic bag thing with the metal tip?" She turned toward me slightly. "I'm going to the bakery to get, like, one of everything."

"Yeah?"

"I can't wait. Not that I want to be a pastry chef. Pastry chefs are the losers of the culinary world."

"Don't you want to keep your weight off?"

Eden shifted in her seat, making herself comfortable. "I don't know. It's not like it will matter."

"Won't it?"

"I don't believe it works. Weight loss. People want to lose weight so badly. People want to be thin. And they're not. Our country's getting fatter and fatter. Did you know that? So whatever we're all doing isn't working. I mean, right? If there was a solution, everyone would be skinny."

"We have to try."

"Why?" Eden asked. "I've tried before. I've eaten nothing but salad. I've done that. It doesn't work. Not in the end. My mom gets all these dumb magazines. There are women who go on these weight-loss plans that sound like lies. Same crap in every issue. Like, 'I started lifting weights three times a week and walking instead of using the escalator. I started adding spinach to my diet. And now look at me! I'm thin!'"

"And it's not that easy, is it?"

"Maybe for some people. Not for me . . . My ears are popping."

"Hold your nose and blow."

"Can't that burst your eardrums?"

"They're just eardrums," I said, smiling. I twisted the radio dial until I found something worth listening to. Lester Young. One of my father's favorites. "Maybe fat camps work," I said. "Maybe you guys will all go home and feel motivated and keep losing weight. Maybe the answer is to get at you while you're young."

"I'm not that young."

"Well . . . maybe the youngest kids will benefit?"

"Or maybe we'll all gain it back and our parents will make us come here again next summer. It could go on forever."

"Do you like jazz?"

"How should I know?"

"You should," I said. "You should like Lester Young. He's in your blood."

Eden was resting against her window, her feet bare on the glove compartment. Her toes were tapping out the rhythm. I could practically see our father slinging one arm around each of us, crushing us into him, saying, "My girls, my girls."

Eden was sucking the gold star on her necklace.

"Who gave you that necklace?" I asked. I swallowed hard and gripped the wheel more tightly.

Eden let the star fall from her mouth. "A woman from one of my cooking classes. She got it in Israel."

"Is she . . . Jewish?"

"Yeah."

"So . . . she brought you . . ."

"I used to really like stars," Eden said. "I used to draw them on everything. I used to wear stars a lot, too. I was obsessed with stars."

"Stars?"

"It was stupid. I don't know."

"The star of David, you mean?"

"This one time, I made little loaves of star-shaped sour-dough bread and brought them to my cooking class. And then this woman went to Israel and brought me this." She lifted the charm from her chest to see it. "Everyone thinks I'm Jewish because of it."

"You have a Jewish name."

"It's not really a Jewish name."

"Isn't it?"

"It's really gross how I got my name." She let the charm drop.

"It was the garden," I said. "It was the most perfect place in the world before Adam and Eve ate the forbidden fruit. And then they became self-conscious about their bodies. And—"

"Yes, Gray, thank you. I know the story of Adam and Eve."

"I hate that story," I said. "I hate that they had to go and do that. They're responsible for everyone's body image issues."

"I was conceived in a town in Minnesota called Eden Prairie. My parents were on a vacation. I think they were skiing. Can you ski in Minnesota?"

"Maybe they were cross-country skiing."

"Do you know what that means?"

"What *what* means?"

"Conceived?"

I took a deep breath. I opened my mouth. I said, "Eden, I have something to—"

And that was when I lost control.

I lost control of my father's car three thousand feet above Peach River Gorge. It was as if an invisible hand—a heavy, desperate, determined hand—yanked the wheel away from me.

It was an old car, yes. And I was told that I hit a rock that flattened the tire, that started the chain of awful events. But I don't know. I know what I felt. I would know my father anywhere.

SIXTY

I intentionally omitted something. Of all the parts of my story I would rather not remember, this part ranks fairly high. It's the part that happened between the time Bennett woke me up and the time I went to the canteen to watch the end of *Bugsy Malone*.

When I stepped outside the dorm, alone, the rain was holding, but the night was wet, as if it had been crying. I meant to go straight to the canteen, to join the group, to chat mindlessly with Mia, as if everything were normal. But I couldn't stop feeling the aloneness beading up on my skin like sweat.

I saw the cabin behind the cafeteria where Lewis had been staying all summer. His car—something blue with tinted windows—was parked in front of it, still and dark. I walked to the car and touched the hood. I walked up the two stone steps to the screen door of his cabin. Behind the screen, the main door was opened wide, so I went inside and turned on the light.

I saw his computer set up on a desk. A shirt had been tossed over it. More clothes had been tossed over the desk chair. And more on the couch, and even more on the floor, but his messiness wasn't what struck me: Strewn around the linoleum were ten or twelve large white pizza boxes. Some were flung open, showcasing grease stains, crumbs, and crumpled napkins. Hershey Kisses wrappers were sprinkled around the floor like currency. I saw a white paper McDonald's bag, a half-eaten bag of Cool Ranch Doritos, an empty box of Milk Duds, and by Lewis's computer where the mouse should have been, a Twinkie, unwrapped, as if he'd been about to eat it when the cops came knocking.

In addition to the mess, there was a stench. Dirty laundry. Old garbage. Sour milk.

I turned out the light and backed over the threshold. I sat on the stoop and looked at the black sky. It was beautiful here in the Blue Ridge Mountains. It was quiet and lush. Slow and calm. But beauty made me skittish. As soon as it peaked, it began to fade. A forehead wrinkling. A photograph yellowing. Muscles melting to fat.

When I was growing up, my family—my parents, my father's brothers, my cousins—used to rent log cabins in New Hampshire for a week in the summertime. At night, we would sit outside under blankets and watch the shooting stars. Someone always had to say, "This is so pretty." Sometimes I was the one to say it, but I always knew it would have been better if no one said it.

I stood and wiped off the back of my shorts. I meant to go to the canteen then. I really did. But I listened to the cicadas and wished I could hush them—the squeaky taunt of their transience. And I walked straight to the cafeteria. I won't say "as if in a hypnotic state." I won't say "as if someone were holding the back of my neck, pushing me toward it." I know how the Ouija board works. I know that nothing is magic.

I walked through the cafeteria to the kitchen. I turned on the light and lifted the part of the tray rails that would allow me behind the food line.

I remembered the tour Lewis had given us on the first day. And I remembered his theatrical warning. I went to the walk-in refrigerator and opened the door, stepped through the heavy plastic strips that hung from the top of the door frame, and felt the cold air on my skin like relief.

I filled my arms with food.

And then I began to eat.

SIXTY-ONE

I woke up feeling as if I had only one eye, and knew immediately that I was in a hospital because rails confined my mattress, white curtains hung on either side of me, and a red box-shaped metal receptacle stood in front of the bed. And then I remembered an ambulance, a low voice saying, "I can't get a vein." Had that happened? When had that happened? I looked at my arms. There were no tubes taped to them, no needles piercing them.

I closed my eyes, remembering what I'd done in the kitchen at camp. I remembered the 100-calorie packs of mini chocolate chip cookies. How many packages had I eaten? Ten? Fifteen? I remembered the leftover sugar-free pudding, remembered polishing off the mixing bowl of it. And then the cereals, straight from their single-serving boxes. And then . . .

My left eye throbbed. When I opened my eyes, a woman in pink scrubs with a stethoscope slung around her neck was leaning over me, inspecting something on my face.

"How we doing?"

We.

And then I remembered. "Is Eden okay?" I grabbed the metal rails and tried to slide into a sitting position, but the strength had been vacuumed from my arms. "The girl in my car. Eden Bellham. The girl in the passenger seat."

The nurse stood up straight. "You let us do our job and you do yours. Your job is to rest . . . Honey, don't sit up. Whew *boy*, did you hit your head. You took some glass in the face, too, but we got it all. You in pain?"

I thought about it. I felt a heavy pain I couldn't locate. I remembered Mikey.

"Yes."

"Figured you must be."

"Wait—"

"Honey, there's nothing in all of creation that you need to worry about at this moment." She bent over a tray on a shelf beside the bed. Then she took my arm. "This'll hardly hurt."

"No shots!" I said. "Pain makes me crazy."

And then darkness.

SIXTY-TWO

The next time I woke up, I could tell it was daytime, but I couldn't see a window, couldn't locate the source of the sunlight. On a table by the bed, a glass vase bloomed yellow roses. Bennett was standing beside me. I looked at him and wished I could fold up into the wall like a Murphy bed, as if his seeing me in a hospital bed were more personal than the times he'd seen me naked.

"What day is it?"

"Saturday."

"What time is it?"

He looked at his watch. "Noon." He was dressed in a button-down shirt. Khaki pants. A brown leather belt. As if he were off to a stuffy Sunday brunch. He was incognito. No one would recognize him as the assistant director of a weight-loss camp. It occurred to me for the millionth time that I didn't know Bennett Milton.

"Did I lose an eye?"

"You've got a patch over one." He touched it gingerly. "But you're going to be as good as new. You just got a little roughed up."

I pulled the blanket tight around me.

"Bet you weren't expecting me to meet your mom anytime soon. I told her, 'Mrs. Lachmann, it's so nice to meet you. I'm the old man who's been banging your daughter.'"

I rubbed my eye and almost smiled. And then I sat up. "You're kidding, right? My mom's not here."

"In the waiting room."

"No. How long have I . . . Where's Eden?"

"She'll wake up soon. Everyone's saying so. You both hit your heads pretty hard, but everyone's going to be just fine. I'll tell you what's not fine is your car."

"It's not my car."

"Well, whose is it?"

I saw my father then, his coffee and doughnut between us on the console.

"What were you doing? Where were you headed?"

I closed my eyes over the heat of tears. "Is Eden's mother here?"

"Yup."

I laid back to rest on the pillow and opened my eyes. "What's going on at camp?"

"Yeah. About that." Bennett's eyes were bloodshot.

"You look exhausted."

"Don't you worry about me, Angeline."

"What's the latest?"

"Hell of a mess. I'll tell you about it later."

I reached for Bennett's face. He bent down a little so I could touch him.

"I'm sorry," I said.

"What for? I'm just glad you're alive. I'm glad you hit a guard-rail instead of falling into the gorge."

"Me, too."

"I went to where you crashed. You could be graveyard dead."

I pulled the blanket tight around my body.

"You sure had a lot of stuff in your car. I brought it all to the post office. It's on the way to your mom's house."

"You did that for me?"

Bennett took one step away from the bed.

I sighed. "I'll pay you back."

"You don't owe me a thing." Bennett studied me for a minute. "How about this?" he said. "Here's how you can pay me back. If I'm ever in New York, you can show me around town. Deal?" He stuck out his hand for me to shake.

I remembered the last time we'd shaken hands, when I'd agreed to a summer of fun. I knew enough to recognize defeat. I knew what an ending looked like.

I took his hand. I held it in my palm. I wanted to tell him this was his loss, which would be proportionate to my gain. But I didn't really believe that. Loss was never so tidy.

"Okay," I said. "It's a deal."

SIXTY-THREE

My mother, her hair a mess, fiddled with one of her pearl earrings. "You're so thin," she said, her voice trembling.

"I'm thin in a good way."

"We all think thin is so *good*."

I remembered her from years before, weighing broccoli on a scale, trying on a light yellow bikini every morning before getting dressed.

"I've been at weight-loss camp all summer. I'm in the best shape of my life. If you saw me without cuts all over my face—do I have cuts all over my face?—if you saw me in workout clothes or in a bathing suit, you'd tell me I look great."

"Are you losing your hair?" She sat at the foot of my bed and held my toes through the faded blue blanket. "You could have told me." She pulled a tissue from her purse and blew her nose. But despite the crying, she looked stronger than she had the last time I'd seen her. There was more color in her face. She filled out her jeans. She looked like a person on the mend.

"Told you?" I tried to rearrange my hair over the bald spot. "What could you have done?"

"I mean, you could have told me why you were coming here for the summer."

I studied her. "What exactly do you mean?"

"Does Mikey know?"

"Mikey doesn't know anything. Mikey . . ."

"Saul told you about Azalea."

"You know about Azalea?"

I floated out of my body, watching us: a mother perched on a hospital bed, holding her daughter's feet.

"He told me he told you her name," she said.

"Why didn't you tell me?"

"Why didn't *you* tell *me*? I know I'm missing something." She pulled one of her earrings off and I saw that they were clip-ons, covering the holes. "Like why you wanted to meet Azalea Bellham's daughter, like why you cared about any of this. I know you miss Dad. You were looking for a connection. Was that it? You wanted a connection to him?"

"You can't be serious."

"I just can't fathom why you—"

"She's my sister!" I said. "Why *wouldn't* I care? You guys never told me she existed!"

My mother cocked her head at me. "Who's your sister?" Her eyes moved over my face.

"Eden," I said, my voice weak.

My mother shook her head. She leaned in to inspect me more closely. She seemed to be searching my eyes for a hint that I was joking. Then she leaned back. "You don't have a . . . Gray! *What*?"

And that was how I learned that I had gotten the whole thing wrong.

Part III | **After**

SIXTY-FOUR

This was what happened at Camp Carolina while Eden and I were unconscious: Friday morning, people with serious faces, sensible shorts, and socks and sneakers arrived in official-looking vehicles. They came from the Department of Environment and Natural Resources and the North Carolina Department of Health. It took them under an hour to announce that the jig was up.

Camp Carolina's kitchen didn't meet the state's sanitation standards. Lewis, sometimes with campers in the car, had been driving around all summer with a revoked driver's license. There were other infractions, too, a list that amounted to seventy-eight; and while the child molester accusation, at least presently, seemed to be fictitious, Lewis was still going to be swimming in lawsuits.

Spider's parents were suing.

The original kitchen ladies were suing.

Kimmy's parents were suing.

Harriet's parents were suing. She'd returned from camp with a staph infection.

From Friday morning until Saturday morning, parents came and collected their children. Because of all the chaos, no one ever took the kids' "after" pictures. All that was left of the summer were the pictures from before.

The kids were either devastated or stoic. Miss and Whitney screamed and sobbed, as if they hadn't just screamed and sobbed about how much they hated camp, as if they hadn't been whining all summer about how badly they wanted to leave. Other campers stepped stone-faced into their parents' minivans and didn't look back.

They rode away from the Blue Ridge Mountains and back to their homes, to the places where they had grown fat. They stepped into their houses and remembered the smells that were trapped in the walls—the years of pancake breakfasts and Sunday night pizza dinners. They lay on their beds and felt happy and thin. They took naps in the middle of the day. Then they woke up and went downstairs, where their parents had ordered feasts of Chinese food, or where their mothers had made them their favorite lemon cake.

In the morning, they had Belgian waffles for breakfast.

They watched television.

They ate Kettle chips straight from the bag.

Sure, some of them tried to keep losing weight. They ran around the block every morning, or attempted the exercises they'd done in cals, or strained to remember what they'd learned in Mia's nutrition class. Some asked their parents to buy them Dance Dance Revolution. But even the ones who wanted to try wound up feeling confused. Was Diet Coke okay? Was pizza healthy if it was covered in vegetables? Was cereal acceptable?

What about a second bowl of cereal? What about apple pie? After all, it was mostly fruit.

Eventually, the trying was replaced with not trying.

Only Pudge would make a drastic change. Nurse would take him home with her, enroll him in school, treat him like a son. In time, she would get her nursing certification, and then she would pay for his gastric bypass surgery. For a while, that surgery would make his life better.

But for most, the successes were extremely short-lived, as if weight loss were a wound, something time was supposed to heal.

SIXTY-FIVE

Here's what I learned from my mother fourteen months after my father's death, in my bed at Falling Rock Hospital: When I was a child, when my father was still a lawyer, a man named Jimmy Hagen fell from a ladder while trying to replace a roof shingle.

After he fell, Jimmy paced around his yard, cradling his aching arm. He cursed for a few minutes, and then popped black-market prescription painkillers, cracked a beer, and passed out. The next morning, his left wrist swollen and throbbing, he drove to see Dr. Koa Bellham, an orthopedic surgeon in Cambridge, a friend of a friend of a friend, who had agreed to see Jimmy free of charge, and who suggested immediate surgery.

Jimmy refused. "Buddy of mine had shoulder surgery and his shoulder was never the same again."

It is important to understand some things about Jimmy Hagen. He was thirty-seven years old. He lived with his mother in the house he'd grown up in. Sometimes he had a job. More often, he did not. When he was nineteen, he lost five thousand dollars in a pyramid scheme. In subsequent years, he attempted his own pyramid schemes, but his attempts were unsuccessful because no one ever trusted him.

"I don't have insurance," Jimmy said. "I have no money."

Dr. Bellham sighed. He looked at Jimmy's wrist again. "Look," he said. "Off the record, maybe you could wait a few months on this. Maybe it will heal on its own. I don't recommend it, though."

"A few months?"

"Could heal without surgery. It's not my recommendation, but it is possible."

Nine months after Jimmy's fall, my father got a call from an old friend. "My cousin needs legal advice. None of us likes the black sheep fuckup, but . . . you know how it is. Family."

Days later, in his office, my father looked across the table at the splint on Jimmy Hagen's wrist.

"So the doctor told you to have surgery immediately."

"My wrist is ruined!" Jimmy cried. "Forever! My life will never be the same." He was desolate, as if his injury spelled the end of his career as a concert pianist. "The medical profession is corrupt. I want to fight for justice."

"You really don't have a case," my father said. "He advised you to have the surgery. You didn't follow his advice."

"He told me 'off the record' that I didn't have to."

"Really?"

"He did! He did! He told me not to tell anyone. He said, 'Don't bother with surgery, Jimmy.'"

My father was suspicious, but—why not?—he did a little research into Dr. Koa Bellham, and this was what he learned: Koa Bellham was thirty-three years old. He had grown up in

Hawaii. His wife was pregnant with their first child. Oh, and his malpractice insurance had lapsed.

Dr. Bellham had let his insurance lapse not because he was unethical (he was not unethical), not because he was trying to pinch pennies (he was meticulous and fair), but because of a fatal oversight. His practice was new. He'd made a mistake. The lapse was only three and a half weeks, but the timing, for Dr. Bellham, could not have been worse. For Jimmy Hagen, it could not have been better.

My father told Dr. Bellham, "I know what you told my client 'off the record.' Bad medical advice? Lapsed insurance? You wanna play rough? Okay. It's on!" Or something to that effect.

"I told him to have surgery!" Dr. Bellham said.

"Oh, yeah? You have that in writing?"

"No. I saw him as a favor."

"You should really get everything in writing," my father said. "If you don't have anything in writing, there's not much we can do now, is there?"

Because of Jimmy Hagen, because of my father, because of Dr. Bellham's oversight, because of bad luck, because of greed, because of fate or the alignment of the stars or God's will or corruption or justice, Dr. Koa Bellham, his wife pregnant and unemployed, turned every penny he owned and then some over to Jimmy Hagen and my father.

My father told my mother, "I might have just done something reprehensible. I've become one of those lawyers I never wanted to become." But then, for a few weeks, he barely thought about Dr. Bellham again.

Perhaps Dr. Bellham, hopelessly in debt, wandered around his house at night, unable to sleep. Perhaps he thumbed through the *Boston Herald* want ads, circling words he could barely read through his panic. Perhaps one day, while drawing these circles, he paused and saw the futility of life—how the best that anyone could do was make loops with a cheap red pen.

He pushed his chair back from the kitchen table, stood, walked down to the basement in his pajamas and socks, entered the garage, sat on the wooden workbench, and shot himself in the mouth.

SIXTY-SIX

I thought of Eden's eyes and her gold Jewish star. Even as I remembered her, she looked different from the way I'd been seeing her. Eden was half-Hawaiian. Not Jewish. Not my half sister. Not my father's daughter.

"You really thought Dad had an affair?"

"I thought he was hiding all this from us. I thought you had no idea. Why didn't you tell me?"

"We always said we wouldn't."

"But Dad must have wanted me to know."

"After you finally spoke with Saul, I kept expecting you to ask me about it. And you didn't. So I figured you didn't want to talk about it. I don't know, Gray. It seems stupid now. I should have brought it up. Of course I should have." My mother fished a tissue from her purse and touched it to the inner corners of her eyes. "Do you remember when Dad couldn't get out of bed?"

"No."

"Good. That's good. We always wondered if you'd remember. We told you he had the flu. I kept telling Dad, 'It's business. Things happen. You didn't kill the man. You just did your job.' But that suicide . . ." She smoothed the tissue out and blew her nose.

I thought of the black-and-white picture I'd seen a few times of my father's father, wearing a white undershirt tucked tightly into his pants, squinting in sunlight, smiling at the camera, holding a baby—my father. He didn't look like a person who would hurl himself off a bridge.

"Whenever Dad thought of Azalea, he imagined his own mother, raising her sons by herself. He set up a trust for Azalea. Not a lot of money, but it was something. He blamed himself completely. The trust will stop when Azalea's daughter turns eighteen." She stood and crossed the room to a wastebasket, and then returned to the bed.

"I've put Azalea's daughter in a coma."

"She's not in a coma. She's fine. She woke up an hour ago. And she said you were driving her to the hospital because she was having stomach pains. You were trying to help her."

"That's not what happened."

"Was she covering for you? Azalea thinks you were trying to save her daughter's life."

"Lying, yes. Covering for *me*? No."

"You kidnapped her."

"That's ridiculous."

"You drove recklessly in an old, unsafe car with a minor in the passenger seat. I'm not saying what I think. I'm just saying . . . if Azalea were angry instead of grateful, these are the things she could accuse you of. She'd have a case. If being married to a lawyer taught me anything, it's that everyone's got a case." She rubbed her temples with the pads of her fingers. Her wedding band twinkled. "That woman. Maybe Dad had a role in her husband's death. *Maybe*. But if you ask me . . ."

"What?"

"She had a bigger role in Dad's."

SIXTY-SEVEN

In the coming weeks, my mother and I talked more than we had in three years. We lounged on the couch in the living room I'd grown up in, sat on the porch my father had built, watched television together in the bed she'd been sleeping in alone. We talked while my scrapes and bruises healed, while I tried to decide what to do with my life. But the only decision I made in those weeks was to stop keeping secrets.

This was how my father—the man whose eyes I'd believed had no tear ducts, the man who called me Brenda Preston, the strict detractor of emotional rhetoric—responded to Dr. Koa Bellham's death: He climbed into bed, drew the blinds, denied the sunlight, and swallowed pills that would keep him asleep. He woke up now and then and thought, *I'll take more pills and sleep more, and when they wear off, I'll take a few more, and I'll sleep and sleep and sleep.*

My mother called a friend of theirs, a doctor, who entered the dark room, tried to speak with my nonresponsive father, and confiscated his pills.

"I'm not seeing a shrink," my father told my mother.

"Fine. Then what?"

"I'll go back to work. I'll plod through life. I'll get to the end of it eventually."

He rose from bed and returned to work. He moved through his life as if dutifully performing a choreographed dance. Until one day, his miracle came.

My father's phone rang at work. A hysterical man with a Yiddish accent had been referred to my father by a friend. He cried that he'd been accused of malpractice in his accounting business. "It's crazy!" he said. "I am nothing if not honest in business. Please help me. My wife is pregnant with our fourth child. If I lose my business, I'm in serious trouble."

My father recognized this second chance. Through his office window, he watched the sun push its way out from behind a cloud. The pane of glass glared gold. "I'll help you," my father said, the weight of depression sliding smoothly off his shoulders. "And then I'm never going to practice law again as long as I live."

"*Baruch Hashem,*" the man whispered.

That was how my father found God.

SIXTY-EIGHT

I meant to call Eden. All of my campers' numbers were still programmed into my cell phone, where they'd been since that day at Adventure Gardens, in case anyone had separated from the group. But when I thought about the conversation we would have to have, when I thought about having to explain myself, to defend my sanity, all I wanted to do was sleep. At my mother's house, I was sleeping a lot. Before bed, I would think, *Tomorrow I'll call Eden. Tomorrow I'll be better. Tomorrow will be the day I start my life anew.*

But after a week, Eden called me.

"You okay?" I asked.

"Yeah. I wasn't hurt."

"Eden," I said. "I'm sorry."

"It's okay. You didn't mean to crash."

"Yeah, but—"

"And you had my back. You didn't tell anyone we were going to eat food that wasn't in the program."

"Right. But." I wondered if I should tell her that I'd lied about that restaurant, that there was no such thing as comfort food, that I hadn't been driving anywhere.

"My mom told me who you are," Eden said.

I was lying prone on my childhood bed, looking at things that had mattered to me—a wooden jewelry box from my father, framed pictures of friends whose names I had to squint to remember, a jar of pennies, a shelf of my college business textbooks.

"It all probably makes no sense to you," I said.

"I heard your dad died."

"You must think I'm off my rocker."

I listened to Eden's silence, to the faint sounds of a television going in the background. When she spoke again, she said, "Remember how I told you about that thing I did? That night when I was so drunk?"

"You only sort of told me."

"I was seriously *wasted*." Eden paused. "But want to know why I did it? Aside from being wasted?"

"You don't have to explain yourself."

"There's this bookstore by my school that I used to go to a lot. I would sit in the self-help section and read all the books. I didn't even care what they were about. I just liked them. I read the cookbooks, too. Maybe this year I won't anymore. I might have more friends this year. Not that I don't have friends. I have friends."

"I read a lot of self-help books last year, too," I said. "I love self-help books. Although I'm not sure they help."

"Well, there was this one I read about how girls without fathers act out. They meant sexually. They meant, girls without fathers might be, like, skanky. So when I did what I did, it was because I thought the book had told me I could. Does that . . . ?"

"It makes a lot of sense."

"I think that's what you were doing, too. You wanted to find me because you felt like you were allowed to."

"Sort of," I said. "Maybe."

"Or maybe you had a descent into madness. I just saw a show about a woman who had a descent into madness."

"That might have been part of it, too."

"But she came back."

"Did she?"

"She's better now. She's a dental hygienist. It happens to lots of women, according to the show."

Above me, the light fixture housed a mass of dead bugs, rendering the room unnecessarily dim. I would have to stand on my bed to unscrew it. I could take it outside and shake it out on the sidewalk. But since I'd left the hospital, even tasks as small as that one felt enormous. Still, I could picture myself doing it. I could practically feel the satisfaction of it—how I would lie on my back afterward and admire my work, basking in new, clean light.

SIXTY-NINE

The diet was over. It had been since the day Mikey showed up at camp. Every morning, while my mother was at work, I walked down the street to the grocery store, hoping I wouldn't see people from my past. (But I constantly saw people from my past.) I bought boxes of Pop-Tarts, family-size bags of Smartfood, cartons of Whoppers, blocks of cheddar, fresh baguettes, packages of Ritz Crackers, and four-for-one frozen pizzas.

I sent e-mails to every friend I had who might tell Mikey about my car accident. Friends sent cards and flowers, called to check on me, and sent e-mails urging me to hurry back to New York. But I never heard from Mikey.

Each morning, I thought, *Today I'll get back on track. I'll go for three runs. I'll order those infomercial diet pills.* I made pot after pot of dark-roast coffee, hoping to re-create the energy I'd had at camp. But a switch had been flipped. The old hunger blazed inside me, stronger than ever. I couldn't even remember what it had felt like to need so little. I remembered how loose my clothes had been. I remembered feeling small and pretty. But how had I gotten through all those days barely thinking of food?

Bennett called.

"Soon as you're better," he said, "I'll fly you down here. I'd like to see your beautiful face."

While we talked, I stuffed my beautiful face with cookies and muffins and corn chips, remembering how at one time Bennett had made me full.

"What are you eating?"

"Celery."

Bennett sighed. "I can't wait to touch your body again."

My body. My tan was fading. My hair kept shedding. My waist, within two weeks, had begun to lose its sucked-in-cheeks shape. I didn't want to see Bennett. I didn't want Bennett to see me.

One night, I mustered unprecedented energy and accepted a dinner invitation from an old friend. We'd lost touch after high school and she'd married young. Her husband shared her name: Micah. They had a baby, and they lived nearby, in a house like the ones in which we'd been raised.

I sat at their kitchen table and observed their grown-up life. A perfect circle of a clock hung on the wall. No one else I knew would have bothered with a wall clock, would have lived beneath the ticking of its steady, predictable hands. I pictured Husband Micah, a dermatology resident, standing on a stool, hanging the clock, while Wife Micah stood back, tapping her lips with her index finger, deciding whether it was straight. She was fatter than she'd once been, and didn't seem to care. Her body resembled her husband's. I wondered if I was missing something. I wondered if they were.

Pictures of the two of them covered the walls. In some, they were thin and young. They'd met in college. They seemed to have taken many ski vacations. In other pictures, they held the baby between them like a trophy.

I asked Husband Micah, "Can you tell me what's happening to my hair?"

He got up from the table and came to stand behind me. He tugged gently at my hair. I closed my eyes. His hands felt like cool rocks. I resisted leaning into his touch. He said, "You're not going bald."

"I think I am."

He inspected my part. "Take vitamins. Do yoga. Remind yourself to breathe."

"I breathe every three to four seconds," I said, a factoid I'd learned from Spider.

"Could just be that we're getting older."

"Twenty-seven?"

"Sometimes hair gets thinner."

"And then grows back?"

"Or not. But no matter what happens, you'll adjust."

I scheduled blood tests anyway. I held out my arm and let the needle in. I didn't flinch. I felt briefly hopeful. A few days later, when the results came back negative, I hung up the phone and put my face in my hands. I wanted a deficiency. I wanted to ingest supplements to restore whatever was missing.

SEVENTY

One night I pulled a box of old pictures out of the attic and asked my mother to tell me stories. I lifted the lid and extracted the pile. At the top, the pictures were from my prom. My high school graduation. But then came the older pictures. My father holding me on his shoulders by the ocean. Me as an infant, asleep on his chest.

"I always forget," I said. "Dad used to be thinner."

"He was svelte."

"He wasn't *svelte*."

We were lying on our stomachs, side by side on the living-room floor, eating peanut M&M's from an oversize yellow bag. This was a new thing—my mother snacking. And while I knew it was an unhealthy habit of mine, it seemed a healthy one for her. She was still skinny, but she had more color in her face. And she looked taller, as if her year as a widow had strengthened her vertebrae.

"When I married him, he looked like a movie star."

I found some pictures of my parents from before I was born—posing in front of some statue, kissing in some park, feeding baby goats. My father looked nothing like a movie star. But it was undeniable: Although he'd always been big, he'd been nowhere near obese.

"Maybe you had your love goggles on," I said.

"Do you?" My mother bumped me with her shoulder.

When I had told her that Mikey and I were finished, she'd asked, "Did you have a fling with that gorgeous man from the camp?"

I thought about Bennett now, about our faces almost touching on a shared pillow, the way we'd stared at each other, and the things we'd said in the dark of his bedroom, hidden away from the campers.

I moved a picture of my parents slow-dancing to the bottom of the pile. "I'm wondering," I said, "how it's possible to love someone for years, and then meet a total stranger and suddenly love him instead. I'm wondering what love even means if it's so fluid."

"Some say love, it is a river," my mother said, and we both giggled. This was new, too—my mother making jokes. Whenever she made one, she looked at me right away, nervous, as if she expected me to tell her she had no business trying to be funny.

"Or is it that if you learn love once, in a particular way, you'll just repeat that version of love again and again for the rest of your life, pinning it on different people wherever you go?"

"You know what your father would say. You're too young to be cynical."

"But doesn't it seem too easy that I could pack love into my car with my clothes, and then drive awhile, and then arrive somewhere and rummage through my trunk and pull the love out and give it to someone else?"

My mother picked lint from my sleeve. "You think that's what happened?"

"I don't know." I set my chin in my hands. "I don't trust anything I've thought for at least a year. I haven't made good decisions in a while. Seems like I keep thinking the wrong things."

My mother straightened the edges of a pile of her honeymoon pictures. "Everyone's been telling me not to trust myself. 'Don't sell the house yet,' 'Don't date too seriously,' 'Don't make any decisions.' But I *want* to make decisions."

"Well, then you should."

My mother ran a hand through my ponytail, and I thought about how one day, she would love another man. Perhaps he would be timid. Perhaps he would be a vegan. A violinist. The kind of man who would cry. Perhaps it would be one of her customers, who loved to watch the bones of her hands whipping up perfect bouquets.

"You know why your father got fat? He started eating that way after that man killed himself. Your father was very sensitive. Like you."

"Ha."

"You are, Gray. You're very sensitive."

I wanted to rest my cheek on the carpet and sob. I wished I could see what my mother saw—a sensitive, innocent child. Instead I saw a grown woman afflicted with questionable judgment.

"Ask Mikey. I'm not sensitive."

"Mikey doesn't know you like your mother does."

"Mikey hates me."

"He has to hate you until he stops loving you."

"I don't want him to stop loving me."

"Eventually, when he heals a bit, he'll love you in a different way. He'll love you the way people love youth. Forgetting the bad parts."

She flipped through a few pictures and paused at one from her wedding. It was a formal picture, everyone posed and young. She tapped it with her fingernail. "I watched what happened to Dad. He started self-medicating with food. I read books about it. He thought those rabbis were showing him the way. But it was food he always turned to. If that woman . . . Azalea . . . if that woman had just told him she forgave him . . . But she never forgave him. She said she recognized his apologies, but she would never forgive him. What the hell kind of a thing is that to say? So he ate until he had a heart attack."

I plunged my hand into the yellow bag, extracting a fistful of peanut M&M's.

"I kept telling him, 'Let it go, Alan. Let. It. Go.' But he couldn't. Wouldn't." She paused. "I guess I shouldn't blame that woman. She's been through the wringer."

I chewed and swallowed. "Do you blame Dad?"

She pursed her lips for a second. "He was depressed. A depressive person. He couldn't let go of things. That was just him. You aren't like that, Gray. You are sensitive. But you know when it's time to let go. People with obsessions . . . they let themselves get eaten alive. Pardon the pun. He even let this whole mess ruin his relationship with you. Those rabbis got it into his head that religion would absolve him. If you'd wound up with Mikey—"

"Well, I didn't."

"But if you had—"

"I know what you're going to say."

"You wouldn't have raised Jewish children."

"Right." I ate a red M&M. A green one. "There are worse crimes," I said. I remembered how I'd once believed that green

M&M's were aphrodisiacs. That Pop Rocks and Coke could make a person explode. That Taco Bell burritos housed cockroach eggs that would hatch in the consumer's stomach. All those childhood legends that acknowledged the power of food.

"Well, I know there are worse crimes. But *I* didn't approve of Mikey, either. I want you to have a husband with a stable job. Mikey would have been traveling all the time. And those clubs are so seedy."

"They're not seedy. Just sad."

"Your kids wouldn't have seen their father. And they would have been so confused!"

"Why do you guys always say that?"

"'Are we Christian? Are we Jewish? Why do we have a Christmas tree? Or why *don't* we have a Christmas tree?' On and on."

"Mom."

"But anyway. It was different for me. If you were in love with Mikey, I wasn't going to intervene."

I looked at my empty palm, now streaked faintly with candy dye. "But you never stuck up for me."

"I kept telling him: 'Don't put this kind of pressure on her.' But you know how your father was. And those rabbis kept hammering away at him." She spread pictures from my first birthday party in a row in front of her. "Well. What's done is done." She pinched a blue M&M from the bag and studied it before pushing it into her mouth. "Or maybe it's all my fault."

"I didn't say that. It's not. Maybe I should have . . . I don't know."

"You could have humored him instead of getting angry."

"Why was that my job? He was the parent."

"If you'd tolerated him, you'd feel better now. You wouldn't be so tortured."

I looked down at the stack of pictures. My young, healthy father was laughing maniacally beneath the spray of a waterfall. "What's done is done," I said. "Right?" I curled my fingers into fists, dug my fingernails into my sticky palms. "Besides, if I'd tolerated him, I would have been agreeing with him that my life was all wrong."

"You're stubborn like he was."

"I didn't want to look at my life. I think that's what stubbornness is."

"Well, the positive flip side to stubbornness is that you know what you want."

"I really don't."

"You do. You will." My mother sat up and started stacking the pictures.

"I'll clean up," I said.

"No, you need your rest."

"That's the last thing I need. I need to figure out what to do." I felt tears starting in my chest. I was thinking about blowing out that candle at Morgan Rye's Steak House, about my obstinate refusal to wish.

"I like having you here," my mother said.

"I can't stay."

"Right. You're an adult. I understand. Maybe you can be a teacher. I always wanted to be a teacher."

"I have nothing to teach. Except water aerobics."

"Not that you should do anything just because I wish I had. Maybe *I* should go back to school. Maybe *I* should be a teacher."

I looked at my mother, at her short ponytail drawn back and secured at the crown of her head, at the silver hairs coming in at the roots, making her temples sparkle. I remembered my father's face more vividly than I had in months, not the face I saw in pictures, but the real, three-dimensional version, the glisten on his lips when he licked them, the way he would blink rapidly when he was arguing a point. There was a time when my parents would lean their faces together, cheekbone to cheekbone, their temples touching. I remembered how they would sigh, as if resting at a filling station.

"I have to tell you something," I said. I drew in a breath. And I told her the story. I recounted the last two hours of her husband's life. I told her every detail I remembered, as if I were under oath. Maybe it was wrong of me, selfish to pick at her scabs. But I felt hot and stuffy inside my secrets.

As I talked, I saw my grandfather reversing his flight, landing on both feet on that suspension bridge. I saw my father closing an open carton of ice cream, returning it to the freezer.

"It's okay," my mother said, putting her skinny arms around me. "It's going to be okay."

SEVENTY-ONE

Dear Fat People,

I'd like to call a truce. If I forgive you, can I exorcise you? I thought I had bested you. I thought that for the rest of my life, I would just become thinner and thinner.

No. Wait. I'm holding back. I've promised not to hold back anymore.

I hoped that for the rest of my life, I would just become thinner and thinner.

One problem is that no one knows what hunger is. How can we defeat what we can't define? Try it: Define hunger. No, desire is different. Wanting is not the same as being hungry. Filling a hole inside you is not the same as filling your stomach. How will we ever learn this? How will we ever make peace?

You wonder why we hate you? You are the visible manifestation of the parts of ourselves we hide.

SEVENTY-TWO

Dear Mikey,
I

SEVENTY-THREE

But before all that. Before I found out that Eden was fine. Before I stopped returning Bennett's calls. Before Bennett stopped calling. Before I closed my eyes and hovered over a map. Before I opened my eyes and found my finger on Colorado. Before I bought a used car and—why not?—moved to Colorado. Before I drove to Mikey's show at the University of Denver. Before I watched his set comprised of jokes I'd never heard. Before I waited for him outside. Before he walked out with his new girlfriend. Before his eyes settled on me. Registered me. Before I thought, *I am looking at a version of Mikey that doesn't love me.* Before he hugged me stiffly. Spoke politely. Walked away. Before I met someone else. And someone else. And someone else. Before I learned that no relationship would have quite the same gravity. Before I spent three months posing nude for an artist in Breckenridge. Before I once and for all lost my beloved fat camp body. And quit nude modeling. And realized how tightly we hold on to things we lose—until sufficient time passes and we can't hold on anymore. Before I applied to medical school. Before my hair stopped shedding (long before baldness, but not before irreversible loss). Before my grief finally broke like a fever. Before I made peace with some things. Before I made peace with the realization that I'd never make peace with some things. Before I began the rest of my life, I had to go back to camp.

I had just been released from the hospital. Bennett drove me, his hand on my knee, my eye in a patch. I had to collect my things, box them up, and mail them to my mother's house.

"It's empty," I said when we drove in. "It's so weird to see it empty."

"What did you expect?"

"It's a shell. It's a body with no life inside it. It's like the summer never happened."

On my floor of the dorm, the doors were flung open. The beds were stripped. The air was silent. Only my room was full.

"Can you believe this?" Bennett said, smiling. "I could take your clothes off right now." He filled his arms with some of my things and walked out to his car. "With the door open," he called over his shoulder. "Right in your dorm room!"

He didn't understand. I'd already left him behind. I sat on my mattress, my limbs weighted with painkillers, and saw all the life through the window. The green that had been there all summer. The trees and the grass. The intimation of mountains beyond. And for just a second, I forgot where I was. I forgot the things I always wished to forget. And I felt a remarkable lightness.

AFTERWORD

While I was writing *Skinny*, I was asked from time to time if the story was "true." Because I, like Gray, worked at a weight-loss camp for kids in North Carolina, taught water aerobics, and spent a summer in unforgettable company, the answer to that question is complicated. My knee-jerk response used to be, "It's fiction." However, "fiction" and "untrue" certainly aren't synonymous.

I didn't feel right including, in the pages of this book, the standard "This is a work of fiction" disclaimer, which states that any similarities between the characters and real people are coincidental. Some similarities might be coincidental, but others are not.

With that said, although many of the characters in *Skinny* were inspired by real people, they are, like most fictional characters, composites—combinations of more than one person, some invented elements, and pieces of the author. It's also worth noting that the plot, including references to dramatic deceptions, illegal activity, abuse, and violence, came entirely from my imagination.

ACKNOWLEDGMENTS

Thanks to all the folks at Harper Perennial and ICM. Special thanks to Jeanette Perez for her brilliance and support, and to my incomparable super-agent Kate Lee. Thanks to Cristina Henriquez and Aryn Kyle, cherished readers and confidantes, and to Chris Iacono, my portal into the New York stand-up circuit. Endless love and gratitude to my friends and family.

About the author

About the book

Read on

Insights,
Interviews
& More . . .

A Conversation with Diana Spechler

1. How did the idea for the plot of Skinny first come to you?

At some point in my early adulthood, it occurred to me that most people I knew had body-image issues or unhealthy relationships with food. People are shackled to sugar or salt or GNC or plastic surgery or their skinny jeans or their elastic-waistband sweatpants. Roomfuls of bodies sit on stationary bikes and pedal nowhere, drenched in sweat. We eat a casual handful of M&M's, and then can't stop looking at the M&M bowl. We weigh ourselves five times a day or have never been on a scale. We call women whose bodies we envy "anorexic," and people with weight problems "lazy." We push seconds and thirds on our loved ones. We eat ice cream that makes us sick and then chase it with Lactaid. We count calories. We count fat grams. We deprive ourselves of carbohydrates until our bodies produce ketones and our mouths taste like nail polish remover. Finally, we binge on croissants. We avoid mirrors. We worship mirrors. We raid the fridge in the middle of the night. We buy Spanx. We celebrate with cake. We drink protein shakes. We Photoshop. Just on the other side of all this effort is a lot of pain. I felt desperate to explore it. Because weight-loss camps are microcosms of the racket that is the diet industry, I thought I should infiltrate one. So I worked at a weight-loss camp for ten weeks. *Skinny* is based partly on that experience.

2. Writers often talk about the difficulty of writing their second novel due to their audience's expectations or perhaps publisher demands. Did you find starting and finishing Skinny **was tough for you at all since it's a sophomore effort?**

After I wrote *Who by Fire*, I was asked a number of times if I thought of myself as a "Jewish writer." Although I don't really consider myself any particular kind of writer, I did worry at times during the writing process that *Skinny* wasn't Jewish enough. But I think I was projecting my own insecurities onto my book because I worry that *I'm* not Jewish enough. There is Judaism in *Skinny*, but mostly it's a book about food and body image, not about Judaism. So I thought I might disappoint people. That gave me pause now and then. Sometimes those pauses distracted me.

3. Judaism and, more important, its role in your characters' lives have influenced the plot in both your books. Are you religious? How does religion help you build a character or story?

Currently, I'm not religious, a fact that is directly connected with my upbringing, my education, my attachments and resentments and life experience. Religion has always intrigued me, less ideologically than ▶

Meet Diana Spechler

DIANA SPECHLER is the author of the novel *Who by Fire*. She has written for the *New York Times*, *GQ*, *Esquire*, Details .com, Nerve.com, *Glimmer Train Stories*, *Moment*, and *Lilith*, among other publications. She received her MFA degree from the University of Montana and was a Steinbeck Fellow at San Jose State University. She lives in New York City. ∽

anthropologically. What a person believes or doesn't believe, how vociferously he asserts his beliefs, how he responds to others' beliefs, and whether or not his stated beliefs contradict his actions provide priceless insight into his character.

4. Both of your books include scenes in which the female characters use sex or perhaps distract themselves with sex in order to deal with other issues in their lives. How does sexuality help you to mold your characters?

When I write, my goal is to make my characters rub up against each other (both emotionally and physically) intensely enough to create friction. I'm sort of a sadistic matchmaker.

Sex can be a powerful, fleeting, often dangerous bond. I do mean "dangerous" in the obvious, high school health class sense—that sex can result in unwanted pregnancies and diseases—but I also mean that people do crazy things for sex, and that sex can make people crazy. It can make one person fall in love and make the other repulsed. It can make strangers speak freely about their darkest desires, sometimes in voices unlike their own. Most of all, sex can be a vice, a distraction from the parts of life that hurt us. I'm interested in what happens when vices stop working—when our zealotry is challenged; when cigarettes stop calming us; when food can't satisfy us; when we need alcohol not to feel better, but to function.

5. *Your first book,* Who by Fire, *examined the guilt felt by a family after their youngest sibling and daughter goes missing.* Skinny *examines the guilt Gray feels after losing her father. What attracts you to stories about blame and guilt?*

One of my pet peeves is that cliché about guilt being "a pointless emotion." Intellectually, I understand that guilt can be pointless or even self-destructive, but so what? Everyone grapples with it, so it deserves to be written about. Besides, what's wrong with engaging in something pointless? I lie awake in the middle of the night, wishing I could sleep. That's pointless. So is paying for the brand name instead of the generic. So is the Magic Eight Ball. So is that game the guys from my high school played at parties—throwing beer bottle caps into cups of warm beer. So is wishing on a star. Farmville. The Macarena. But we all do the Macarena sometimes.

6. *Do you have any writing rituals? Or perhaps any vices that help you get through the process of writing a novel?*

Coffee, yoga, crying, running, trusting the process, hating the ▶

process, wishing I were a different kind of writer, shielding my ego, ignoring my ego, rewriting, rewriting, rewriting.

7. If you were not a writer, what would be your dream job?

The alternate careers that pop into my head excite me solely because I'd like to write about them—handwriting analyst, astronaut, pimp. But if writing were off the table, none of them would interest me much.

8. Who are some of your writing influences?

I am influenced by countless writers. I love so many, and who's exerting the most influence changes all the time. A few writers that accompanied me while I was writing *Skinny* were Aimee Bender, Robert Boswell (particularly the title story in his collection *The Heyday of the Insensitive Bastards*), Antonya Nelson, and Amy Bloom.

9. When you are writing, do you have a particular audience in mind? Are you writing for someone in particular?

I write most passionately and prolifically when I have a muse, but muses come along rarely, and they never stick around. They often take the form of someone whose approval I long for, someone I feel a little bit in love with from afar.

Because I can never sustain that dynamic, the best, most reliable substitute is fiction. I always keep short story collections that I love near my computer. I page through them when I'm looking for inspiration. In a way, I'm writing for those writers, or to those writers. ⤳

Ten of My Favorite Not-Entirely-Likable Protagonists

by Diana Spechler

IT MADE ME SELF-CONSCIOUS, writing a novel about a woman who feels fat, but isn't. What's more annoying than *that girl*? Ugh. So it occurred to me that some people might not like my protagonist, Gray Lachmann. At times, I didn't. But I love many unlikable protagonists. I've compiled a list of some of them. My hope is that Gray, who condemns overweight people, who's a little self-absorbed, a little whiny, and maybe a little delusional, is in good company.

1. Humbert Humbert of Vladimir Nabokov's *Lolita*

What would a list of controversial protagonists be without Humbert Humbert at the top? When *Lolita* was published, readers liked Humbert Humbert so much, they felt ashamed. At least, that's my theory on why the book was banned, and on why the prettiest girl in high school is always labeled a slut, and on why it's trendy to rail against McDonald's. (Well, maybe that last one is an oversimplification.) Even Nabokov wanted to divorce himself from Humbert Humbert, calling *Lolita*'s themes "so distant, so remote, from my own emotional life that it gave me a special pleasure to use my combinational talent to make it real." Incidentally, I find

Nabokov's claim questionable, mostly because who besides Nabokov would casually drop the word "combinational"? No one, except Humbert Humbert.

2. The unnamed narrator of Tobias Wolff's *Old School*

He's a plagiarizer. Yet he's vulnerable and hungry in the most human ways. When he gets caught, and life as he knows it is about to crumble around him, he notes, "During our worst dreams we are assured by a dog barking somewhere, a refrigerator motor kicking on, that we will soon wake to true life."

3. Lee Fiora of Curtis Sittenfeld's *Prep*

She has no social graces. She's lazy. She's ungrateful. She's rude to her parents. She underachieves. But she's hilarious and authentic. I read this book as soon as it came out, and have often thought of Lee since. I remember her the way I remember old friends. And I love her particular sense of nostalgia: "Did we believe we could pick and choose what passed quickly? Today, even the boring parts, even when it was freezing outside and half the girls were barefoot—all of it was a long time ago."

4. Holden Caulfield of J. D. Salinger's *The Catcher in the Rye*

Apparently, I love boarding school novels and their entitled protagonists. Why should we feel sympathy for a privileged teenager who gets expelled from his elite prep school? Because ▶

he's Holden, and as readers, we get so deep inside his head, we're thinking his thoughts with him, seeing things as he sees them, and his worldview is convincing and timeless: "Don't ever tell anybody anything. If you do, you start missing everybody."

5. Arthur Camden of Michael Dahlie's *A Gentleman's Guide to Graceful Living*

This is a novel about a wealthy older man whose wife has left him. He is socially inept and is the butt of every joke, but he doesn't quite know it. He has horrendous judgment. He steals and gets caught. He accidentally burns down a house. He leaves the country and runs into trouble with the French police. And if I knew him in person, I can imagine everyone saying about him, "But he means well!" That's the tragedy of him, and what makes him lovable.

6. Alex of Anthony Burgess's *A Clockwork Orange*

Alex is a classic sociopath, inflicting the worst sorts of harm on others, showing no remorse. But how can anyone hate the narrator who says things like, "The Korova milkbar sold milk-plus, milk plus vellocet or synthemesc or drencrom, which is what we were drinking. This would sharpen you up and make you ready for a bit of the old ultraviolence"?

7. Siddhartha of Hermann Hesse's *Siddhartha*

Admitting to liking this book, and this protagonist, makes me feel like a college boy with a lava lamp and a crush on my Introduction to World Religions professor. In fact, because that association has always existed in my head, I didn't even get around to reading the book until about a year ago, at which point it became one of my favorite novels. What sets me apart from the college boys (not that there's anything wrong with being a college boy, and I'd be lying if I denied swooning over a Siddhartha-loving college boy or two back when I was a lava lamp-owning college girl) is that I find Siddhartha, as portrayed by Hesse, to be an insufferable egomaniac. College boys can't be expected to see that; they're still working on *becoming* insufferable egomaniacs. (Okay, I'll stop with the man-bashing; it's a relic from my college women's lit class anyway.) What a great irony: the egomaniac who shuns egomania. I love Siddhartha.

8. Marie of Marcy Dermansky's *Bad Marie*

Bad Marie is the most contemporary of the books on my list, and the one I read most recently. Marie, as the title implies, is bad. She's a thief, a kidnapper, and a husband-stealer. But she's unapologetic about it. And she genuinely loves the ▶

girl she's kidnapped. I kept feeling guilty for rooting for her.

9. Esther Greenwood of Sylvia Plath's *The Bell Jar*

Few novels are as unnerving as Plath's thinly veiled account of her own depression, and few protagonists in contemporary literature are as frustratingly self-defeating as Esther Greenwood, but her fragility is intoxicating: "I didn't want my picture taken because I was going to cry. I didn't know why I was going to cry, but I knew that if anybody spoke to me or looked at me too closely the tears would fly out of my eyes and the sobs would fly out of my throat and I'd cry for a week. I could feel the tears brimming and sloshing in me like water in a glass that is unsteady and too full."

10. Medea of Euripides's *Medea*

Medea, though not a novel, deserves inclusion on this list. Although Medea commits the most despicable of crimes—killing her own children—she does it to hurt her husband who left her for another woman. Who doesn't love a good revenge story? Who doesn't love a character who exacts the kind of revenge most people wouldn't even fantasize about? There's a gulf between the tire-slashers of the world and the people who wish they could slash someone's tires. Every now and then, I like to give some credit to the tire-slashers. ∼

Have You Read?
More from Diana Spechler

WHO BY FIRE

Bits and Ash were children when the kidnapping of their younger sister, Alena—an incident for which Ash blames himself—caused an irreparable family rift. Thirteen years later, Ash is living as an Orthodox Jew in Israel, cutting himself off from his mother, Ellie, and his wild-child sister, Bits. But soon he may have to face them again; Alena's remains have finally been uncovered. Now Bits is traveling across the world in a bold and desperate attempt to bring her brother home and salvage what's left of their family.

Sharp and captivating, *Who by Fire* deftly explores what happens when people try to rescue one another.

"Impressively executed. . . . [The characters'] voices are strong and convincing. . . . Spechler is a talented writer who transcends melodrama and cliché with striking sensitivity and delicate touch."   —*Boston Globe*

An Excerpt from
Who by Fire

Prologue

April 24, 2002

AT THE BACK OF THE PLANE, twelve men bow and mumble and sway, masked by thick beards and crowned by black hats. They wear angelic white shawls over demon-black suits. Their eyes are shut. They hold their prayer books closed, using their thumbs as bookmarks. I face the front of the plane again, and return to the article my mother e-mailed me: "How to Cope When Your Loved One Joins a Cult." For peace of mind, I'm supposed to get a support group, to eat whole wheat bread and peas, to breathe deeply and remind myself that I'm not to blame. I inhale sharply through my nose. The air smells stagnant—transatlantic airplane air. I try to exhale some blame.

After Alena disappeared, my mother was brimming with blame. She blamed the state police for not making enough effort. She blamed other families for not understanding. If my father sat down to watch TV, she would say, "You think your daughter has the luxury of watching television?" She started grinding her teeth so hard, she had to wear a mouth guard. For a year, she dragged Ash and me all over New Jersey, making us tape flyers to telephone poles, as if we had lost her favorite cat. She never directly blamed us, her two remaining children, but she often began a thought with, "If it had been you, instead of Alena . . ." Of course, she always followed that up with "Don't give me that look. I never said I *wished* it had been you. God forbid. What do you take me for?" But we have always understood: Alena was the baby. Alena was the favorite. Six-year-old Alena, with the paintbrush-black hair and the chin dimple and the jeans rolled halfway up her calves, Alena imitating our eighty-four-year-old neighbor's smoker voice, Alena whizzing through the kitchen on roller skates with pink wheels—Alena was the irreplaceable one.

After losing its baby, its best member, especially if a family can't properly mourn, it begins to decay like a corpse. At ten years old, I didn't know yet that my father would leave us, that my mother would grow old while she was still young, or that Ash would swing from obsession to obsession like a child crossing the monkey bars. All I knew for sure was this: We had lost everything we had been.

Ash might remember it differently. Perhaps he remembers the voice of God saying, *No one will ever forgive you*. I wait a while before unbuckling my seat belt and making my way to the bathroom at the back of the plane. The praying men have dispersed, but as I walk down the aisle, I can pick them out. I can see their hats towering over the seat backs. I can see their plain wives, their squirmy broods of children. I want to tell them that they are no match for me, that for ten days now they have been no match ▶

for me, ever since I heard the news that I know will get Ash to come home.

I plan to catch Ash off guard, to show up at his yeshiva, to tell everyone there that he used to eat baseball stadium hotdogs that couldn't possibly have been kosher; that he fidgeted restlessly during *Schindler's List*; that at Yom Kippur services, he used to fart on purpose during the silent meditation. I will tell them, *This is my brother you've taken! And now I'm taking him back.* ∾

Don't miss the next book by your favorite author. Sign up now for AuthorTracker by visiting www.AuthorTracker.com.